STEALING CINDERELLA

THE SINISTER FAIRY TALES COLLECTION

A. ZAVARELLI

DISCLAIMER

This is a work of fiction. Names, characters, businesses, places, events and incidents are either the product of the author's imagination or used in a fictitious manner. Any resemblance to actual persons, living or dead, or actual events is purely coincidental.

GLOSSARY OF TERMS

GLOSSARY OF TERMS:
Glossary of Terms:
Akevitt- A Norwegian Spirit
Mor- Mother
Min Gudinne- My Goddess

PROLOGUE

"WHERE ARE WE GOING, PAPA?"

He squeezes my hand in his as we walk alongside a bustling London street. All around us, there are new sights and smells and sounds. A double-decker bus whizzes by, and a group of women in heels scurries past as they rush to catch it. England is so different from the tiny village in France where I come from, and I want to absorb every detail while I can.

"I promised you we would explore the city." He smiles down at me. "Now we're here, so let's explore."

"It's getting late." Narcissa glances at her watch, her eyebrows pinching together. "And it's a long ride back to Kent. We should call the driver soon."

"Ahh, but I dismissed the driver for the evening." My father offers me a mischievous wink. "Ella wants to take the train."

"The train?" my stepsisters cry out in unison. "You've got to be joking."

Even though they don't seem to have the same sense of adventure, I can't help admiring the girls as they go on to discount all the reasons we should avoid a train. With their posh British accents and smart red dresses, they remind me of the Parisian fashionistas on TV.

Magnolia's hair is long and dark while Lavinia's is blonde like mine. But theirs contradict my wild curls by flowing like a silky river over their dainty shoulders. Their skin is fair and smooth, complexions Narcissa insists they maintain by avoiding the sun. It's easy to see they take after their mother, who I've already decided is the most beautiful of all. Even more stunning than the actresses from the old French films my father used to watch.

Narcissa is tall and willowy with a grace I could only ever hope to possess, and I often find myself imitating her accent when she's not around. It's not difficult to see why my father fell in love with her. Whenever she looks at him, his eyes shine with admiration for her. But whenever she looks at me, her eyes fade to pools of black, and I shrink back into my invisible shell.

"Henri." Narcissa pouts. "The train is filthy. It's been such a lovely evening in the city. Let's not spoil it with this silly nonsense."

My father glances down at me, and the smile slips from my face. I do want to ride the train, but I also want to make my stepmother happy because it seems as if I never do.

When my father moved us from the only village I'd ever known to make a home with Narcissa and her daughters, he said it would be our grandest adventure yet. But so far, I have not managed to find my place within the family.

Narcissa is the queen of our household, shopping and primping to keep herself beautiful at all times. And my father is the king because he makes all the money to support us. Magnolia and Lavinia are definitely the princesses with their lavish wardrobes and lofty aspirations.

But when it comes to me, nothing makes me particularly special or notable, and truthfully, I'm not really sure where I fit in.

"It's one train ride," my father insists, urging us forward. "A little adventure will be good for all of us."

Behind my father's back, Narcissa's icy gaze slips to me, and it chills me to the bone. Turning my attention to the pavement, I focus on the cracks as we trudge on. The smell of kebab shops and hot fries lingers in the air, and even though we just ate, my stomach rumbles for more. Someday, I want to try those restaurants too. As we get closer to the train station, those smells disappear, and a quiet stillness settles over the group as my father directs us to the ticket station and then to the platform.

"It's freezing up here," Lavinia wails. "Do we have to wait outside?"

"Are you sure the train even comes this late?" Narcissa peers around the empty platform uncertainly.

The conversation that follows fades away as I study the Overground map, checking off all the places we'll stop on the way back to Cranbrook. A thrill shoots through my veins as I consider what the train will look like inside. Perhaps like one of my father's old movies where everyone is dressed in fancy clothing, the men carrying their briefcases and the women in those funny hats. Papa and I never had any reason to take the train back in France, but now that we live in England, he promises we'll take it often to see the places around us.

Papa's voice sneaks back into my consciousness as he appears at my side, and I'm on the verge of pointing out some of the stops when he grabs me by the arm and shoves me behind him. My heart thrashes like crazy when I feel the tremor in his grip. Instinctively, I know something is wrong before I tune back into my senses, and everything blasts me all at once, like radio static.

"Just give us your wallet and the jewelry, and we'll be on our way."

"Papa?" I peek around his arm and then freeze when my gaze collides with the two men standing in front of us, blades drawn.

"Here, take it." My father fishes his wallet out of his trousers and tosses it onto the platform.

"The watch too." One of the guys uses his blade to point at my father's wrist. "And ladies, you can start taking off that jewelry any second now."

"Not my engagement ring!" Narcissa protests as she stares at my father.

"It's okay," Papa assures her. "Just give the men what they want so they can be on their way."

Lavinia and Magnolia shed tears as they discard their matching gold bracelets into the heap that's accumulating on the platform. Narcissa is equally teary-eyed as she delicately sets her ring on top of my father's wallet.

"Now, the little girl." One of the men steps toward us, and my father pushes me back.

"She doesn't have anything. We've given you what we've got, now please just go."

"Nah, I don't think so." The scary-looking stranger tilts his head, examining me. "We'll have to see for ourselves."

My father shoves me back against the cold metal fence, shielding me with his body as I frantically tuck my necklace beneath the collar of my dress, hoping they won't spot it. This was the last gift my mother gave to me, and I know that's why he's trying to protect it. But as their footsteps slap against the concrete, I consider that there might not be a choice.

Before I can make that final decision, both men lunge forward at the same time, yanking my father away from me. He doesn't go without a fight, and when he knocks one of the men down, the other swings straight for his throat.

Papa stumbles back, coughing and sputtering as he brings his hands up to his throat. A scream pierces the air as he falls back onto the pavement, and it takes my brain a second to understand what that crimson liquid is on his fingers.

"Papa!" I collapse onto my knees and crawl toward him, terror vibrating through my entire body.

My limbs are too stiff, and everything seems to be happening so fast. Narcissa is frozen, her eyes unfocused as she watches me slip through my father's blood. There's so much of it, and I don't know how to help him. When I bring my hands to his, warmth oozes from his wound into the crevices of my fingers. His eyes are glazed and weak as I clutch at his shirt, pleading with him.

"Papa, please be okay! Please, someone, help us!"

With what little strength he seems to have left, he curls his fingers around mine and offers me a sad, strange smile.

"I love you, Ella," he croaks.

"No!" I cling to him, refusing to believe this is real. He can't leave me. I won't let him. But even as I tell him that, his body falls limp beneath me, his head lolling to the side as the life fades from his eyes.

"Please!" I look at Narcissa, a frantic, desperate energy making my voice too high. "You have to do something!"

Her trembling hands fall to her sides, and in the span of a few seconds, her face morphs from horror to hatred.

"I think you've done enough for us all, Ella."

1

ELLA

"THAT'S A GOOD GIRL, MABEL." My fingers dance over her glossy black mane. "Look at how far you've come."

She dips her head and nudges me with her nose, offering me a cheeky little kiss. Mabel is a former racehorse who was abused at the hands of her owners, and when she first arrived at Hilliard, she was so skittish we feared she might never recover. But time and patience have given her space to trust again, and now she spends her days happily lazing around the English countryside. I love to work with her whenever I get the chance, and while I try not to pick favorites, I think I've developed a soft spot in my heart for the jet-black Arabian mare.

"I wish I could stay a little longer, but I have to go." I nuzzle her face one last time. "Enjoy your dinner."

She swishes her tail and turns her attention to the hay as I scurry off through the pasture, counting off the feed stations to make sure I got them all. When I get to the gate, Olivia is already waiting for me, shaking her head with amusement. She's the owner of Hilliard Animal Sanctuary, and she's been kind enough to let me volunteer my time here whenever I get a chance to slip away from home.

"All the other horses are going to get jealous if you keep giving her smooches." She laughs.

A grin splits across my face. "I don't pick favorites, and you know that."

"Sure, you don't." She smirks. "Try telling that to your shadow."

On cue, the tiny kitten appears and paws at my leg to get my attention. Alfred's just a little ball of gray fluff with the prettiest blue eyes I've ever seen, and I'd be lying if I said he hadn't stolen my heart. When I scoop him up into my arms, he curls against my chest and starts to purr.

"Any word on the puppies?" I ask.

Anxiety swirls in Olivia's eyes as she nods. "The vet wants to keep them for a while longer before he releases them."

I scratch Alfred's ears, contemplating what else I can do to help. A couple of weeks ago, someone dumped a litter of gravely sick puppies at Olivia's doorstep in the middle of the night. They'll require a lot of care upfront unless we can find someone willing to adopt them, which seems unlikely. The animals who need more attention rarely get adopted. Olivia is worried about the vet bills, and it's hard not to feel helpless. It seems like every week someone else is asking her to save another abandoned animal. Meanwhile, the vet is pressuring her to pay off her existing balance before he provides any more care.

"I have five alteration orders this week," I tell her. "One of the neighbors bought some dresses that need hemming. I'll come right over on Sunday and give you whatever I earn from those."

"Thank you, Ella." Her face softens. "I appreciate it, but

you better get home now. It's past four already."

"Crap!" I set Alfred down, and he swishes his tail as he meows up at me.

"You know you don't have to come here every day." Olivia studies me with concern. "Not if it's going to get you into trouble."

My chest deflates, and a desperate sorrow unfurls inside me. "This is the only sanctuary I have. If I couldn't come here—"

"I know." She squeezes my shoulder. "And I wouldn't ever want you to stop. But I don't want to get you in trouble, and truthfully, I'm not sure how much longer I'll be able to keep this up."

"I'm still trying to get funding," I insist. "More donations are coming in every week."

She placates me with a smile, but deep down, I know the sanctuary is in big trouble. As it stands, we are relying on donations for food to get by from week to week. Not to mention all the other costs involved with running such a vast operation. Olivia has a kind heart, but unfortunately, there are more irresponsible pet owners in this world then there are dollars in her bank account.

When I look around this place that has become home to so many animals, the thought of it disappearing brings tears to my eyes. If we can't take care of them, I don't know what their futures will hold. It's a bitter fact that many of these babies who have already had such difficult lives will likely end up in places where they'll be euthanized.

"We'll figure something out," I promise, but my voice cracks. "I'll write another letter to the royal secretary."

"I don't know what I would do without your help." Olivia pulls me in for a hug, only to be interrupted by a tiny mew from below.

"Oh, Alfred." I reach down and pat him on the head. "I wish I could take you home too. But unfortunately, our visits here will have to do for now."

Alfred doesn't seem to agree, opting to weave between my feet to convince me otherwise. If I had any confidence he could go undetected at the manor, I would take him. But it's safer for him to stay here for now.

"You better get home." Olivia nudges me. "Narcissa is probably coming unglued."

I cringe at the very thought. "I don't know where my head is at lately."

"Up in the clouds," she calls after me as I set out for the path home. "As always."

———

"Where in the bloody hell have you been?" Lavinia snarls as soon as I slip into the entryway.

"Sorry, I'm late." I toe off my muddy shoes and leave them by the door, rushing to clear the cups on the table in front of them.

"Oh, God." Magnolia waves a hand in front of her face. "You smell like a horse's ass."

"I had to make my own tea!" Lavinia glares at me. "And I'm starving. I want dinner now."

"I'll get it started right away," I assure them. But before I can get that far, Narcissa appears in the hallway, blocking my path.

Her eyes roam over me, cold and critical as she shakes her head. "Disappointment. That's what I should call you. Honestly, Ella, look at you. Roaming the countryside in those rags you call clothes. Do you have no shame?"

I glance down at the faded jeans I scored from a thrift

shop, hoping she doesn't notice the hole in the knee that I still need to mend. While Narcissa is quick to criticize my wardrobe, she's even faster in refusing assistance to correct the sad state of my clothing. She squandered every last penny of my father's life insurance on London's finest for her and my stepsisters while I've made do with scraps of fabric and my mother's old pieces.

"I'm sorry." My head dips under the weight of her scrutiny. There's no point in arguing. I learned that the hard way. This life is my punishment for taking my father away. I caused his death and ruined all our lives.

"Sorry, sorry, sorry," she mimics. "That's all I ever hear. Do you think I don't know where you spend all your time? On that godforsaken shamble of a farm with all those critters. You seem to have trouble performing the most basic of tasks here, and I'm starting to wonder if it's because I've given you too much freedom."

The cups in my hands wobble as I look up at her, hoping she will just dismiss me. But I'm not so lucky.

"Perhaps you need a refresher course," she says. "Is that it? Do I need to forbid you from going there to wake you up to your obligations at home?"

"Please don't!" I blurt.

A sinister smile curls across her lips as she watches me squirm. Realistically, we both know she can't truly forbid me from doing anything. I'm twenty years old. But given that she spent all my father's money and has never allowed me to work outside the manor, my options are limited. She hates me, but she isn't willing to let me live a life free of her demands, either. To Narcissa, I have only ever been a prisoner, working my debt off with a life sentence.

"Girls, what do you think will inspire Ella to be on time?" she muses.

"We could bring back medieval punishment." Magnolia twirls a strand of dark hair around her finger with a cruel smile.

Narcissa laughs casually as if they are discussing the weather.

"Maybe Cinderella could tend to the fire tonight." Lavinia holds me hostage with her shrewd eyes, taunting me with the nickname.

Without thinking, my attention drifts to the sleeves covering the scars on my arms, and Lavinia doesn't miss it. A wicked gleam flashes in her eyes, and I shudder at the memory. The way she tells the story, I slipped and fell into the fire, but the truth is, she flew into a fit of rage when I'd refused to do her homework. She'd pushed me straight into the fireplace with so much force I was convinced she never wanted me to crawl back out. To this day, I can't forget the expression on her face when I dragged myself out of there, pleading for her help. The pleasure she reaped from my suffering was nothing short of psychotic. I've done my best to steer clear of her tantrums since then, but I always wonder what evil is lurking just beneath the surface.

"What do you think, Ella?" Narcissa asks. "Are you up for the task?"

"Please, no." I shake my head. "I'll do anything else. I won't be late again, I swear it."

"Very well." She sighs. "In that case, you can give me whatever you earn from your little sewing projects this week."

The protest tumbles from my lips before I can think better of it. "I can't. I've already promised that money to Olivia."

Narcissa whips her hand out, snatching a handful of my

hair and tugging until it feels like she's going to rip it from the roots. "Did I just hear you tell me no?"

I stare through her, biting my tongue before I say something else I'll regret. Already, the dishes in my hands are about to topple over, and God knows I don't want to provoke her again.

"Answer me!" She leans into my face, eyes piercing mine.

"You can have the money," I reply bitterly. "I'll give it to you just as soon as I have it."

"You disgust me." She shoves my head away, and I stumble back, nearly losing the dishes as I try to steady myself. "Pathetic, ungrateful little bitch. All these years, I've had to support you. I could have sent you to an orphanage, you know. It's times like these I wish I had."

Biting back the sting of my emotions, I try again to move past her, but she isn't done yet.

"You can forget about going to the farm this week," she adds. "You'll be doing chores at the manor from sunup to sundown."

"Okay." I force myself to reply before she makes it two weeks.

"And while you're enjoying that, we'll be getting ready for the ball," Lavinia chimes in. "You'll need to steam all my dresses so I can decide which one I want to wear."

"What ball?" My gaze whips to her.

"The royal family is hosting a masked charity ball." She speaks as if I'm too slow to comprehend such a thing. "All the eligible royals from around the world have been invited. And this morning, our dearest mummy managed to secure us tickets."

"Us?" My belly flutters as I consider what this could mean.

"Don't be daft." Narcissa slices her red clawed hand

through the air with a sense of finality as she points at her daughters. "Lavinia and Magnolia will attend the ball with me. These tickets are very exclusive, and you would just embarrass us."

"That's right," Lavinia snarls. "We need everything to go perfectly for the next two weeks, so you better not do anything to muck it up."

"Yes, your responsibilities here are what's important," Narcissa echoes. "There isn't any time to be sitting around on your arse, do you understand?"

"Of course." The hope I'd dared to have dies swiftly.

In all honesty, I couldn't care less about attending a royal ball. But if I could just speak with the British Prince for a few moments, I'm convinced I could get him on board with helping the sanctuary.

"Well, what are you waiting for?" Narcissa shoos me away. "Go fix dinner. And then get to your chores. We have a lot of planning to do."

For the rest of the evening, my stepsisters concoct a detailed plan of attack on every royal bachelor they deem worthy. There are notebooks and newspaper clippings and photographs spread across the kitchen table as they dissect every potential weakness for the singletons they aim to snag.

"No, not him," Magnolia whines as I clear away the last of the dishes. "He looks too cross. But his brother Calder, on the other hand—"

"They're twins." Lavinia rolls her eyes. "They look the same, apart from the hair. And it doesn't matter if Thorsen is too cross. He's the heir apparent, which means he's rich, and he's going to be king someday."

"Good thinking," Narcissa praises her. "We can't rule

anyone out just because they might not have a sunny disposition."

I disappear into the kitchen and scrub the dishes and floors before retiring to the attic. When my father died, Narcissa exiled me to the small space with nothing more than a bed and a solitary window to call my own. It might be a little drafty and dark up here, but I don't mind. This is the only place in the whole manor that still reminds me of my father, and there are even a few boxes of his belongings she hasn't managed to get rid of yet. Everything else was sold before she redecorated the place with gaudy furniture and horrible wallpaper.

When I collapse onto the bed, I'm exhausted, but my guilt won't let me rest. I promised Olivia I'd give her the money from my sewing projects this week, and now I have to break that promise. That money was supposed to go toward food or vet bills, but instead, it will probably go straight into a Botox injection for Narcissa's face.

Reaching for the notepad on the bedside table, I consider writing another letter to the prince's secretary. During my research some time ago, I'd discovered that I could nominate a charity for the royal family to review. But first, it has to go through the secretary, and the secretary will only pass it on if they believe it to be something of interest. I've been trying for months, but so far, it's gotten me nowhere. While I've submitted to several members of the royal family, I believe Prince Aston is my best bet. He seems to be more approachable, and I noticed he's already working with several other animal charities.

My pillow vibrates, and I peek at the door to make sure I'm in the clear before I retrieve the phone Charlotte gave me. My best friend since primary school, Charlotte comes from a well-to-do family. She has a weekly allowance from her parents and a brand-new car, and she insisted that I had to have a mobile phone at the very least. I accepted it reluctantly, but Narcissa can never know I have it.

When I check the notifications, I find two texts from Charlotte, both asking me to video chat her when I'm not busy. Pulling up the app we use to communicate, I click on her name. After two rings, her face pops into view, her blue eyes wild with excitement.

"Oh my God, Ella!" she squeals. "I have the biggest news ever. You aren't going to believe it!"

"Bigger than your engagement last week?" I arch a brow at her. "That seems unlikely."

"Even bigger than that." She nods eagerly. "Did you hear about the royal ball?"

"All night long." I roll my eyes. "Narcissa and the girls are planning their attack as we speak."

"Okay, well, forget them for a second and picture this." She waves the phone around as she speaks, making me dizzy. "You're in a beautiful ballgown at the royal palace, chatting up Prince Aston himself."

"Are you high? Did you get into your father's edibles again?"

"No, I'm not high." Her eyes sparkle with laughter. "Ella, this is real. I wouldn't even tease you like that."

"What are you talking about?" I ask reluctantly.

"I got an invitation to the masked charity ball!" she sings. "And as much as I'd love to go, Oliver and I have plans that night."

"So, you think I'm going to go?" I stare at her as though she's lost her mind. Forget the edibles. I think she's on an acid trip.

"Obviously!" She fluffs her hair in the reflection of the

screen. "How many chances do you think you'll get to talk to the prince about Hilliard Sanctuary in person?"

"I wouldn't get within ten feet of him." I laugh. "I'm sure he's just there to make an appearance."

"No." Charlotte wags her finger. "He's on the list of eligible royal bachelors. And I bought you a charity ticket for a speed date. So, if you play your cards right, you can have a full uninterrupted five minutes to pour your heart out to him."

"What do you mean you bought me a charity ticket?" I can't hide my shock. "That must have cost—"

"A fortune," she finishes for me. "It did. So, this is why you HAVE to go. No backing out."

"Charlotte, why would you do that?"

"Because I love you, and you never get to do anything like this. That's what BFFs are for. Besides, I know how much that sanctuary means to you. I can't stand the thought of it going under either. This is what you've been working toward. This is your golden opportunity."

It sounds like the craziest idea ever. But even as I tell myself that, I'm nodding along because she's right. When will I ever have a chance like this again? There's a real possibility I could put an end to the sanctuary's financial troubles for good. I could save everything Olivia's been working for and ensure the animals have a place to stay.

"There's just one problem," I say.

"What?" Charlotte quirks her brow.

"The whole family is going. Somehow, they managed to get tickets too."

"Don't worry." She grins. "I have a plan, Ella. I always do."

2

THORSEN

"How are you feeling today, Thorsen?"

Dr. Blom studies me as I tinker with the scattered pieces of the model sailing ship on my desk. I'd imagine he's tired of this routine by now, but there isn't a Tuesday when he doesn't show up. Every week for eight years, just like clockwork. Dr. Blom is my father's solution for my unfavorable mental state or more aptly, my disagreeability.

"I feel fine." I adjust the hull, sliding another piece into position.

"You're making some progress there," he notes.

My eyes skim over the pieces in search of the cannons. I manage to retrieve one from the pile before he fires off another question.

"Can you tell me what you've been doing this week?"

"Meetings." I squint as I try to secure the cannon into the designated slot. "The usual."

"I see. And have you been to visit your mother?"

The force of my grip severs the plastic mount from the cannon, sending it flying across the desk. In a split second, the entire ship has been rendered useless. For a long moment, I stare at the broken piece, pressure building up inside me like a steam engine. Dr. Blom senses the impending explosion and attempts to intervene.

"It's okay, Thorsen. It doesn't have to be perfect."

But it does. Scooping the unfinished ship from my desk, I dump it into the garbage, followed by handfuls of the unassembled pieces.

Dr. Blom frowns. "I'm sorry if I upset you with the question about your mother. But it is something I'd like to address. It's my job to make sure you're handling the circumstances in a healthy way. This situation would be difficult for anyone."

"I'm fine." I turn my focus to the window, watching the storm clouds roll in outside. It's unusually gray for the spring in Norway. Perhaps Mother Nature is grieving too.

"These events can be challenging to navigate," Dr. Blom explains in his clinical way. "It wouldn't be uncommon to feel a wide range of emotions, even if you aren't always able to identify them. What's important is how we decide to address them. And I want you to know that you can speak with me anytime."

"I don't want to talk about that today." I return my attention to the man across from me. He's thin and tall with graying hair and wire-rimmed glasses. An unassuming character if I ever saw one. He's become a permanent fixture in my life, but lately, I find myself simply staring through him.

"Okay." He folds his hands across his lap. "Then perhaps we can circle back to the topic we didn't finish last week."

Pinching the bridge of my nose, I lean back in my chair and stare up at the ceiling. "Fine."

"Have you given any more thought to the proposal from your father regarding the arranged marriage?"

"I'm not marrying Princess Yasmine," I answer. "I don't want to marry at all."

The clock on the wall ticks off the seconds as he ponders my statement. My position on this topic hasn't changed, but he seems content to revisit it often.

"I understand it's difficult for you to form attachments," he says. "It's not unusual for those who have experienced trauma to avoid intimate relationships. Being vulnerable doesn't come easily for many of us."

I reach for the pencil on my desk, tapping the eraser against the edge four times. It doesn't go unnoticed.

"Can you tell me about the last time you had sex?" he asks. "How long ago was it?"

"Two months, maybe." *Tap. Tap. Tap. Tap.* "Calder found the woman."

"And you both had sex with her?"

"Yes."

"This arrangement has always been easy for you," he observes. "But have there been any occasions when you've ever taken a woman home by yourself?"

"No."

"I see." He studies me, and the silence penetrates my nerves. "I'm going to make an observation that might be uncomfortable, and I want you to hear me out."

Tap. Tap. Tap. Tap.

"Calder was the first person to help you, wasn't he? He brought a woman back home for you, introducing the possibility of sex in a way that gave you control. You didn't have to speak to her. You didn't have to interact. You simply did what came naturally."

The eraser snaps off the end of the pencil when it butts against the desk, and I toss it aside, opting for a pen instead.

Click. Click. Click. Click.

"Have you ever considered that you might be using this situation with Calder as a crutch?"

"Sex doesn't mean anything to me," I tell him. "It's just a release. There's no need to complicate it."

The clock ticks in time with my pen, and I contemplate how much damage I could really do with the tip. Is it strong enough to pierce an artery?

"What about your first girlfriend? You never had her on your own?"

"No." My vision clouds. "We shared her too."

"Has there ever been a time you simply wanted someone for yourself?"

The minute hand on the clock revolves twice as I consider his question. I don't know what it's like to have something for myself. Something I can control without the investment of societal expectations. Talking. Dating. Feeling. Caring. Those things require too much work and energy that I don't have the time or capacity to offer.

"It couldn't ever work," I say. "Women have too many expectations. And even if they didn't, they aren't trustworthy."

"Because you think they will betray you since that has been your experience in the past?"

My eyes fall shut, and I think of the trees. The dark, cold, quiet trees.

"Have you ever heard of the Aokigahara Forest?"

"No," Dr. Blom answers. "Why do you ask?"

"It's at the base of Mount Fuji in Japan. They call it the sea of trees."

He silently dismisses my topic as a derailment from more important things. "What would it feel like to have an authentic conversation with a woman who doesn't judge you, Thorsen? How would that feel to you?"

"I imagine it would feel like this."

His brows pinch together. "What do you mean?"

"There is no authenticity in conversations." *Click. Click. Click. Click.* "Most people are too self-involved to listen. I think you're the only one who tries, but you still don't hear me."

He shifts in the chair, trying to hide his discomfort at my observation. "I'm sorry you feel that way. Is there something you'd like to discuss in particular?"

"Our time is almost up."

He glances at the clock and nods reluctantly. "Before I go, you know I have to ask. Have you had any more intrusive thoughts?"

Yes. "No."

"Are you still taking your medication?"

No. "Yes."

"Your mother suggested I come by twice a week," he says, rising from his chair. "How would you feel about that?"

"I don't have the time right now for more than one visit."

"Give it some thought," he suggests. "We'll revisit it another time."

"Lisbet will see you out now. Thank you, Dr. Blom."

"How is she?"

Astrid, my mother's nurse, offers me a pitiful expression as she shuts the door to the suite and steps into the hall.

"She had another headache this morning. We managed to get it under control, but she's drained. That's normal at this stage. You'll notice she needs to rest more."

Normal. I balk at the word used to describe the hell of my mother's reality. Every day, her life gradually slips away from her. Her body shrinks down to an empty shell as she fights to hold onto the mind that's always shone like a sunbeam on a dark, cloudy day. Nothing about this situation is normal, and I resent the term ever being associated with this illness.

"Perhaps you can check back tomorrow," Astrid suggests. "She'll probably feel a little better in the morning, and I know she'd love to see you."

My eyes drift to the door separating me from the woman who brought me into this world. A deluge of agony hits me all over again, and it feels as though the dead organ in my chest has been strapped into an electric chair, forcing me back to life just to torture me. She has been my only solace in this existence, and soon, she will fade away. I can't do anything to make her stay a little longer, but I'm not ready to accept that she's leaving either.

"Thorsen." My father's deafening voice booms from behind me, and every muscle fiber in my body knits together, bracing for his impact.

He's striding down the hall with two of his personal staff in tow and my brother not far behind. Calder gives me a warning glance, silently alerting me our father is already on the warpath.

"Your mother is resting today." His lips twist into a sneer. "She doesn't need any visitors. And I need a word with you now."

"Regarding what?" I provoke him. It's no secret what the king wants to speak to me about.

His nostrils flare as his eyes cut to Astrid, and with a single look, he dismisses her. There are more appropriate places in the palace to discuss these matters, but my father has never given a second thought to airing his grievances in front of the staff.

"You know damned well what I'm referring to." He

narrows his eyes at me. "King Lars wants to know why Princess Yasmine has not yet received an official offer of marriage."

"I have already discussed this with you at length. I'm not marrying Princess Yasmine, and if you have failed to inform King Lars of my decision, that's your problem, not mine."

His face mottles with red, hands curling into weapons at his sides. Right now, I imagine he wants to lodge one of those fists into my noncompliant mouth. It wouldn't be the first time.

"You seem to think you have a choice," he growls. "But you forget that it merely takes one signature from me to alter your life forever."

"And what, you'll drag me down the aisle in chains?" I challenge. "What would the media think?"

He launches himself at me, slamming me back against the wall as his fingers twist around my throat. His resentment for me blots out the color in his eyes like the moon eclipsing the sun. He wishes I was never born, and he doesn't bother to hide it anymore.

"I am your king!" he roars. "And you will fall into line, so help me, Odin."

"Father." Calder attempts to intervene by grabbing his arm, only to be shoved aside.

Elias Lykken doesn't look like much of a king as he crushes my trachea between his fingers, taunting me with his eyes. He wants me to fight back. He wants me to protest and beg, and if he knew me at all, he would understand there are no protests left in me. He'd do me a favor if he simply finished the job, right here and now.

"Thorsen." Calder's voice penetrates my dark thoughts, and when I search his eyes, the fear I witness there wakes me up to my cold reality. He always wants me to fight, even with the demons weighing me down.

"Elias!" The sharpness in my mother's voice startles all of us as she appears in the doorway. "What is happening here?"

I shove my father's hand away and move toward her, preparing to catch her if she falls.

"You shouldn't be up without your chair," I admonish her.

"Thorsen." She reaches out with a trembling hand, clearly shaken by what she's just witnessed. "What are you two fighting about?"

The king is uncharacteristically quiet as he studies her, his jaw working. He can't tell her what he really wants to say, and I don't want them to fight about it again.

"It's nothing," I assure her. "Let me help you back to your bed."

She shrugs me off, swaying slightly but refusing to allow any of our help. "Don't treat me as if I can't understand what's happening right in front of me," she says. "Now, one of you tell me the truth."

"There was a disagreement about Thorsen's impending marriage," Calder explains. "He doesn't accept the idea, and the king is displeased."

My mother looks at my father, confusion shining in her eyes. "I thought you said he'd agreed to marry Princess Yasmine."

My head throbs as I imagine the contents of his skull splattered across the floor. A bloody and violent death is what he deserves. It's one thing for him to hound me, but it's another for him to lie to her. The disappointment in my mother's eyes is unmistakable. She wants to see me settled and happy before she goes. In her mind, the cure for all my problems is a woman with a soft heart. It's a grand notion, albeit unrealistic, and I regret that I can't give her the peace of mind she desperately wants.

"I'm sorry, *Mor*." I dip my head to hide my frustration. "I can't marry Yasmine."

"If not her, then who?" she asks, her voice wavering.

"This is something to work out between us, Frida," the king tells her. "You have no need to worry. I assure you we will find a suitable match for Thorsen."

It's impossible to miss the murderous scowl leveled at me, but Calder is quick to take on the role of mediator.

"I have a suggestion."

Our parents turn their attention to him, and the mischievous smile on his face tells me I should humor him.

"What is it?" Mother reaches for him, gesturing him to her side.

"First, let's get you back to your room," he says. "You can sit down while we have this conversation."

She nods, and we help her back into her suite, easing her into her favorite chair by the window. She's pale today, and I can't help noticing that she can barely move her left arm at all anymore. But she tries to hide it as she gently folds it across her lap with her other hand.

"Right." She smiles up at us softly, her eyebrows pinching together. "Now, where were we again?"

"As you both know, Thorsen and I received an invitation to attend the royal ball in London," Calder says. "It's a charity event."

"Of course." My mother gestures for the notepad on the table. "Can somebody write this down for me?"

"It already is," Calder answers gently. "It's in your planner."

She frowns and shakes her head, attempting levity as

her eyes shine with sadness. "I'm sorry, I forgot. This pain medication makes everything so fuzzy."

"What is the point of all this?" the king demands. "Your mother needs to rest, and I have work to do."

Calder sighs. "My point is that perhaps Thorsen should find his own match. The ball would be a good starting point, with women you'd likely approve of."

I cringe, and he shrugs as if to say he's sorry, but he's just trying to help. Calder knows the last thing on my agenda is finding a wife, but he's also aware that if I don't go along with this idea, it's very likely I'll be walking down the aisle with Princess Yasmine any day now.

"And what am I to tell Lars?" My father scoffs. "His daughter has been crying for weeks over this situation."

"I find that highly improbable." I glare at him. "Considering we've scarcely spent more than thirty minutes together alone."

"Thirty minutes with you would be all it takes to make her cry," Calder jests.

My mother sighs, watching all of us intently. "I think it's a wonderful idea. Thorsen, will you consider it? For me?"

Any protests I may have had fall to pieces under her anxious plea. Denying her would wreck her, but I also don't want to give her hope where none lives. I'll never be able to make her understand that it's too late to fix me. In her eyes, I'm still salvageable, and as long as she's here, she will always believe that.

"I've heard enough." The king interjects, deciding for me. "You will attend the ball and find a suitable match there. But mark my words, Thor, this is the last opportunity I'm giving you."

3

THORSEN

"REMIND me why we're doing this again."

Calder drags his attention away from the flight attendant on our private jet to meet my gaze. "I bought you some time to find a wife." His lips tilt into a sarcastic grin. "And besides, it's for charity."

"Ah, right." I sip from a glass of *akevitt* as I stare out the window. "A charitable grand gesture you will certainly be praised for."

"And you punished for." Calder salutes me with his glass. "What a fucking world we live in."

Though Calder is my twin, I was born first, which makes me the heir apparent to the Norwegian throne. And almost as if fate was having a laugh, she blessed me with dark hair and dark looks, while he is lighter in features and humor. In short, the media has always loved him. Calder Lykken can do no wrong, and I can do no right.

"It will make *Mor* happy," he says. "And we both know you'd never deny her."

A bitter taste coats my tongue as the suffocating weight of the impending crown threatens to crush me. I've been trapped, caged my entire life by expectations and a title I can't shake. I'm not just the future king of Norway. I'm also one of the most hated men in Scandinavia. Reality is frigid, but Calder is right. I want my mother's last months on this earth to be peaceful. I want her to be happy, but more than anything, I just want to escape.

"Who knows?" Calder shrugs. "Maybe you could actually meet someone at this ball. Someone who doesn't even hate you yet."

"She'd have to be deaf or blind."

"Who gives a fuck what the media says about you?" His eyes dim with frustration he can't hide. "You just need to relax a little. Maybe try a smile every now and then, just to see if you still can."

"I think you should leave the head shrinking for Dr. Blom," I answer dryly. "Personality aside, there isn't a woman on this earth who could tempt me into marriage."

"They aren't all like Anja." Calder watches me carefully as he mentions the woman I haven't spoken of in six years.

My blood pressure rises as the barrage of her deception plays through my mind like a bad home movie. She represents everything I've come to loathe about my position. A snake in the grass, waiting for the right moment to strike. I was bitten once, poisoned by the venom I thought was love. Now, I cut their heads off with vicious words and erect a shield of cruelty that ensure they'll never get close enough to sink their teeth in again.

"No, they aren't all like her." My head pounds with the onslaught of a headache. "They are even worse."

Calder glances around the cabin to make sure our security detail isn't listening. A sign that I'm not going to like whatever he's about to say next.

"I won't pretend to understand what it must have been

like," he says. "The first woman you finally took a chance on after everything that happened—"

"Calder." My voice is a warning, but unlike most people, my brother has never heeded the caution flags in front of him.

"You shut down. You isolate yourself, and you tell everyone you're okay, but I know you aren't. I hate to say it, but *Mor* is right. You need someone in your life. If you can't talk to me, and you can't be honest with Dr. Blom, then it needs to be someone else. These secrets you're keeping, they're going to poison you, Thor."

"I have no secrets." I look out the window, watching the clouds swirl around me. "Only lies."

Calder falls quiet, but I know his mind is still working. He is always thinking. Planning. Trying to save me somehow. He cares, and that is his only fault. Sometimes, I think it would be so much easier if he didn't. If he could just hate me like everyone else, I wouldn't have to worry about disappointing him.

"Want to tag team the flight attendant?" He changes the subject. "I bet she'd love to have a royal cock up her ass."

"You can have this one," I reply somberly, my mood darkening as we get closer to England.

"That's right. You only like the ones who hate fuck you."

He leaves me alone with my thoughts and disappears into the back where the flight attendant is supposed to be gathering snacks. A moment later, she laughs, and it isn't long before she's moaning.

I tune it out, retrieving the phone from my pocket and scanning the email Prince Aston sent with the details of the masked charity ball. If I had to rate on a scale of one to ten how many fucks I give about attending, zero wouldn't be a low enough number. But this is the life of an heir. I am doomed to be paraded in front of the masses to perform my royal duties because I had the unfortunate luck of being born first.

Something rattles in the back of the plane, and Calder groans. The sound of skin slapping against skin distracts me from my thoughts for a moment as I try to recall the last time I fucked a woman. Was it the hotel maid in Barcelona? Or the stewardess on the latest yacht trip? Their faces blend, but one thing is for certain. I haven't dipped my cock in a woman for far too long. Calder's offer to join them should have tempted me, but those games don't have as much appeal as they used to. So, instead, I focus on my email, trying to absorb the details for whatever the fuck it is I'm supposed to do. I'm near the end of the list when Calder returns, tucking his shirt in and flopping back into the seat with a satisfied grin.

"She'll be needing a new uniform."

"You never mentioned anything about this." I glare at him.

"What?"

I shove the phone toward him, pointing out the clause that states we are participating in the speed dating event.

"They're only five-minute slots." He laughs. "Who gives a fuck? You might even get your cock wet if you play nice."

"We have to talk to them." I stare at him as though he doesn't know me at all. "What the fuck am I supposed to say to a group of gold-digging socialites for two hours?"

"Climate change." Calder smirks. "I don't know. But I'm sure you'll think of something. Regardless, it won't matter. They'll be too busy fawning all over you to speak much."

"Not likely," I growl.

"They won't know who you are," he argues. "Behind the

mask, you'll just be a prince. When they choose their line, they'll have no idea who's waiting for them."

"I may as well start writing refund checks now." I close my eyes and rest my head against the seat.

"Or maybe you could make an effort," Calder nags, mimicking our father's voice.

"Don't remind me."

"It's either this or go back home to find another princess waiting at the palace."

"Perhaps you could just carry the burden of producing all the heirs," I reply. "Who knows, you may have a few running around already."

"Ha, very funny," he answers with a cagey sharpness to his voice. "But you won't be laughing when Father springs a wedding on you."

"Asshole," I mutter under my breath.

The pilot's voice crackles over the speaker, announcing our descent into London, and my chest feels like a vise is squeezing it. I'm already counting down the hours until we can leave again.

Prince Aston greets us the moment we step off the plane. "Thorsen. Calder. Always a pleasure to see you."

"The pleasure is all yours," I answer testily.

"Ah, yes, I know you'd probably rather sit at home washing your royal hair," he says with a laugh, "but it's for a good cause. And if that isn't motivation enough, there will be some hot women there. I vetted most of them myself."

"We better make a pit stop at the service station," I tell him. "Calder will need a bulk-sized box of condoms."

"Not necessary." Prince Aston pulls a handful of foil packets from his coat. "I came prepared."

I tug at the collar of my dress shirt, itching to loosen my tie. "Aren't we going back to the palace?"

"Palace schmalace," he says. "I'm taking all my lads to the castle tonight. It's ours for the evening, and I have a spread you won't want to miss. Booze, poker, and tits galore."

"Sounds like my kind of evening." Calder slaps him on the back. "Let's get this party started."

The drive to the castle goes quicker than I'd hoped, and once I'm there, amongst all my royal peers, I find myself a secluded chair and a glass of whiskey. Calder makes the rounds, charming everyone as he always does. I spend the evening replying to emails and glaring at every woman who dares to come my way. There are an abundance of them, and God only knows where Prince Aston dug them up. If I had to guess, I'd say they were escorts, but who the fuck knows.

"Hey, you're that prince." A drunken brunette stumbles over to me. "The Norwegian one, right?"

I stare through her, hoping she'll get the point, but she doesn't.

"You know, everyone always says how horrible you are." She offers me a sly smile. "But I bet they're wrong."

"They aren't wrong," I answer dryly.

She frowns, twirling her hair around her finger. "I could suck your dick if you want. I bet that would put a smile on your face."

For a minute, I consider the offer, just to give me something to do. But when her eyes betray the wheels turning in her mind, it smells like another scandal waiting to happen. She wouldn't be the first woman trying to be sneaky by recording me, or snapping a photo, or going to the media when it's over. Selling their story about how I took advantage of them, broke their heart, mistreated them, or whatever wild tale they can spew to the press that day.

"Go find someone else to please." I wave her away. "I'm not interested."

In a flash, her face morphs from doe-eyed to spiteful, proving my point. "You are an asshole!"

"That's right," I call after her as she turns away. "Tell all your friends. Tell the tabloids too while you're at it."

After all, I have a reputation to protect.

ELLA

"I'm here," Charlotte whispers as she taps on my door. "Is the coast clear?"

Pivoting away from the mess on my bed, I use the heels of my hands to wipe away the evidence of my tears. But it's too late.

"What's wrong?" She pushes her way inside, rushing over to me.

"The dress." I point at the scraps of what's left lying on the bed. "I spent all week piecing it together. It was so beautiful, but then... Lavinia and Magnolia found it."

"Oh, Ella." Charlotte pulls me in for a hug. "I'm so sorry. They are wretched, evil women."

"They tore it to shreds. There's no way I can go to the ball now."

"Don't worry." She holds me at arm's length and flashes me her most beautiful smile. "I came prepared."

"What?" I call after her as she holds up a finger and slips out the door. When she returns a moment later, she's carrying a dress bag.

"I thought I'd bring it just in case, and I'm glad I did. We can't risk anything going wrong tonight."

"Charlotte, you've done too much already—"

"No protests," she says. "It's from my closet. I haven't worn it in years, but I think it will be perfect with your complexion."

She unzips the bag, revealing the most stunning icy blue ball gown I've ever laid eyes on. The butterfly accents are hand stitched, and the beading is impeccable. I can tell just by looking at it that it must have cost a fortune.

"I can't." I shake my head. "What if I spill something on it? Or rip it? Or—"

"It's yours," she insists. "Don't worry about any of that. For tonight, you are a princess, and I want you to act like one. And look, I even had my seamstress add lace sleeves, so you'll feel comfortable."

Her eyes inadvertently drift to the scars on my arms, the ones she knows I often try to hide.

"You deserve this, Ella. It's time to stop punishing yourself. For one night, I just want you to enjoy the best of everything. And if you find that too difficult, remember what you're doing it for."

"The sanctuary," I whisper.

"Yes, the sanctuary," she repeats. "Now, where are these heels of yours?"

Retrieving the silver heels that belonged to my mother, I lay them on the bed next to the dress. I've always loved these shoes, but I've never had an occasion to wear them. It's a miracle I've managed to keep them hidden from Narcissa all these years, and I can't imagine wearing anything else tonight. Charlotte examines them, and I know right away she loves them too.

"They're perfect!" she shrieks. "Okay, come along now.

We need to do something with that hair of yours. I brought makeup too."

An hour later, she's applying the finishing touches to my face. She tells me it's a frosty ice queen look, whatever that means. But when she turns me around so I can see my reflection in the mirror, I feel the opposite of frosty. In fact, I'm not convinced that I won't melt all over the floor as I hold back my tears of gratitude.

My eyes are sparkling with a glittering silvery shadow and black mascara that makes my lashes look a mile long. And in place of the long, wild blonde hair I'm used to seeing is a sleek updo with tendrils escaping in just the right places.

"Charlotte, it's beautiful." My fingers dance over the braided bun. "You are an artist."

"The canvas makes all the difference." She winks, holding out the mask for me. "Now you can't forget this. Oh, and my license."

"Are you sure I'm going to pass for you?" I swallow nervously. "This seems like a big risk."

"It will be fine." She waves off my concerns. "We could be sisters."

At least that much is true. We both have blonde hair and similar complexions. All I can do is hope she's right and that the license and invitation will be enough to pass for her tonight.

"Okay. We've got the ID, your ticket, your phone." She stuffs everything into the beaded clutch she's loaning me for the evening. "I think that's it. There's just one more thing. You need to meet my driver outside the palace by midnight so he can get you back here before Narcissa discovers you were ever gone."

"Got it." I nod. "But what about you? Don't you need Rupert this evening?"

"No." She hands me the clutch. "Oliver has a business dinner at a fancy hotel. I'm going with him. He's picking me up at the corner. In fact..." She checks her watch and hurries me out the door. "They should be there right now."

Rupert navigates the streets of London with ease, making attempts at friendly conversation while I choke back my nerves. I'm still not convinced I can do this. But then I think of the animals at the sanctuary who depend on Olivia. She's already scrambling to get enough food to last them the week. I can't allow my nerves to get in the way of what's right.

I have a mission tonight. Find Prince Aston and get in his line. Talk to him politely, but firmly. Inform him that Olivia and I have both made several requests for his patronage, and don't take no for an answer.

It seemed a lot easier in my mind when I was rehearsing that speech, but when Rupert drops me off at the entrance, my legs feel like they've turned to mush.

"I'll be waiting down the street for you at midnight." He points ahead. "But if you have any trouble or wish to leave early, don't hesitate to call me."

"Thank you, Rupert. You're very kind."

He gives me a gracious nod and shuts the door behind me, leaving me to follow the herd into the security line. Even though I'm already technically an hour late to the event, there is still a long line waiting to get in. By the time my turn comes around, I'm a nervous wreck, and my fingers tremble when I fork over the license and invitation. I'm so convinced the security team is going to tackle me to the dirt and announce that I'm an imposter, I can scarcely catch my breath. But instead, they simply wave me on to the metal detectors.

It all seems too easy for a second as I scurry into the grand entryway of the palace. But then I remember the hard part is still yet to come. After securing my mask, I pin the clutch to my side and do my best to walk gracefully in my mother's heels.

Music and laughter float out from the ballroom as I draw near. The delicate tune calms my racing heart, if only for a moment. When I step inside, an usher greets me and points out the locations of the refreshments. I head over to the linen tables and grab a glass of punch, praying I don't spill it on myself as I look around the room. For the past week, Charlotte and I have both done our homework, trying to devise a plan that would give me the best chances of picking Prince Aston's line. But I can already tell it's not going to be as easy as I'd hoped.

All the men are dressed in smart suits, in varying shades of black or blue or gray. And with the masks on, it's difficult to tell them apart. But I remember that Prince Aston had dark hair, and he was a strapping six feet, three inches tall. That detail alone should make him easy to spot, but as it turns out, there are a lot of tall men here this evening.

I find a few potentials that I suspect might be him, but I still can't be sure. For all I know, those men might not even be princes. They could just be regular old Joes.

Across the room, I spot Narcissa and the girls in the dresses they picked out for the ball, and I freeze. They're scanning the room, faces obscured by masks, but no doubt their eyes are just as shrewd. I'm convinced when they pass over me, the whole charade will come to an abrupt end, but their attention only lingers on me for a second before they move onto someone else.

Just to be safe, I slip behind a group of people to avoid their attention until the speed dating begins. But it isn't likely they'd recognize me anyway. Lavinia made a point to ensure I wouldn't get any bright ideas by tearing my dress to shreds. But with my hair and makeup done, I could be just about anyone. The truth is, Narcissa would never expect me to disobey her like this. In her mind, I'm still home scrubbing the floors. And as soon as I get back to the manor, that's exactly what I'll have to do.

Pushing those thoughts aside, I listen carefully when the king makes an appearance at the podium they've set up just for him. Like magic, a hush falls over the entire room in a matter of seconds.

"Ladies and gentlemen, welcome to our first ever charity bachelor event. As you are aware, we have gathered here this evening to raise money for the worthwhile cause of feeding impoverished communities around the world. Every donation made this evening will be distributed amongst the Sky Relief Project recipients, and your pounds can make a great deal of difference in a family's life. Throughout the evening, we will be collecting donations, and I hope you'll enjoy yourselves as we dine, drink, and dance in celebration of this event.

"We are about to commence the speed dating, so at this time, I would like to invite those who have purchased a charity ticket for a bachelor to form a line in the corridor. From there, you will be escorted into the white drawing room on your turn. For everyone else, let's commence the evening with our first dance, shall we?"

A throng of masked women rush toward the corridor, attempting to maintain their grace while they quietly gush over which prince they are hoping to meet this evening. I slip into the crowd, noting that Narcissa, Lavinia, and Magnolia have already pushed their way to the front. That comes as a relief because it means they'll be so focused on meeting the prince that their attention won't be on me when it's my turn.

The royal security checks our tickets, allowing us to enter the line in the corridor just outside the white drawing room. Leading the women in batches of twenty at a time, the line slowly crawls forward as I listen to the eager chatter around me. There are a lot of us, and I never considered how that could put me at a disadvantage. The prince will have spoken with a large number of women before he even gets to me. He's likely to be tired and maybe not as receptive as I'd hoped. This plan seems to be less certain with every passing minute, but I'm trying my best to stay positive.

When my group is finally called forward, a million fleeting thoughts enter my mind as they lead us inside, and I get a glimpse of the bachelors. At the front of the room, ten royal princes from around the world are already sitting with their current dates in the staging area. The sections are divided by gold partitions with a small ornate table and a chair for the women beside each man. We can see enough of them to discern general features like skin tone and hair color, but the mystery beneath the mask remains. This is our time to choose a line, and we must all choose wisely.

I study the princes while other women push their way through, determined to get to the line they've decided on. But the longer I examine the men myself, the less sure I am. They're all sitting down, and at this angle, it's difficult to discern their height. Six of them have dark hair, a couple of which I eliminate straight away based on the shade alone. But the rest is uncertain.

"That's him." A woman in front of me hisses to her friend. "I think that's Prince Aston. I've seen him wear those shoes before."

"Are you sure?"

"Yes." She nods enthusiastically.

"You better be right."

For lack of a better plan, I follow them into the line they believe to be Prince Aston's. There are still a handful of women in front of me, which means I won't see the prince for a while. I use every minute of that time to tweak and rehearse the speech I've prepared. And before I know it, I'm only one person away from meeting the man himself. But when I notice the woman in front of me, I don't recognize her. At some point, the other two women disappeared. They were certain this was Prince Aston's line, but now I can't see them anywhere. I'm starting to second-guess myself when the line facilitator gestures me forward.

"Your turn, madam."

"What? Oh..." I stumble forward—not gracefully, I might add—and force my legs to move in the direction of the prince. But now I'm questioning everything. *Is this really him?*

He stands to greet me, his frame towering over me like a skyscraper. When he doesn't bother to extend his hand as I've seen some of the other princes do, I try to remember royal etiquette. In the process, I wind up doing the most awkward curtsy of all time while I struggle to find my voice.

"Pleasure to make your acquaintance, Your Royal Highness."

I swear I could almost see him grimace, and he doesn't reply in kind, but instead, simply nods. I find it odd, and as we sit down opposite each other, I'm not sure if I should just blurt out why I'm really here or wait for him to speak first.

As it turns out, the latter doesn't seem to be an option. Judging by his tense posture and the raw disinterest radiating off him, I'm convinced he couldn't care less about any of this.

It irks me, but at the same time, I'm flushing under his intense regard. The eyes peering down at me through the mask are a sharp, steely gray, and suddenly, I can't seem to recall the color of Prince Aston's eyes.

Aware that the clock is ticking, and we still haven't spoken, I cross my legs and force myself to get on with what I came here to do.

"Your Royal Highness, I must confess that I came here this evening with an ulterior motive."

He cocks his head to the side, narrowing his eyes at me. Or is that my imagination? It's difficult to tell from beneath the shadow of the mask. He's so much more intimidating than I thought he would be.

"As honored as I am to meet you, our time together is limited, so I'm afraid I must get straight to the point. You see, I've written to your royal secretary several times with the hope that my letter would be passed on to you. But it seems as though it has not, or perhaps, it has, but you did not take care to consider it carefully."

Beneath the mask, I notice his eyebrows rising. He seems surprised by my candor, but it can't be helped. Prince Aston might be royalty, but he's no better than the rest of us if he cannot find it in his heart to do something charitable for those who desperately need it.

"There is an animal sanctuary in Kent, Your Highness..."

He doesn't show any signs of life. I can't even be sure he's blinking, and I don't know what to make of this man. But my frustration is snowballing, and desperation colors my voice as I make my declaration.

"The sanctuary is on the verge of going under, and it is the duty of the people, of all British people, to care for those who cannot help themselves. And these animals cannot help the fact that they have been neglected or abandoned. So I came here tonight to ask if you could find it in your heart to help this organization. Securing your patronage could mean the difference between life and death for thousands of animals. Will you consider helping us?"

Silence.

That is his only response after I poured my heart out. After all the planning, and the risk, and the help from Charlotte it took to get me here. The heat radiating up my neck burns as the prince continues to study me, apathetic to my request or the plight of the sanctuary. I'm on the verge of tears, hopelessness threatening to swallow me whole, but more importantly, I'm angry.

"Do you care so little about this country?" I swipe at the tears that are already starting to spill. "Is that it? Are you such a wretched man that you no longer have a heart?"

He flinches at my accusation, and I'm well aware I'm probably about to get tossed out on my arse. But it's clear I'm getting nowhere with him. And now, our time is almost up.

"Thank you for nothing." I stand and glare at him. "I think I'll just excuse myself now—"

Before I can even blink, his hand whips toward me and latches around my wrist.

"I haven't dismissed you yet." The unmistakable accent that does not belong to Prince Aston sends a shiver down my spine. "Now *kindly*, sit your ass back down."

5

THORSEN

THE PETITE BEAUTY shrinks back into her seat under my command, her expression morphing from one of horror to despair when she recognizes that I am not her beloved British prince.

The entire evening, I've been listening to women drone on and on about themselves, scarcely bothered that I never said a word myself. They presumed me to be whoever they wanted in their imaginations, running wild with offers to bake my favorite treats, attend upcoming events, or do my bidding in the royal bedroom. It left me contemplating throwing myself off the palace roof just to get it over with.

And then she came along with her sky-blue eyes and champagne hair and a pair of pouty lips she wielded like a weapon. She was captivating, but I suspected beneath her nerves, she didn't have the faintest idea about it. There was something different about her, but I couldn't figure out what it was. She smelled like sunshine and wildflowers. Freedom. An escape from the monotony of my everyday life. When I looked into her eyes, I found myself getting lost there. Maybe it was the passion with which she spoke. Or maybe it was her complete honesty that she had no intention of snagging herself a prince tonight. Regardless of what drew me in, I was suddenly hyper-focused on everything this woman had to say.

When she confessed that she came here with an ulterior motive, the first spark of life I'd felt in months nearly suffocated. I anticipated she was about to propose a scheme in which she would lead me by my dick. But instead, she blurted out the most ridiculously impassioned speech I'd ever heard. About a charity, nonetheless. And while I sit here, trying to make sense of what's happening, I still can't find it in me to accept she could be that selfless. If I am to believe her, she came here with the sole intention of gaining support for her furry friends.

"Your Highness." My line facilitator steps forward, subtly nodding at his watch. "Time is up."

"Time's up when I say it's up." I shoot him a withering glare and turn my attention back to the mysterious woman in front of me.

"I should go," she says, trying unsuccessfully to excuse herself again.

"No, you won't." I squeeze her wrist in my grip. I don't know why I'm still holding onto her, or why I can't seem to stop staring at her. People are starting to take notice, and it makes me irrationally angry. I'm the prince who everyone loves to hate. The man the media can never print a kind word about. And now she's making a spectacle of me in front of the entire room.

"You came in here and presumed me to be someone else." I lean into her, my voice low and dark. "You accused me of being wretched and heartless. And now you think you're just going to walk away?"

"I didn't know," she whispers. "I thought you were Prince Aston."

"That isn't an apology," I muse.

"An apology?" She blinks, startled by the notion. "Why would I offer you an apology? You've been rude to me from the start. You couldn't even deign to speak to the likes of me, and now you want an apology for observations that were only the truth? Do you think I don't know who you are?"

My spine steels at her remark. Has my accent already betrayed the truth?

"I may be nobody in your eyes, Prince Thorsen, but I've seen what the media prints about you. And having made your acquaintance, I am now convinced it is all true. You really are as heartless as they say."

My hand falls away from her, but inside, I can't temper the rage churning in my gut. I should be accustomed to it. Every day of my life, I have heard nothing less, but from her, it burns worse than all the others, and I can't understand why.

She stands up again, not bothering with a curtsy this time. "Excuse me."

When she rushes to the exit and down the corridor, I'm not thinking clearly as I give chase. My security detail attempts to stop me as I wade through the crowd, but my focus is on the blue dress slipping out the palace doors.

"Is everything alright, sir?" My secretary intervenes, trying to block my path.

"Everything is fine." I wave him away. "Let me be for a minute."

He doesn't argue, and I follow the mystery woman onto the lawn. She's trying to outrun me, but my legs are longer, and she has the disadvantage of heels, which she's clearly not accustomed to wearing.

When we both spill out into the garden, her heel gets caught in the grass, and she tumbles forward onto her knees. The next time she looks up, she's at eye level with my cock. She swallows her nerves, and I tug her up into my grasp.

"What is your name?" I demand.

"Why?" she asks breathlessly. "Are you going to have me arrested?"

The streak of fear in her eyes is enough to make me question everything. I can't figure out what it is about this woman, or why I even give a fuck, but I can't let her leave without knowing more. It irritates me, and it fascinates me, and I can't rationalize this senseless hunger to strip her bare and force her to reveal her secrets. But when I reach for her mask, she gasps, shaking her head.

"I can't. I can't, Your Highness, please forgive me."

"It's too late for forgiveness. Give me a name."

"Cinderella!" she cries out. "That's what I'm known by, and now I really must go."

My eyes drift to her lips, and my cock stirs to life in my trousers. It's a pity she's so beautiful. I'm tempted to drag her around the corner of the palace and hate fuck her right here on the lawn, smearing her lipstick and ruining that pretty dress of hers when I spray my come across her tits.

"Thor?" Calder's voice startles me, bringing order back to the chaos in my mind. "What are you doing out here?"

When I turn toward him, the mystery woman slips out of my grasp, and it takes all of my restraint not to chase after her again as she glances at me one last time.

"Who was that?" my brother asks.

"Nobody."

"It didn't look like nobody." He arches a brow at me.

"She was offensive and needed a reminder of her manners."

"They are all offensive." He chuckles darkly. "Isn't that the entire point?"

I nod and turn to go back inside, but the reflection of her heel stuck in the grass captures my attention. She left it behind. Calder watches me curiously as I kneel to examine it, tugging it from the dirt and tucking it against my side.

"What are you doing with that?"

"I don't know," I admit. "Perhaps she'll want it back someday."

———

The rest of the evening passes in a blur of faces and grating laughter. By the time I leave the white drawing room, I'm far past ready to retire.

"Surely, you must have found someone who would suit your dick for the evening." Calder blocks the escape path to my quarters. "The night is still young."

"Another time." I shrug him off. "I'm not in the mood to return to the party."

"You are never in the mood." Concern seeps into his features as he studies me. "Do I need to worry about you, brother?"

"No." I disregard the pity in his eyes, opting not to react to it. While my brother's intentions might be honorable, he should know he's treading on thin ice.

"Perhaps we need to make another appointment with Dr. Blom when we return home," he suggests. "We can speak to him together."

"That's unnecessary." I narrow my eyes at him. "Regardless, this is not the time nor the place to discuss such matters."

"I'm sorry." He bows his head and shrugs. "I just wanted you to have a good weekend before we return to your royal duties."

"There is no escaping my royal duties," I remind him. "Only through death."

Calder grabs my arm, his expression morphing to one of despair. "Don't even joke about that. It isn't funny."

The hard outer shell of my heart softens, if only a little. "I know. I'm sorry."

We study each other, allowing the tension to ebb away before more words are spoken between us.

"Please return to the party," I implore him. "Enjoy your evening. Don't hold back on my account."

He sighs and gives me a resigned nod. "As you wish. Just promise me you won't sit in your room brooding all weekend."

My focus inadvertently moves to the heel in my possession, and a sinister seed plants itself in my mind. "I can assure you I have no intentions of that."

6

THORSEN

"As much as I love slacking off in England and partying every night, I think Father might blow a gasket if we don't get you back to your royal cage soon."

I tear my attention away from the list of names in front of me to meet his gaze. "I only need a couple more days. My engagements can wait until then."

"What are you even looking for?" He leans closer, trying to peek at the names Prince Aston's secretary gave me.

"Nothing." I stuff them back into the folder from which they came.

Recognition dawns in Calder's eyes. "Dare I venture a guess that she has a blue dress and might be missing a heel, perhaps?"

A sigh escapes me as I turn my head toward the window, observing the children playing out on the palace lawn. I don't want Calder to think this is more than it is. And I certainly can't admit that I haven't stopped thinking about the way she spoke to me. People might hate me, but they are always dignified to my face. It's only when I turn my back that the knives come out. But that isn't the case with the little fire-breather, whoever the hell she is.

As it turns out, Cinderella was a bogus name, and there are hundreds of real names on the guest list to sort through. That could take weeks, and so far, my search for her has turned up nothing. As much as I'd like to keep this to myself, I'll have to get my secretary involved.

"I'm just planning to return her shoe," I tell Calder. "And pay a visit to some animal sanctuary she rambled on about. She was trying to secure patronage for the charity."

"You haven't done a charitable thing in your life." Calder muses. "Why start now?"

His words burn, particularly because it seems my entire life has been one charitable endeavor after another. However, he is right about one thing. None of it has been my choice, and therefore, I suppose I am due none of the credit.

"If you'd like to go back without me, I'm not holding you hostage here."

"I'm not going anywhere." He stretches out on the chair and kicks his feet up onto the coffee table. "Aston is taking me shooting this afternoon if you'd like to join us."

"Another time, maybe." I grab the folder and head for my private room. "Hayes and I have a few things to discuss."

———

"Your Highness?" Hayes knocks on the door to the study, interrupting me mid-email. "I have that information you requested. Would you like to schedule a time to go over it?"

"Now." I set my phone aside and gesture him in.

Hayes has been my secretary for five years. He's polite, studious, and respectful. But his loyalties lie first and foremost with the crown. I can trust that everything we say to each other will be leaked back to my father at some point.

"Charlotte Duncan." He sits down across from the desk and slides a folder in my direction. "That is the name that was on the ticket. However, my research tells me she didn't actually attend the ball. She was across the city at a business dinner with her fiancé."

Fiancé?

My pulse thrums as I flip open the file and shuffle through the paperwork on Charlotte Duncan. At first glance, the woman in the photograph could be her. Their features are similar, but it's the eyes that give her away. This is not the mystery woman in the blue ball gown. Whoever she was used Charlotte's ticket if what Hayes discovered is true.

"You are certain this Charlotte was elsewhere that evening?"

"Yes, sir." He points at the additional photographs printed out from the society section. Indeed, this is Charlotte Duncan, which makes my shoeless runaway a liar. Cinderella, as she referred to herself, used Charlotte's ticket to gain entry to the bachelors.

"Should we alert Aston to this?" Hayes asks cautiously.

"No." I shut the folder. "There is no need for concern. She probably just gave her ticket to someone else. Not exactly cause for the royal lynch mob to come and haul her away."

Hayes frowns but gives me a stiff nod. "As for your other request, I have gone through the list of potentials and narrowed down the pool to five. But I believe this one is likely to be the woman you're searching for, based on the fact she lives in Kent, and she's blonde."

I look at the name, Lavinia Maddison, and then the face.

While she is a beautiful woman, this is not my mystery woman either. But if she lives in Kent, there's a possibility she knows the woman I'm searching for.

"Thank you, Hayes. I will take it from here."

"Is there anything else I can do for you, sir?" he asks.

"No, that will be all."

He hesitates, and I know I'm not going to like whatever he has to say next. "Your father requested that you schedule a return flight home tomorrow."

Absently, I nod. "Of course. Thank you, Hayes. You are dismissed."

7

ELLA

"WHAT IN THE bloody hell took you so long?" Narcissa snarls at me as I set her cup down in front of her. "Did you have to go to China to source the tea yourself?"

"I'm sorry." I avoid her gaze. "I had some trouble with the kettle."

"Sorry doesn't cut it," she snaps. "There's nothing wrong with the kettle. Do you know what I think, Ella? I think you're a liar."

I bite my tongue, forcing myself not to reply in a way that might provoke her anger. I'm already exhausted from her constantly barking orders and giving me more chores than ever. To her bitter disappointment, neither Lavinia or Magnolia seemed to snag themselves a prince at the ball, and Narcissa has been in a foul mood ever since.

"Did you hear me?" Her arm whips out, icy fingers wrapping around my wrist. "Or are you so daft you can't think of another excuse?"

"I'll take the kettle to the shop tomorrow and have Mr. Burnaby look at it."

"You will do no such thing." Her nails dig into my skin. "Do you want the whole town to think we are so poor we can't afford a new kettle?"

"No, of course not."

"You are nothing but an embarrassment to this family. It's no wonder your sisters can't find a decent man. Who would want to associate themselves with the likes of you?"

She shoves my hand away, and in the process, I bump the teacup, watching in horror as the hot liquid splashes into her lap. Narcissa screams, knocking over the saucer and half of the silverware on the table as she stands up and pulls her dress away from her body. Everything else happens so fast I barely have time to react.

Her eyes latch onto mine, and I take a step back, but she snatches my wrist again and drags me forward. Her other hand rears back, and she smacks me across the face so hard, I stumble into the table, dazed, only for her to thrust me back until I fall on my arse.

"You wretched, jealous little bitch!" she screams, reaching for the teapot.

My hands fly up to shield my face as I curl into a ball, but it does me little good when she pours the scalding hot water over me, eliciting a scream from my throat when it seeps into my skin. White-hot pain electrifies my nerves, and I can't muster the energy to beg her to stop as I try to crawl away from her. I only make it three feet, my fingers digging into the wooden floorboards, when she smashes the teapot beside my head, splintering shards of glass all around me.

"Clean that up, you miserable cow. And then go upstairs. I don't want to see your face for the rest of the day."

After spending the afternoon nursing my splotchy red skin, I tidy up the attic so Narcissa can't find another reason to come unglued. When the sound of trashy reality TV filters up from the floor below, I'm relieved they seem to be settling in for the evening.

With the coast clear, I reach for my phone and call Charlotte. She answers on the third ring, hair mussed and rosy cheeks glowing with satisfaction.

"Do I even want to know?" I ask.

"You mean, do you want to know that Oliver just gave me four bloody orgasms." She grins. "I can dish if you can take it."

Her playful mood disappears when she takes a closer look at my face. "Ella, what's wrong? Have you been crying?"

"Nothing's wrong." I force a smile, secretly wishing I had someone who could make me feel the way Oliver makes Charlotte feel. But that can only ever be a fantasy for me. Why should I get to have a happy life when my father didn't? He died because of me, and every time I think about trying to better my situation, that voice in my head whispers I don't deserve it.

"It's not nothing." Charlotte's pretty face scrunches up in anger. "Did that bitch do something to you again?"

"Shh." I peek over at the door. "She's been in a foul mood for days. I don't need to give her another reason to lose her shit."

Charlotte shakes her head, quietly mulling over her thoughts before she seems to decide on something. "Oliver and I are moving into our flat in just a couple of months. We'll have a spare bedroom. You could come and stay with us. It won't be an imposition, Ella. I can help you find a job. You can check out some local trade schools. Whatever you want."

Her offer sounds like a dream come true, but at the same time, I'm already reasoning it away as too much. I don't want to put her out anymore. She's done so much for me over the years, and it's never been her responsibility to help me. But logically, I don't know how much more of Narcissa and the girls I can tolerate. It's only a matter of time before I break completely.

"I'll think about it," I say, hoping to placate her for now.

She nods eagerly. "That's practically a yes. Now tell me something good. Any news from the prince?"

Warmth flushes my cheeks as I shake my head. I was too mortified by the mix-up to confess the truth to Charlotte. As far as she knows, I spoke to the prince I thought was Aston but never got a firm answer. After all the trouble she went through to get me a ticket, I mucked it up completely by getting in the wrong line. And then to make matters worse, I yelled at the Prince of Norway and lost my mother's shoe.

"No news." I shrug. "I don't think he's going to help."

"What an asshole," she mutters under her breath.

If only she knew. Thorsen Lykken is known for being an asshole. His reputation in the media has never been a favorable one, not that I believe half of what the papers print. But after meeting him in person, I'm convinced at least some of it must be true. Still, I can't seem to stop thinking about the way he chased after me. Tall, dark, and too handsome for his own good. The man might have a horrible disposition, but he has the body of a Nordic god. Long after I left the palace that night, I could still feel his touch branded into my skin. I've never been touched by a man, and Thorsen is all man. A strapping, virile, muscular brute of a dark prince. I'd be lying if I said those stormy gray eyes haven't continued to haunt me in my sleep. His temperament might be pitch black, but there's something undeniably attractive about that enigma. My imagination has taken that image of him and run wild with it. In my dreams, he isn't just holding my arm. He's caging me in with his body. Branding me with his lips. Moving inside me, altering me forever as he infects me with his darkness.

"What are you doing this weekend?" Charlotte's voice stirs me from the depths of my depravity. "Do you have time to hang out?"

"I don't know." I frown. "Narcissa has been adamant that the manor is spotless. She's still convinced the prince is going to knock on our door any day, intent to carry Lavinia off into the sunset."

A strangled laugh bursts from Charlotte's lips. "Poor miserable bastard he would be."

A commotion from downstairs catches my attention as a herd of footsteps clomps across the floor. Someone squeals, and then there's a knock on the front door.

"Shit, I gotta go," I tell Charlotte. "I'll call you later."

"Okay," she answers frantically. "Go, go."

We both hang up, and I stuff the phone beneath my pillow just as I hear a masculine voice at the front door. Running to the window in the attic, I press my face against the pane, hoping to catch a glimpse of the mysterious visitor, but all I can see is a fancy car sitting in the drive.

My curiosity gets the best of me, and I know it's a risk, but I crack open the door to the attic and hold my ear against the gap. Narcissa is speaking with someone, insisting they come in while she offers tea, coffee, or anything their heart desires. She's being far too kind for a regular guest, and my heart leaps into my throat when I recognize the voice that responds. Masculine. Accented. *Unmistakably Nordic.*

Holy freaking shit.

"I can't stay," Thorsen answers. "I just came here to ask if you are familiar with any other women from Kent who attended the ball on Saturday as well."

A sour note colors Narcissa's voice. "Another woman?"

"Yes, a blonde. Petite. Blue dress. She left her shoe behind, and I don't know much about her, only that she was from Kent, and—"

"That's my shoe!" Lavinia interjects. "I can't believe how silly I was to leave it behind. I've been looking everywhere for it!"

"Your shoe?" Thorsen answers with a biting note. He knows she's lying, but Lavinia is too self-involved to notice. Meanwhile, I can scarcely breathe, praying he doesn't say anything that will incriminate me. *What is he even doing here?*

"Yes, it's mine," Lavinia assures him. "And I was wearing a blue dress that evening as well, Your Highness."

"In that case, you wouldn't mind showing me the other shoe," he suggests.

There's a pause of silence, and then Narcissa answers. "We would, Your Highness, but unfortunately, it's at the repair shop. Her heel broke."

Another silence. "Then perhaps I can return another day when you have the shoe in your possession."

"We would be so honored," Narcissa replies coyly.

"There isn't anyone else from this area who might have attended?" Thorsen repeats.

"I can't think of a single person," Narcissa says. "To my knowledge, we were the only family from Cranbrook with the honor to attend."

"Very well." He clears his throat, but the undercurrent of hostility remains. "I'll be on my way then."

"You must come back." Narcissa follows him out the door, their voices disappearing from my reach.

I shut the attic door and run to the window again, peeking through the glass. My stomach roils when I spot the familiar heel in his possession. It's definitely mine. But why is he bothering to return it? And why does my heart feel like it's going to explode when I lay eyes on him?

Today, he's in a navy sports coat and matching trousers, a pair of shiny brown Oxfords jutting out from beneath the hem. And right now, it's not difficult to understand why I got him mixed up with Prince Aston. He's incredibly tall, and every part of his body seems extraordinarily large, from his hands to his feet. If I had to venture a guess, I would bet money he's an actual descendant of Odin himself.

My breath seems to get caught in my throat when I look at his face. He's wearing the customary scowl I've noticed in all his media pictures. From their perspectives, he's moody and reclusive. The articles paint him as someone who rarely speaks unless he's forced to, which explains his behavior at the ball. Yet I can't help but wonder what made him that way? I don't believe anyone would choose to be so miserable all the time.

Narcissa continues to fawn all over him, touching his arm and admiring his car. She's probably making offers to sacrifice Lavinia's firstborn and send him straight to Valhalla if she can have some sort of royal title herself.

With every passing second, tension bleeds into Thorsen's face until inevitably, he shrugs her off and locks himself in his car, speeding away. It isn't but a moment later when Narcissa returns to the entry, where Lavinia assaults her with questions.

"Do you think he'll come back? What are we going to do about the shoe?"

"We'll have one made," Narcissa conspires. "Whatever it costs. Don't you worry, darling. We'll get us a prince yet."

8

ELLA

TWO WEEKS HAVE PASSED since the excitement of the ball, and I've fallen back into my routine with the exception of Narcissa breathing down my neck. She's been making me work triple duty every day, insistent that the Norwegian prince will return at any moment to haul Lavinia back to his kingdom. I've hardly had a moment for myself, and worse yet, I haven't been able to get to the sanctuary in days.

"House bitch!" Lavinia summons me. "I spilled some crumbs. You better clean them up. His Royal Highness could be here at any moment."

I refrain from rolling my eyes and grab the broom while she and Magnolia flip through a magazine with a few articles on Thorsen. They've been doing so much research on the man I might actually find it in my heart to feel sorry for him if he ever does cross their paths again.

"I don't know." Magnolia studies his photograph. "He seems so stuffy to me. He'd hardly be tolerable with that cold demeanor."

"You're just jealous," Lavinia snaps. "I'd hardly have to worry about tolerating him. I'd be rich, you daft cow. That means I could spend my time however I want. Besides, I think that broody, silent thing he has going on is hot. All women love a bad boy."

"Maybe I could take up with his brother," Magnolia muses. "Imagine that. Two royal sisters."

"Not likely." Lavinia shoots laser beams into the competition. "I'm going to be queen someday, which means you would be there to serve me. I'd get to tell you what to do, and you'd have to do it. Same with you, house bitch."

"Maybe your job at the palace can be tending the fire," Magnolia adds bitterly. "Since we know how much you love it."

Fear licks at my throat, and warmth tickles the mangled skin on my arms where white-hot pain once singed my nerves. I can still feel it every time I see a flame, and much to their amusement, I've never fully recovered from the incident. But reacting would just give them what they want.

As far as I'm concerned, Lavinia can run off with her prince and take the whole lot of them with her. Even though the idea makes my chest feel weird, I refuse to give it too much thought. I won't be going anywhere. In fact, it would be the best day of my life if they moved away.

"Do you think she's gone mad?" Magnolia snaps her fingers at me. "She looks odd."

"She hasn't gone mad." Lavinia sighs. "She's just a moron, like you."

I put away the broom and finish the rest of my chores for the afternoon, and by some miracle, I have an hour to spare before dinner. It isn't much, but I know exactly where I want to go.

"Hello, Alfred." The tiny kitten greets me with a head bop, purring as he nestles into my arms.

I find a comfy place on a hay bale in the barn, letting Alfred snuggle up against me as I close my eyes and soak up his comfort. People have often accused me of being too much of a bleeding heart when it comes to animals, but I can't help who I am. Something about how these innocent creatures depend on us wrings every ounce of love and compassion from my heart.

My mother told me when I was young that when the world carries on around me, I should look for the magic. Love blooming between a new couple, the breeze stirring the leaves, a butterfly emerging from the cocoon. What she didn't realize was she never needed to tell me because I inherited her empathic heart too. I see everything. I feel everything too, often much too deeply for my own good. It's exhausting to live in such a shallow world when I can only ever swim in deep waters.

It has been many years since I've felt love. So long, I can't even remember what that was like. I often find myself wondering if I merely dreamed about having a family who cared for me, but then I look into Alfred's eyes, and I know that I am loved. When I'm here, feeding the horses or playing with the dogs or cuddling the kittens, nothing else in the world matters. And to me, these pets are my family.

I know they'll all have to go to new homes eventually, and I'm heartbroken every time they do. But I'm also happy for them because they deserve the best, and right now, I simply can't give that to them.

Tears streak down my cheeks, and it hits me all at once how helpless I feel. For so long, I've barely kept my head above water, and now I'm certain I might drown. I don't have anything else to look forward to. I don't have anything else of value in my life. This place is it. These furry babies and Olivia's kindness in letting me be a part of it. And I'm failing them.

Last week, she told me again she can't keep it up anymore. She's trying to find other shelters for the animals because she can no longer afford to feed them, and she's going bankrupt as it stands. Every source of funding has dried up, and my pathetic little fundraisers have only managed to buy a little food every now and then. It's so depressing I can't bear the thought of not having this place around anymore. It isn't just their sanctuary. It's mine.

"I don't know what we're going to do, Alfred." I stroke his fur and kiss him on the head. "I wish more than anything I could take you home with me."

He meows, and my heart shatters a little more. We might not have much longer together, but I'm going to cherish every moment we do. Curling up into a ball, Alfred and I both close our eyes, and I soak in his warmth as exhaustion settles into my bones. I should probably set the alarm on my phone. It's the last thought I have before sleep swiftly carries me away.

THORSEN

FROM THE SHADOWS, I watch her sleep, the scraggly gray kitten curled against her like it's his favorite home. He opens his sleepy eyes and blinks at me, dazed but completely unaware there's a predator in his midst.

It's been two weeks since the ball, and for the entirety of that time, I've been thinking about what I would find when I came back here. After doing my research, I concluded this was one of a handful of animal sanctuaries in Kent, and over the past few days, I've already been to all the others.

I came here with little hope. But there she was, asleep in the hay like the furry critters she seems so intent to protect. At first glance, I wasn't quite convinced this is the same woman I chased from the ball. In place of the blue gown is a faded sweatshirt that looks like it's on its last life and a pair of jeans two sizes too large for her slight frame. Her shoes have holes in them as well. Half of the rubber soles are worn off the bottoms. But beneath the grime and obvious exhaustion, her champagne hair and ivory skin are still the same.

As if she can sense me, her eyes snap open, and my

heart beats wild, rattling its cage when she looks up at me in distress.

"What are you doing here?"

She cringes at the sight of me, and all the blood in my body courses toward my cock, reminding me how much I'd like to fuck that hate right out of her.

"I think you left something behind." The heel dangles from my finger, and she eyes the glittering shoe with a nervousness that betrays her wish to escape this situation.

"I don't know what you're talking about," she says. "That isn't mine."

The vein in my neck hums. If there's one thing I refuse to tolerate, it's a liar, and I can't figure out how in the matter of a few moments, she's already sentenced me to her dishonesty.

"If it's not your shoe, then you won't mind me testing that theory." I take a step forward, and she shrinks beneath my shadow.

"But why?" she challenges. "What does it matter one way or the other if it is my shoe?"

"Because you're a little liar." I glare down at her. "And I don't have patience for liars."

"I'm not," she declares, shaking her head so righteously, I'm tempted to beat her ass black and blue right now to teach her a lesson.

"So, you're telling me that you didn't use a ticket with someone else's name to gain entry to the ball?" I demand. "You didn't lie to the palace guards, and me, about who you really were?"

Her face pales, and when I kneel before her, reaching for her leg, she tries to scoot away from me. My fingers clamp down around her ankle and drag her back, and she shrieks about the same time the kitten darts away.

"This won't take long." I pry off her pathetic little shoe and slip the heel onto her right foot. Sure enough, it fits like a glove, and she's practically quaking with fear when she opens her mouth again.

"Please don't tell anyone," she begs. "I didn't mean any harm. I was only trying to help the sanctuary, and if you tell anyone—"

"I'm not going to tell anyone. But you have to do something for me."

Her eyes widen, and she considers my words carefully, awareness coloring her voice when she speaks again. "What would I need to do?"

"What are you willing to do?" Against my better judgment, my fingers caress the soft, creamy skin around her ankle as I remove the heel and replace her shoe.

"I... I don't know," she says. "Do you have something specific in mind?"

"Have you always been so naïve?" I lean into her, my fingers gripping her jaw. A breathless sound escapes her lips, and her pulse comes alive for me, throbbing with panic.

My cock is so hard I could fuck her for hours, but not yet. There's a time and a place for my depravity, and they are both elements I need to be able to control. Reluctantly, I let her go and stand.

"I have a proposition for you," I tell her. "Something that can save you from the repercussions of your deception and help your precious sanctuary too."

Her eyes light up, hope shining like a beacon in the darkest ocean. "You're going to help me?"

"I can help you. But you have to do something for me."

"What is it?" She rises and grabs the kitten, who has snuck back into her orbit.

"Come with me, and I'll tell you."

She hesitates, eyeing me like a shark in the water. Little does she know how true that is. "I can't come with you. I have to get home, in fact..." She checks the time on her phone, and alarm seeps into her features. "I'm so late."

"Who's waiting for you at home?" I ask, not out of curiosity but necessity.

She hesitates but thinks better than to lie to me again. "My stepmother and stepsisters."

"I'm sure they won't mind your absence a while longer."

"No, you don't understand." Her panic rises. "I'm sorry, but whatever it is will have to wait."

"I think you must have me confused with someone else." I laugh darkly. "I don't wait for anyone."

Indecision paralyzes her, and if I had to guess, I'd say she was weighing the balance of her indiscretions. It doesn't take her long to figure out that whatever strife is waiting for her at home can't be worse than the potential for punishment of her actions at the royal palace.

"Tell me what you want," she pleads.

"Tell me your real name."

She considers it for a moment, and I'm half expecting another lie to spill from her pretty lips before she finally answers.

"Ella," she says. "My name is Ella Laurent."

"Ella," I repeat, rolling the word over my tongue. "Good. Now, Ella, I'm going to give you a ride home. Where are you going?"

She chews on her lip, holding the kitten hostage against her chest. "I only live a few streets away. I usually just cut through the field."

"And today, you won't."

She glares at me, and there is a spark of fire in her that I already know I'm going to enjoy stoking. When she concedes, I almost regret the battle being won so easily.

"Okay, but only to the end of the lane. I don't want my family to see."

"Of course, you wouldn't," I sneer. "How dreadful it would be for you to be seen with the Prince of Norway."

Her shoulders fall under the weight of my wrath, and she follows me wordlessly out to my car, which is parked on the street outside of the sanctuary. The kitten trails her after she sets him down, and she looks grief-stricken that she can't take him with her.

When she sees the BMW, she pauses. Judging by her clothes, I would venture a guess that she isn't used to such luxuries, which leaves me to question how she managed to acquire the dress for the ball.

I open the passenger door for her, and she carefully slides into the seat, glancing at her dirty jeans. She's worried about filthying up the car, but she has no idea that's the least of her worries.

"Allow me." I lean over her and grab her seat belt.

She sucks in a breath when her eyes collide with mine, and for a minute, I almost regret what I'm about to do. But then I look at her face, so fucking pretty, and I don't think I've ever had something so pretty to call my own. Her innocence speaks to me on a primal level, and I can't wait to destroy it.

My hand moves quickly, and she doesn't even notice the syringe until it's lodged into her thigh. She flinches, and I slap my palm over her mouth, smothering her scream as she stares at me with terrified eyes. Her instincts are telling her to fight back, but she's no match for me. I secure her wrists with my other hand, forcing her to stay where she is.

Ketamine can take a few minutes to be effective, but

luckily for me, she's small, so it doesn't take long to flood her body. After about a minute has passed, she's rendered immobile, but her eyes are still open. She's sedated but conscious. Using the buttons beneath her seat, I lean her back enough that I won't have to worry about her choking.

I leave her hands folded on her lap and wrap my fingers around her jaw, forcing her to look at me. She stares absently, trapped in her own mind as I brush the hair away from her eyes. The pulse in her throat is a wild drumbeat against my fingers, a stampede of horses in a lightning storm. She's fucking terrified of me, and I'm harder than I've ever been.

The kitten meows from behind me, and when I turn, he's watching me like a silent witness. His eyes wise and brave as he comes closer, daring to pass the monster who took his human mother. Without much of thought, I scoop him up and haul him back to the barn. Today, he will have to learn to share.

ELLA

I'M COMPLETELY IMMOBILE. Frozen in my body, my mind swirling with strange and terrifying images. Am I drunk? High? I can't seem to recall what happened to make me feel this way. But the hallucinations continue, and I could swear I was on an airplane. The rumble of the engines vibrates my eardrums, and it's difficult to distinguish reality from my imagination.

"She's just had a little too much to drink," someone says.

Another seat belt clicks, and something brushes against my face. Is it Alfred? Am I still at the sanctuary?

Seconds and minutes drag on for what feels like an eternity. Everything is so slow. Time has never felt this expansive. For a while, I think I drift off. Or am I just staring at the sky? A pill squeezes past my lips, and it seems familiar. How many of these pills have I had?

The next thing I see is a pair of dark gray eyes. The eyes that have haunted me for weeks. *Thorsen Lykken.* Is he real too, or just a figment of my imagination? He hoists me into his arms, and my face collapses against his chest, hard as steel. He smells clean, like mint and expensive cologne, but not overwhelming. I want to inhale that scent, and I think I do. But then it all starts coming back to me.

The sanctuary. My heel. His threat. *The needle.*

My mouth falls open, and I try to ask where he's taking me, but my lips refuse to move. My muscles are starting to twitch, and it feels like the life is coming back to me. Soon, I can fight him off. I can run away. These are my best-laid plans until he drops me into the seat of another car, securing me before he gets behind the wheel himself. I don't know where we are. That becomes abundantly clear when I observe the passing scenery outside.

Colorful houses dot the landscape as the car speeds along the road, and I catch glimpses of hills and water off in the distance. This isn't England. That much, I know. I'm beginning to wonder if he actually brought me back to Norway. A million different thoughts bounce around my mind, giving me a pounding headache. Or is that the drug?

What will Narcissa do when I don't come home? Will anyone even look for me? No, I don't think they will. She will be angry, but I can't see her actually bothering to worry about my absence. What about Olivia? Relief springs up inside me, only to be dimmed when I remember that she wasn't even home. She didn't know I was there and probably never will. But I remember I had my phone and my purse. Where are they? Did he take those too?

My head flops over to study him, and it occurs to me that whatever he's given me is wearing off. Maybe I shouldn't be so obvious. Maybe I should wait until I'm certain I can move my body and then strike. But how?

The man is a towering steel frame and royalty at that. Which is about the time it occurs to me that none of this makes sense. Why would he take me? How can any of this even be real?

I lick my lips, desperate for water, and then try again. "Why?"

This time, the word comes out as a throaty whisper, and I'm not imagining that I really spoke because Thorsen turns to look at me.

"Why?" he repeats. "Because I can. You asked me what I wanted, Ella. Remember?"

His words should terrify me. I think that would be the normal reaction. But I don't know if it's the drugs or the fact that my entire life has been a series of unfortunate events that's left me numb to my fate. If it isn't one monster, there's always another lurking around the corner. The men who killed my father. Narcissa. Lavinia. Magnolia. And now, Thorsen.

What can he do to me that hasn't already been done?

Grief, so dark and deep, sinks into the chambers of my heart like lava, snuffing out the last flickering flame of hope I held. For me, survival mode has always meant abandoning my feelings and icing over my heart. Numbness is the only way I can function through the bad days anymore. But I think what scares me the most is that when I look at Thorsen, I can't go to that safe place in my mind. I can't turn off my fears, and I feel... *too much.*

I wonder if he can sense that weakness in me when his eyes clash with mine. A bolt of lightning strikes my heart, and adrenaline floods my veins as he narrows his gaze like I'm the enemy. I couldn't see it before, but I see it now. This man hates me.

I shrink into my seat as he turns the car down a private lane, coming to a stop at a secure gate. It's dark outside, and I can't be sure, but I think he punches in a code. When the car lurches forward again, and the gates lock us in from behind, a lump forms in my throat.

I'm likely never getting out of here alive.

"This will be your quarters." Thorsen drapes my body onto the bed, his massive figure blotting me out beneath the soft glow of the lamplight. "Tomorrow, we will discuss expectations."

Expectations?

He lingers for a moment longer than necessary, his eyes burning a path over my face. There isn't a single ounce of warmth radiating from this man, and I understand now why they call him the coldhearted future king. Every word he utters is like a biting wind in a tundra. There is no escape from his hostility.

"Go to sleep," he commands. "You're going to need it."

With that ominous threat, he turns away, his back rigid as he retreats from the room. My blurry eyes dart around the space, trying to determine the next logical step. I should seek out a weapon and prepare myself. But the exhaustion of the day hits me all at once as I sink into the bed, and before I can do anything, my eyes are already drifting shut.

11

THORSEN

"You seem agitated," Calder observes.

It's unnerving how easily he can read me sometimes. But agitated isn't the word I'd use to describe the frantic energy electrifying my veins. I spent half the night pacing the floors of my estate, and in my sleep-addled brain, paranoia takes root. Does he know about my dirty little secret locked up in the guest room? Does he know that I've come completely unhinged?

"I'm just tired," I tell him.

"In that case, you better start mainlining coffee now."

"Why?"

"*Mor* has requested a meeting with you," he says. "And I've been sent here as a carrier pigeon to inform you that if you don't come to her by noon today, she will materialize here instead."

A groan rumbles from my chest. "I can't imagine Father letting her out onto the palace grounds, let alone here. Do you know what this is about?"

"I don't know." Calder tosses a grape into his mouth. "But she said it was important."

I open the fridge and pour myself a glass of orange juice right before Lisbet, my housekeeper, comes scurrying over.

"Can I get you anything else, Your Highness?"

"No."

She shrinks before me and disappears just as fast as she arrived.

"You certainly have a way with women." Calder snorts.

"She doesn't need to like me," I answer bitterly.

He tosses another grape into his mouth and shrugs. "Nobody does."

Ignoring his jab, I rummage through the fridge until I find the fruit and yogurt that has been set aside for this morning's breakfast.

"I have some work to do in my office," I tell him. "Are you going to stay?"

"No." He stands up and stretches. "I have a fencing match this morning. But I'll be at the palace this afternoon."

"I'll see you there."

We part ways, and I take the tray of food down the hall to the row of guest suites that have rarely seen use before. Ella's is the closest in proximity to my master suite. On the off chance she decided to throw a fit last night, I wanted to be able to hear her. But so far, there has been no disturbance whatsoever. When I turn the key in the lock and push open the door, I'm expecting more of the same.

The first thing that registers is a lamp swinging at my head, and when I duck backward, Ella stumbles forward, losing her balance and nearly toppling over completely. But it doesn't stop her from swinging again. Maybe I'm off my game, or maybe I just want to see what she's capable of when she smashes the lamp into my head. It bounces off my skull, the tray in my hands clattering to the ground, food spilling everywhere.

I'm stunned, but more than anything, I'm fucking pissed, and she recognizes that as she tries to bolt. But little Cinderella is no match for me. She hits like a girl, and she runs like one too. She may as well be trying to outrun a cheetah.

My fingers wrap around her arm, dragging her back to me just as she lets out a bloodcurdling scream for help. I curl my palm around her mouth, only for her to bite me as she kicks me in the shin.

I'm a raging fucking bull, nostrils full of steam when I tug her back into the bedroom and slam the door behind me. She continues to fight in my grasp, using every possible weapon at her disposal, including her nails as she rakes them down my arms.

It takes me a full minute to get her under control, pinning her hands behind her back and turning her in my arms to face me as I force her back onto the bed. She's breathing hard, eyes wild as she stares up at the beast she's just awoken.

"You have a fire in you, don't you?" I straddle her body and pinch her face in my fingers. "But you should know you're only making my cock harder when you fight."

She stills, her baby blue eyes drifting down my body. When they land on the weapon stabbing painfully against the zipper of my trousers, she sucks in a breath.

"That's right." I lean into her and hover above her lips. "I'm going to fuck you."

Her chest heaves as she shakes her head, a pitiful denial. But that fear, that hatred emanating from her is like an aphrodisiac stronger than any other. I don't know what it is about this woman who triggers this depravity in me, but she should know better than to provoke it.

Her claw marks burn into my arms as blood drips from

the side of my temple. When it splashes onto her, she wiggles in my grasp, and for a split second, regret lingers in her eyes.

"Too soft." I drag my bloody fingers over her lips. "Don't you know you should never feel sorry for me?"

She whimpers as I lower my mouth to hers, just enough to inhale her breath. And then I cave, drawing her lip between my teeth and tugging until I taste her blood mingled with mine.

She hisses, and I lick her wound, metallic and biting against my tongue. My cock rests against her hip, deadly, and wanting. I want to squeeze that rigid flesh into her body, claiming every orifice. I want to fuck her and fill her with come until she understands exactly who owns her. But right now, I don't have time for all the things I want to do to her. And we still have a deal to make.

Reaching into the nightstand, I find the length of rope I stashed there in my preparations. When she sees it, it reignites the fire in her, and it's cute how she struggles against me. A valiant effort for someone so small, but she couldn't overtake me even on my worst day.

Within seconds, I have her wrists secured in a column tie, and I take a moment to admire her delicate flesh, wrapped up like a gift for me. But the abrasive rope isn't the only thing that captures my attention. The scars peeking out from beneath her sleeves give me pause. Has she been hiding them from me? And more importantly, how did she get them?

I want to reach out and touch them. I want to ask her what they are, but that conversation will have to wait for another day.

"Word of warning." I fondle the delicate skin on her

wrists. "If you try to resist now, you can expect an unpleasant rope burn."

She flinches at the mention of the word burn, and I take note of it. I like to know the weaknesses of everyone around me, and I can already tell this is hers. But when I remove the knife from my pocket and tease the hem of her shirt, she forgets my warning and thrashes against the restraints, only to cringe a moment later.

"Told you." I dip the blade beneath her shirt, bunch the material up in my hands, and with a solid yank, it splits in half. "The quicker you learn, the easier this will be."

"Why are you doing this?" she demands. "What did I do to make you hate me?"

"You want to know what you did, Ella?" I remove the scraps of her shirt, cutting at any pieces that don't give way freely. "You came to the ball, and you got in my line, and you sat beside me. That is what you did."

"You are an asshole!" she shrieks. "Everything they say is true."

"Tell me something I don't know." I drag the blade of my knife over her beating pulse. "Until then, you can keep your mouth shut."

Her lip quivers, and she tries to hide it, but she can't hide the tears ready to leak from her eyes at any second. The depraved part of me wants to taste those tears. I want to soak them into my tongue, absorb them with my body, and remember what it's like to feel such human emotions.

"You tricked me," she accuses. "You lied to me about the sanctuary."

"I didn't lie to you." I turn my attention to her jeans, unbuttoning them and dragging them down over her hips while she bucks beneath me. "I meant what I said about the sanctuary. I can help, but you have to do something for me."

"What?" She stills, and I use the opportunity to yank her jeans over her ankles and toss them aside.

"I should think that would be obvious now," I say.

"You want me to have... sex with you?" she croaks.

"No." The blade of my knife moves to her panties, swiftly cutting the band in two. "I want to fuck you."

She shakes her head automatically as if the thought is so abominable, she can't even consider it. It only makes me more eager to turn her into my little slut, begging on her knees for my cock.

"You're... insane." She blinks. "You can't really mean this."

"Oh, I do." I tear the scraps of her panties away, and she squeezes her thighs together, horrified by the fact that she's almost naked. But there's still one last piece left, and when I bring the blade to her bra, her tears finally break free.

She's a shivering mess of nerves when I lean back to examine my new toy. Just as I suspected, she's soft and feminine and so perfect, it almost hurts to look at her. She's a goddess of fire, a force of nature who hasn't yet been awoken to her power. Her only defect is the soft heart beating beneath her ribs. It makes her weak. It makes her the perfect snack for men like me. I just can't believe I'd be the first to exploit her this way.

My fingers dip to the fine patch of hair between her thighs. "Has anyone ever touched you here?"

Her pulse skitters, and she presses her legs together as only a virgin would, but it still feels too good to be true. I can't believe it until I hear the words from her lips. And even then, I still won't believe it until I split her wide open, bathing my cock in the blood of her innocence. There's no way somebody else hasn't already done it. One look at her, and I would be a fool to believe she could be *that* pure.

"I'd rather not say." She lifts her chin, steeling herself.

"Fine." I reach down and tug her nipple between my fingers. "That's just fine, little fire-breather. I have other ways of finding out."

The clock on the mantel confirms I'm running out of time, and the last thing I need is my mother showing up here. So, for now, I have to put my toy away. Lock her in a gilded cage until I can come back and admire her again.

"It's almost time for me to leave you, *min gudinne*. But first, we need to make sure we don't have another incident like this morning."

Her eyes widen, and she struggles against me as I hoist her naked body up over my shoulders. She's so slight it takes very little effort, and I wonder about her ability to take all the darkness I have to give as I carry her to the St. Andrew's Cross on the other side of the suite. I wonder if Ella has even had time to notice the contraption or the wall of tools designed for pleasure and pain.

"What are you doing?" she shrieks as I set her down in front of the apparatus and force her legs apart to secure her ankles.

"You misbehaved this morning," I inform her. "And now you have a punishment coming your way."

"Please—"

Her cries fall on deaf ears as I loosen the rope around her wrists and jerk her arms up above her head to secure them in the last two restraints. When I step back to examine my masterpiece, I'm not quite certain I ever want to take her down. She's a deity up on my altar, and it would be just as tempting to worship her, which leaves me feeling unsettled.

Yes, she's pretty, but she's just a toy. A vessel to provide me a distraction and a release. If this is going to work, I can't allow myself to think otherwise. But I'm having difficulty remembering that with her blue eyes staring deep into my soul, rattling me on a level I'm not accustomed to.

"Where is Alfred?" she chokes out.

"Alfred?"

"The kitten." Her voice wavers. "You didn't... hurt him... did you?"

Her assumption prickles more than it should. To hear that her opinion of me is really that low irritates me more than all the others. I've been accused of many things in my life, but barbarity toward innocent animals isn't one of them.

"The kitten is fine," I answer sharply. "He was safely tucked away in the barn when we left."

She eyes me suspiciously but seems to accept what I'm telling her as the truth. "Are you going to leave me here like this?"

"Did you have any doubts that I wouldn't?" I trace the line of her jaw beneath my fingers, and she shivers. "That is the point of punishment. You will grasp this concept soon enough, should you accept my offer."

"Are you telling me I have a choice?" she challenges.

"You always have a choice." I shrug. "You chose to sneak into the palace and lie about your identity. You chose to get into my line with an ulterior motive, passionately delivering a speech for those animals you wish to help. And finally, you chose to get into my car, and now here you are. You've come this far in your pursuit. You just have one last decision to make."

"What is it?" She swallows.

"You can go back to England to face the consequences of your fraudulent actions at the palace, or you can choose to save your precious sanctuary."

Her shoulders cave inward, but she lifts her chin, determined to show her bravery. "What would I have to do?"

The words sound like sweet music to my ears, but I refuse to let my victory show. I already know what she will choose. This woman doesn't have an ounce of self-preservation in her body. She isn't capable of being selfish, and despite the light that shines out of her like sunbeams, I can recognize the darkness in her too.

"Two months," I tell her. "Two months of doing whatever I want, whenever I say. You will submit to me, and you will please me. And for every day you spend in my captivity, serving me, I will donate a sum of three thousand pounds to the Hilliard Animal Sanctuary. And when our time comes to an end, I will donate one additional lump sum based on how satisfied I am with our time together."

Silently, she does the math in her head, calculating how many animals she could save with this money she so desperately wants. But doubt still lingers in her eyes. She doesn't know if she can trust me.

"I will make the first donation by the end of the day, should you choose to accept, and you will have the evidence of each receipt delivered to your room by morning."

She doesn't answer me right away. It's taking longer than I anticipated as she debates her options, and I can't have that.

I check my watch and issue an ultimatum. "You have thirty seconds to accept or decline my offer before I remove it entirely."

"Yes!" she blurts, horrified by her response. "I accept."

"Very well." I give her one last lingering touch before I turn my back on her. "I'll be back later, *gudinne*."

12

THORSEN

"THORSEN!" My mother gasps when I walk into the room. "What on earth happened to you?"

Calder raises a brow at me, doing a poor job of hiding his curiosity. He knows the gash on my head wasn't there this morning when he saw me, but he won't argue when I give my mother an excuse.

"It's nothing. I slipped and hit my head on my morning run."

My mother gestures for her nurse to wheel her closer so she can fuss over my wound, inspecting it as if I might bleed out before her eyes. She worries too much, but I never deny her these moments to show she cares because this is what she lives for.

"Calder said you requested to meet with me." I take a seat beside her, and she offers me a warm smile.

"Indeed." She reaches out for my hand, and I resist the urge to recoil from human touch as I usually do, for her sake.

"How are you feeling today?" I ask.

"I'm just fine." She waves my concerns away. "Nothing to worry about."

"Oh, good, you're here." My father enters the room with the subtlety of a hurricane. "Have you told him yet, Frida?"

"Told me what?"

He takes a seat beside my mother, narrowing his focus on me. My mother looks worried, and she removes her hand to touch his arm, her gentle way of letting him know she wants to deliver this news, whatever it is. Still, he chooses to disregard her.

"We have been informed by your secretary that you've been gallivanting around England to find some mystery woman from the ball."

My body becomes unnaturally still, and I glance at Calder, who seems just as concerned as I am about where this conversation might be heading.

"It seems she made quite an impression on you," my mother adds softly. "So, I think you will be happy to hear we have discovered the very woman you were looking for."

"You have?" Alarm stirs inside me.

The king nods briskly, a lingering note of bitterness in his tone that I never accepted Princess Yasmine. "We have invited her and her family to stay at the palace for a length of one month. Adequate time for you to get to know her in a controlled setting. After which, we can announce your engagement."

"Engagement?" I scoff. "You want me to marry... who exactly?"

"It's the woman from London," my mother answers hopefully. "Lavinia Maddison."

The air in my lungs turns to ice as the consequences of my behavior comes back to haunt me. I was aware that Hayes would run back to my parents with this information, but I could never have imagined they would bring that dreadful woman here.

"Don't you think you're getting a little ahead of yourselves?" Calder asks. "He barely knows this woman. You can't expect him to marry her after one month—"

"I have been patient for long enough!" My father slams his fist down onto the table. "Your mother has gone to a lot of trouble to bring this woman here. I've given you time and space. I've indulged your refusals of perfectly suitable women. But you can no longer afford to shun your responsibilities. I will see you married in three months, and this is not negotiable."

I bite my tongue as my mother's face crumples. She's visibly shaken, and I seem to be the only one who remembers that stress can aggravate her condition.

"Don't get yourself so worked up, Elias." She pleads with the king. "It isn't good for your heart."

"My heart will give out before the New Year if the gods have anything to say about it. And then where will we be? A son who is woefully unprepared to take his place at the throne, let alone take care of his ailing mother."

"Don't ever question my abilities to take care of her," I snarl, rising to my feet. "She will never want for anything."

"Please," my mother begs with tears in her eyes as she reaches out to touch my arm. "Let's not fight today. A beautiful woman is waiting to meet you this afternoon. And I'm certain you will be pleased to see her again."

My eyes drift over her face, and she seems thinner than the last time I saw her, only a week ago. Maybe it's my imagination, or maybe she truly is getting frailer every day. But I know I can't afford to crush her spirits now. Her only desire is to see me at peace, and I can't fault her for that.

Leaning in, I place a gentle kiss on her cheek. "I'm sorry, *Mor*. I don't mean to upset you."

"You could never upset me." She squeezes my hand in hers and then releases me. "Now, come. Let's put this stress behind us and meet this lovely woman and her family."

"Your Royal Highness." Lavinia offers an overly exaggerated curtsy as I enter the room. "What a pleasure it is to see you again."

She's wearing a yellow floor-length gown that's entirely too formal for this afternoon's tea session, and it does nothing for her ghostly complexion.

My mother prods me along, encouraging my manners as I greet her mechanically.

"I believe the last we met, you were telling me how you'd lost your shoe."

"Of course." She turns her attention to her mother, who seems to be preserved by plastic as she forces a tight smile.

"Your Highness." Narcissa greets me in a slightly less dramatic fashion. "It's such a pleasure. I think you'll be amused to learn we brought her heel with us for the occasion. We thought it would provide a bit of humor."

"I don't doubt that," I remark dryly, wondering what they will produce.

"Magnolia." Narcissa snaps her fingers. "Go and fetch your sister's shoe, will you, darling?"

"Is that really necessary?" My mother arches a brow at me. "We're about to have tea."

"It won't take long, I'm sure." I nod and help my mother to her seat at the table while Narcissa and Lavinia follow suit. Calder isn't far behind, but my father has willfully chosen to abandon this mission, given that we can barely tolerate each other for longer than twenty minutes.

My mother gestures for the steward to prepare our tea, and I look at Calder, who seems far too amused by this turn of events.

"I thought perhaps you could show Lavinia some of our beautiful city this week?" My mother opens the conversation.

Lavinia does her best to remain poised, but her eyes betray her satisfaction. She already feels like she's won, and I don't have the patience to deal with this situation. But the alternative is to send her away only to have the king produce someone else to fill her place. The question is, how long can I tolerate Lavinia before things implode?

"I have a busy schedule this week," I answer stiffly. "But I could find some time on Friday, perhaps."

"Perfect!" Narcissa exclaims.

"In the meantime, I've organized for them to tour the palace grounds and see a few highlights around the city," my mother says. "Then I thought if the weather improves over the next few weeks, we could take them out onto the yacht."

"That sounds amazing." Lavinia plays her role perfectly, vying for an Academy Award. "I can't think of anything I'd love more."

The steward appears with our tea and an assortment of finger sandwiches, scones, and pastries about the same time Magnolia enters the room. Unlike her sister, she isn't quite as skilled at hiding her true colors as she forks over the silver heel.

"See?" Lavinia displays it with an unwavering confidence that she's fooling everyone. "Just like the other one."

"Is it?" I challenge.

She holds my gaze as her mother lets out a nervous

laugh. "Well, they did have to add some additional crystals, since the others had fallen off."

"It's a lovely shoe." My mother nods. "I've never seen one quite like that."

"I don't suppose I have either."

My words leave an unsettling silence in the room, which my mother quickly covers by asking the steward to pour the tea. After selecting our preferences and filling our plates, I sit through another hour of conversation, answering questions and nodding along as Lavinia and her family attempt to charm the queen.

"I have to leave," I interrupt the women as my watch signals the new hour. "Calder and I have a sporting match we promised to attend this evening."

"Oh, I didn't realize." My mother frowns. "Both of you?"

"Yes," Calder covers smoothly. "Thor has been invited to do some sport shooting over at the Eriksen estate, and I said I would join him as well."

"I see." She sets down her teacup. "Well, Thor, please do let me know about your schedule this week. I like to plan ahead, as you know."

Her words cast a gloomy shadow over the room. My mother doesn't like to plan ahead. She's always been known for her lively spirit of adventure. But the truth is, she doesn't want anyone to know how advanced her cancer is, and the only way she can control that is to organize everything around her.

"I'll let you know." I kiss her on the cheek, and Lavinia rises, expecting a similar farewell. I dismiss her with a nod.

"Lavinia, Narcissa, Magnolia. Until next time."

13

ELLA

I WIGGLE my fingers against the restraints, attempting to bring some blood flow back to my limbs. It feels like hours have passed, but the clock on the mantel is too far away to tell for certain. Several times, I've considered screaming for help, but the fact that nobody came to my rescue during my great escape this morning makes me believe I'm in a part of the house that isn't easily heard.

The quarters I'm in, as Thorsen called them, consists of a bedroom, a bathroom, and an office. Each room is decorated in shades of white and gold, and it's surprisingly light and airy. Every piece of furniture seems more expensive than the last, and I can't imagine what the rest of the estate must look like. But right now, I'm more concerned about all the instruments of torture around me. Whips and paddles and ropes of varying lengths. Half of the room is outfitted like a tool shed with strange apparatuses carefully hung from hooks. Beneath those, a white apothecary cabinet spans the length of the entire wall. It would have been convenient if I had noticed those things this morning before I heard the door unlock. But in my rush, I grabbed the first thing I could, which turned out to be a bedside lamp. When I close my eyes, I can still recall the sickening thud it made when it came in contact with Thorsen's skull.

I've never hurt anybody in my life, and I don't think I've ever been so horrified as I was when I saw the blood dripping from his temple. But I was little more than a wild animal at that point, fighting for my life. My freedom. Whatever waited outside these grand walls for me.

Then he came in here and flipped everything on its head with his offer. It was so much money. So easily disposable to this powerful man, like it would mean nothing for him to write those checks every day. But it comes at a cost to me. To my soul. And I still can't believe I said yes.

For the entirety of his absence, I have debated whether I've lost my mind, swinging wildly from one extreme to the next. I should tell him I changed my mind. But every time I consider that I imagine the sanctuary... gone. Olivia bankrupt. Animals without homes.

Is it really so awful to give myself to this man for two months? The same man I dreamed about in this way? I've already imagined him inside me. I've considered what he'd taste like, how his hands would feel on my body when he touched me.

I don't have to like him to enjoy his touch, right? And it's easy to reason that he couldn't do anything worse than what I've already experienced at the hands of Narcissa and her daughters. He could hit me, bruise me, torment me, and it wouldn't be anything outside the realm of what I've already lived. But he can never truly hurt me. Not where it counts. Not if I steel myself to withstand whatever challenge he throws at me. Except, the truth is, I don't know what to expect from this wicked prince. Because I have never been touched by a man; the kiss he gave me this morning was my first. It was dark, and it was violent, and still, shame lingers within me as I squeeze my thighs together and feel the sticky residue of my arousal there.

How is it possible that I could be so affected by my fight with him? There must be something wrong with me. That's the only conclusion I'm able to draw.

Logical or not, what he's offering me is too good to be true, and I can't turn it down. Not when it means I could save the sanctuary.

The lock on the door turns, and my head whips toward it, the breath catching in my lungs. Is it possible that anyone else has a key? Or is it him? I don't know which possibility is worse, but when the door opens, and Prince Thorsen's shadow falls over the floor, a strange sense of relief floods my muscles. Better the devil you know, I guess.

Across the room, his eyes capture mine as he shuts the door behind him and turns the key in the lock. His shoes clip across the floor as he comes to stand in front of me, a towering amalgamation of flesh and bone.

"Have you learned anything in my absence, little fire-breather?" He reaches out to caress my face.

I bite my lip and hope I'm not betraying myself when goose bumps break out along my skin. How long has it been since I've felt human touch? How long have I been starving for such a simple gesture of affection that I would lean into the very palm of the man who has taken me captive?

"I asked you a question." His voice is a warning. "And I expect an answer."

"My arms are numb." I force the words from my dry lips. "And my feet hurt. I'm thirsty, tired, and hungry."

"Good girl." He reaches down to pinch my nipple between his fingers again, and I arch back into the frame of the cross. "I'm going to let you down in a moment. But first, tell me who Charlotte is to you. And before you consider lying to me, remember that I have your phone."

Shit. My phone. How had I forgotten about that? Has Charlotte called me? Will she start to worry when she doesn't hear from me? These are things I'll need to address, but first, I have to deal with the man in front of me. The man who holds my fate in his hands.

"She's my friend," I tell him. "We met at school."

"And does Charlotte know you spend time at the sanctuary?"

I don't understand why it matters, so I nod.

"Good. Then she won't have any problem believing you've gone away to earn money."

He begins the task of removing my arms from the restraints, carefully examining my wrists and rubbing them as blood rushes back into my fingers. It feels like a thousand pins stabbing me at once, and I fight back a grimace as he soothes the pain that he inflicted. How can one man be so divided by darkness and light? How can he possibly soothe the wounds he caused? I don't know, but I'm more nervous than ever about our arrangement when I look up into his eyes, getting lost in those desolate pools.

"Will I be able to talk to my friends myself?" I ask.

"Olivia will receive a letter from you in the morning," he informs me. "The same goes for your friend Charlotte. As far as both of them are concerned, you've found a job overseas to help the sanctuary, and you went to work on a ship where you won't have any service. A limited opportunity presented itself, and you didn't have any time to allow a proper goodbye."

My heart palpates as I consider what he's telling me. "You sent that letter before I even agreed?"

"Like you wouldn't have." He flashes his teeth as his lips

curl into a sinister smile. "Ella, we both know you were never going to tell me no. In time, I think you will even come to realize that it's the last thing you want to tell me."

"I'm here because I care about the sanctuary." I glare at him. "But I will never derive pleasure from your twisted games."

He laughs, dipping his head to my neck, inhaling me before his lips graze the shell of my ear.

"Mark my words, *gudinne*. You'll beg for my cock. My touch. My violence. And when I've finished with you, you'll wish it had never ended."

A shock of pain spreads through me, and it takes me a moment to realize he bit my ear. On instinct, my hands come up to shove him away, but he catches my wrists, pinning them between us as he leans into my body.

"Think twice," he warns. "You won't like the consequences."

"You already punished me." My lip quivers as I dare to meet his eyes.

"Punished you?" He arches a brow. "I haven't even begun to punish you yet."

Fear licks along my veins, and my nerves come to life as he removes the last of my restraints and drags me over to the bed. I don't know what to expect when he pins me face down in his lap, holding me in place with one hand clamped around my thigh while the other pushes into the center of my back.

"Tell me, little fire-breather." His palm comes to stroke the curve of my ass. "Are you a virgin?"

I bite my lip, resolving not to answer that question, only to yelp when he smacks my ass so hard, I swear I see the bright lights of heaven just ahead. Before I can even gulp in another breath, he smacks me again, forcing my legs apart when I try to squeeze them together. It isn't just the pain, but the fact that he can see all of me that's terrifying.

"Ow!" I hiss.

"Does it hurt already?" he mocks. "I'm just getting warmed up. Now answer the question."

Another slap. I jolt in his arms, desperate to get away, but he rains down blow after blow, smacking my thighs, my ass, and even my pussy at one point. When he drags his fingers over my back and smears my arousal into my skin, the humiliation threatens to swallow me whole.

How can I possibly be turned on by this? I hate him. I hate him for making me so confused and turning me into his pet because he has no heart. That anger blackens every cell in my body and turns into a raging pit of lava in my stomach. At some point, it all bubbles to the surface, spewing from my lips like a volcano. I call him every nasty word I can think of, and when that does nothing, I resort to my baser, childlike instincts.

"I hate you! I hate you! I hate you!"

He laughs, thrusting his fingers into the slippery mess between my thighs.

"You hate me?" His voice is rough and hungry, and it does something to my insides, twisting them up until I'm so unhinged, I can't think straight. "I think your body disagrees, Ella. Don't toy with me, or you'll discover exactly what all ten inches of my royal cock feels like when I bury it deep inside you. Your first time can be gentle or rough. The choice is yours."

That notion terrifies the rebellion right out of me.

"Okay, fine," I blurt. "I'm a virgin! Are you happy now?"

"Ecstatic," he growls, an undercurrent of primal possession in his tone. "You just bought yourself a few days. But don't expect that means you'll be lying around relaxing."

I don't know what he means by that until he unceremoniously dumps me onto the carpet and makes himself comfortable on the edge of the bed.

"Have you ever sucked a cock?" He stares down at me as he unzips his trousers.

"No." I swallow, my eyes darting to the massive bulge between his thighs.

"So innocent," he murmurs. "When this week is through, *gudinne*, you'll know how to suck cock like it's your sole purpose in life. Now fetch mine."

I freeze, my eyes on his, and I can't bring myself to do it. More than anything, I think I'm scared to see it. I knew this was coming when I agreed to our deal, but I was brave this morning, and now, between his spread thighs, my courage has abandoned me.

"Fetch my cock," he orders, the muscles in his throat working. "Or I'll get it myself and shove it down your throat."

His threat spurs me into action, and my fingers shake as they graze the black briefs peeking out from his open zipper. When his heat radiates into my palm, I gasp, and Thorsen groans. It catches me off guard, but when I look up at him, his eyes are liquid pools of fire, and I can see something in them I didn't before. He wants this. He wants it so badly his whole body is ablaze beneath my touch. It's something I didn't expect, and the power is intoxicating.

My fingers curl around the cotton fabric and gradually slip the band down, unveiling his royal manhood. And though I have nothing to compare it to, I'm fairly certain the hulking beast of flesh pointing directly at my face isn't normal by any standards. As if Thorsen can read my mind, he strokes my hair, gentle again, while he murmurs his only assurance.

"You'll get used to it."

I can't be sure whether it's curiosity or contempt that has me reaching out to pet the large cock on display. His skin is so soft it surprises me. I don't know what I expected, but it certainly wasn't this silky flesh wrapped around the steely girth.

"Taste it," he orders, his voice hoarse.

When I hesitate, he cups the back of my head and urges me forward. I lick my lips, opening them just as his cock bumps against my teeth.

Thorsen tangles his fingers into the long strands of my hair, but to my relief, he gives me room to explore this on my own. I've read plenty of Lavinia's women's magazines before. There were always quizzes and tips about spicing up the bedroom. But it was more of a form of entertainment than actual study for me, and now, suddenly, I'm aware that my execution won't be as smooth as he probably anticipates. When I look up, I expect to find disappointment on his face, but to my surprise, all I see is hunger reflected at me along with a growing level of impatience.

I wrap my hand around the thick base, and his cock throbs in my palm as I draw the head forward and smooth it over my lips. It's salty and musky, and I'm not sure what to think of it, but when Thorsen rumbles his approval, it spurs me on.

My tongue darts out and swirls around the head, and his entire body contracts beneath me. His muscles are so taut it feels like I'm leaning into a brick wall. When I peek up at him, his lips are parted in what I can only describe as visceral pleasure.

"Keep going." He twists his grip on my hair, harnessing his restraint, and it occurs to me that's what this really is. If he had his way, he'd already have his cock lodged into my throat, pumping away at my face. The image makes my nipples tight, and I try not to think too much about the reasons as I slip his cock past my lips and draw the tip farther into my mouth.

My illusion of control swiftly disintegrates when Thorsen palms the back of my head and forces himself deeper with a groan. Panic makes me dig my nails into his trousers as my eyes water, and I fight the urge to gag. Just when I'm convinced this is how I'm going to die... with a cock in my throat... he pulls back and allows me to take a breath.

"You're so pretty, *min gudinne.*" He massages my jaw beneath his fingers. "I'm going to wreck you."

I whimper as he drags my mouth back to his cock, gentler this time, easing me into a comfortable rhythm as my lips glide over his shaft. Thorsen closes his eyes, his fingers going lax in my hair, and for the briefest of seconds, I catch a glimpse of him not as a monster, but a man. A man who's been starving for this.

Logically, I know it doesn't make any sense. He could get any woman he wants, asshole or not. In Lavinia's own words, he's hot, rich, and royal. Nothing else matters to a lot of the women he comes across, I'm sure. And at this moment, as I kneel before him, worshipping his royal cock, I actually feel a fraction of sympathy for him.

What kind of life he must live, never knowing who to trust. Is this why he came for me? He saw my weakness, and he exploited it, but is it because he's tired of being exploited too? I shake away those thoughts and suck him harder, deeper. His grunts of pleasure are my reward, and I don't know why my body seems to respond every time I hear them.

I keep reminding myself that I'm not here because I

want to be. But those lines become blurred when Thorsen's fingers kiss my face, playing me like an instrument only he understands. His eyes are fixated on me when his body goes rigid, his cock pulsating while his grip intensifies.

"Deeper," he urges, but it isn't a request. It's a command, followed by him forcing his cock into the back of my throat and holding me there as he growls, hot jets of come shooting into my mouth.

I gag, and he softens his grip, withdrawing his cock and leaving me to wipe my face as he studies me. I rub my jaw, peeking up at him as I swallow the last of his release, and in his eyes, I recognize his confusion. But I can't understand the cause of it. Whatever relief he may have felt at the moment has been replaced by a renewed tension.

"Do better next time." He tucks himself away and zips his trousers back up, standing abruptly. "You'll have the week to practice until your patch is in effect."

"Patch?" I question.

But he doesn't acknowledge me. He's already walking toward the door.

14

THORSEN

"WHAT THE HELL is going on with you?" Calder removes the fencing mask and tosses his sabre aside. "You're not even paying attention."

"Nothing's going on." I tear off my own mask and chuck it onto the mat as I reach for a bottle of water.

"Talk to me." He scowls. "Or you know I'm going to assume the worst."

When I meet my brother's gaze, a part of me feels guilty for hiding the little fire breathing animal worshipper in my guest room. Calder and I have never had secrets. Not since the first one almost tore us apart. But I'm aware of what will happen if he discovers her, and maybe I'm just selfish. We've had a history of sharing women. He helped me through my formative years, paving the way for the only semblance of a normal sex life I've known. For years, that situation has worked. He did the talking and charming, and I could just get a release. But when it comes to Ella, I want her only for myself. It's a thought I don't want to examine too closely. For now, it's just better if Calder doesn't know.

"You have no need to worry," I tell him. "I'm just... distracted."

Sorrow settles into his features. "The last time you told me I didn't need to worry, I almost lost you."

My throat squeezes at the memory of that dark day. Calder was the one who found me with the noose around my neck. If I learned anything from that experience, it was that it almost destroyed him to see me like that. Next time, I won't make the same mistake.

"I've spoken with Dr. Blom," he says. "He agrees that I should attend one of your sessions. *Mor* thinks it's a good idea as well."

I pivot, my palm twitching with the urge to deck my brother. "You told *Mor* about this?"

"She was concerned." He cocks his head to the side. "You didn't seem as excited as she thought you would about Lavinia."

"That's because I'm not."

"If she isn't the woman you've been looking for, then who is?"

I crane my neck from side to side, attempting to release the pent-up pressure that seems to be a permanent resident there. "It makes no difference."

"I've never seen you so out of sorts. And then you showed up with a gash on your head, which I still don't believe happened on your run."

"Believe what you want." I reach for my bag and start stripping out of my uniform. "I'd rather not meet with the inquisition every time I see you."

"Then stop lying to me," he growls.

"I have to go."

"Thor." He snatches my arm, halting me. "Just promise me... you aren't going back to that hole again."

My eyes cloud over, and my brother becomes little more than a blurry shape as I stare back at him. "I'm tired of this conversation. Don't ask me again."

"I have your lunch."

Ella turns away from the wall, dropping the flogger in her hand with a guilty expression. She's more curious than I expected her to be, and I'm not quite certain what to make of her behavior. I can't imagine what her thoughts are. She isn't easy to read like other women, and she never does what I expect. It fascinates me, and it irritates me.

"Thank you."

She watches me as I set the tray down onto the small table near the door. Her arms are folded, and she's in the robe from her bathroom. I should scold her for that, but I think maybe I like this small act of defiance just as much as she does.

I'm still thinking of her lips wrapped around my cock, and it's unsettling how much upheaval she's created in my sense of normalcy. I've had blow jobs before. I've had releases before. But I've never had someone worship me the way that Ella did. I've never felt... *so much*. Her passion. Her pretty eyes staring up at me with the desire to please me. The warmth seeping back into my veins and reminding me that I'm human. I don't know what the fuck she's doing to me, but I don't like it. And still, I'm considering how long is reasonable before I make her do it again.

"Come eat," I order.

Her eyes dart to the food, and she hesitates. I can't understand why. She's hardly eaten since she's been here, and I don't want the added task of forcing food down her throat.

"I don't think I can sit," she says finally.

"Your ass is still sore?"

She nods, and something like guilt settles into my gut. I've never had to take care of someone before. I don't even know where to begin. She's mine now, and if I were a true dominant, I would know how to take care of my toys. But Ella is the first who's only ever been mine, and this is new for me.

I think I should tell her to deal with it because I can't afford to be soft with her. But even as I'm telling myself that, I'm walking into the bathroom and digging through the cupboard. When I find the aloe, I return and try to appear as if I know what the hell I'm doing.

"Come here." I sit down on the edge of the bed, and Ella obeys me, padding over to me softly.

Setting the bottle aside, I reach for the knot on her robe and untie it, pushing the seams apart until the silky material slides off her shoulders and pools on the floor. Her nipples are tight, and I want to bury my face in the softness of her tits right now.

I need to focus on what it is I'm meant to be doing, so I tug her closer and hoist her body up, laying her across my thighs. The soft, rounded curves of her ass still bear the marks of my handprints, and I'm not surprised that she's hesitant to sit. She will feel me every time she does, and the idea is far too agreeable for my own liking.

Squeezing some aloe from the bottle, I smear it over her ass cheeks, and she sucks in a breath between her teeth. My hand pauses, and I try to gentle my touch for her benefit, which has the immediate effect of making her relax against me.

I continue to massage the aloe into her skin, long after it's even necessary. But my eyes are on her face, studying the lines and slopes. Her eyes flutter in appreciation when my fingers skim over her curves. I didn't see it before, but I can see it now. She likes my affection.

I should stop. I shouldn't ever give her what she wants. But instead, my fingers slip between her thighs. Ella whimpers when I touch her clit, and her eyes fly open, snaring mine into a holding pattern I can't seem to break. Neither one of us can look away as I continue to stroke her. Within seconds, her lips part and her body responds to me. I've never experienced someone so reactive to my touch, and I want more. I want all of it.

I pull her up, startling her as I flip her onto her back and lower my body over hers. My fingers find their home between her thighs again, and I latch onto her breast with my mouth, sucking at her until she arches up into me, her fingers curling into my hair. It's an unwritten rule that she isn't supposed to touch me, but I don't stop her. I don't stop her because it feels strangely comfortable.

When I'm done assaulting her tits with my mouth, I do the next illogical thing, which is to bring my lips to hers. Ella kisses me back, and I swallow her pleasure as I bring her closer to climax. Our faces are a breath apart, and it's an intimacy I've never known. But I can't stop touching her, tasting her, inhaling her. I feel drunk and feverish when she comes with a strangled cry. Her fingers dig into my scalp, and it only intensifies the manic energy surging through my body. Long after I've milked the last of her release from her, I'm still kissing her. Branding her with my hands and teeth and lips. I don't know what the fuck she's doing to me.

"Ella, stop," I demand, but I'm the one who can't stop.

She looks up at me, confusion shining in her eyes, and I

know I've betrayed the war inside my head. She can see how she's affecting me. When I rear back with a ragged breath, the ice fortress I've built around me freezes her out again. Nobody gets inside. Not even her.

"Eat your goddamn lunch." I stagger away from her and head for the door. When I slam it behind me, I collapse against the wall outside, trying to figure out what the fuck just happened.

15

THORSEN

RESTLESSNESS BREEDS with every passing second of the afternoon as Hayes shuttles me from one royal obligation to the next. Meetings, tea appointments, agendas to discuss. It never ends. And when he tells me that my father would like to meet with me, my blood pressure skyrockets.

"What for?" I demand.

Hayes blinks as if he can't imagine how I could ever question the king's requests. "I'm not certain. But he asked that you come now."

The threat is left unspoken. There will be consequences if I don't go. Consequences I'm not prepared to deal with. If I don't show up, my father isn't above sending a pair of royal guards to drag me to the palace to present me before him. This is just one way he likes to remind everyone he's in control. He's the king, and whatever he says, we all must do. For thirty years, he's controlled my life. And I'm officially fucking over it. But every time I consider the alternative, I think of my mother.

Hayes signals for the driver to take us to the palace, and I lean my head against the seat and imagine Ella back at my estate. Locked in her room, naked and waiting for me. I picture her on her knees, worshiping me, and for one second, I can pretend that it isn't all fake.

For one blissful second, I can even admit that it felt real. When she looked up at me, so innocent and uncertain, I saw something in her eyes I'm convinced I've never seen before. She wanted to please me. Not for the money. Not because I'm using her for my own twisted purposes. But because there's something so inherently good in her, it feels like she can see right through me.

Delusion. That's what it is. She's doing this because I'm a sick fuck who saw the first opportunity to capitalize on her, and I took it. I would be a fool to believe otherwise, and it's something I can't even consider. Two months. That's what we have together. Two months to use her and wring every ounce of pleasure out of her until I let her fly away. It's the only way this can ever work.

The car pulls to a stop, and a guard opens our doors. Hayes walks beside me, silent, ensuring that he delivers me to my father's office just as he said he would. The palace is quiet today, and I wonder if my mother is entertaining Lavinia and her sniveling relations elsewhere. It's a notion that makes me irrationally angry, considering how frail she already is. I don't want her spending time with them. I don't want her getting attached to women who are merely attempting to scheme their way into the palace. But I also know my mother sees the best in everyone. That's the only way she's managed to stay married to my father for all these years.

"Enter," my father commands after Hayes knocks and announces our presence.

"I'll wait for you in the parlor." Hayes bows and dismisses himself as I open the door and step inside.

My father is at his desk, and his face is pinched as he studies the document in front of him. I take a seat across from him, waiting silently for several moments before he finally spares a glance at me.

"I've rescheduled some of your engagements for the coming weeks," he says.

"Why?" I stare back at him with dead eyes.

"I want you to focus on your guests," he decrees. "Specifically, Lavinia. You will have three dates with her each week. This is non-negotiable."

My jaw flexes so hard my teeth ache. "No."

"No?" My father arches a brow at me. "Do you forget who you're speaking to?"

"I know exactly who I'm speaking to." I challenge him. "And I refuse to spend time with that woman. She is a liar, and a schemer—"

"As are all the women you will encounter in your position," he cuts me off. "You need to learn to make the most of it."

"You speak of things which you can't possibly understand. My mother was never like that."

"Your mother and I married out of duty, and you will do the same. I have given you ample time to find a partner, and I refuse to wait any longer."

"You fail to understand that I haven't found a partner because I don't want one."

"Enough." He slams his fist down onto the desk, rattling the contents on top of it. "I will not be challenged on this, Thorsen. You have an obligation to this family, and your country, to set an example. It's far past time you settle down and show the world you are capable of committing to your royal obligations and a marriage. Your image of a brooding, miserable bastard can no longer be tolerated by me or the media."

"And if I refuse? What then? Will you dress Calder up and parade him around for the masses instead? Find him a wife? Or perhaps you'll suggest that Lavinia is perfectly suited to him as well?"

"You want to know what happens if you refuse?" he snarls. "I will forbid you from the palace grounds, and your mother will be none the wiser. I will cut off all contact between the two of you, and she will spend the last of her days wondering how her son turned out to be so pathetic—"

I launch myself across the desk before I can consider the consequences of my actions, and when my fist smashes into his face, it feels cathartic. For all of two seconds, until he slams me back onto the desk and returns three solid blows himself. I take them, not because I respect him, but because I know I always have to let him win. If I don't, he'll make my life hell.

As I peel myself up off the desk and we glare at each other in the aftermath, I don't doubt for a second that he'll do exactly as he said. My father controls every employee in this palace and every member of our family. If he were to ban me from the grounds, I'd have no recourse to see my mother. And I'd sooner die a slow, miserable death than allow her for one second to believe I wasn't there for her in these final months.

"Three dates a week with Lavinia." The king hurls the words out, breathless. "And you will marry her if it's the last declaration I make. She will be a suitable partner, someone the people can respect, which is more than I can say for you."

He fails to add that he's already excavated her entire background and unearthed everything there is to know about the woman, including her bloodline. After all, it would never suit to have a Lykken married to someone without merit.

"Three dates." I reiterate the words that will continue to haunt me. "For *Mor*."

16

ELLA

MY FINGERS GRAZE the length of the whip hanging on the wall, and I study it with uncertainty. It appears to be hung for decorative purposes, but could it be possible that he intends to use it on me? Will he want to use any of these things on me?

I don't know the exact purpose of all the different floggers and paddles and restraints on display. My knowledge on this subject originates from the few bits and pieces I read in a *Cosmo* magazine. After Lavinia read the article, she whined for a whole month about how she would never let a man do those things to her. And that's when I realized for the first time just how messed up I was.

It wasn't that I wanted these things, exactly, but there were parts of the dynamic between a powerful man and a submissive woman that made me recognize something depraved in myself. I was no stranger to pain. Narcissa had been doling it out my entire life. So, when I examine Thorsen's tools of torture, I can only wonder what it would feel like when he uses them on me.

He's already spanked me. He's already fucked my mouth.

And soon, he will destroy the only innocence I have left. True to his word, he delivered the first receipt with proof of his donation to Hilliard, along with a new pack of birth control patches and instructions on how to use them. I put the first patch on yesterday, which means in six more days, it will be effective, and he'll come for me again. When he does, I can't help wondering what will be left of me.

Will he be rough? Will he be gentle, at least for the first time? I swallow as I recall the size of his cock. It's at that moment, the door to my suite opens, and the man himself appears.

Our eyes clash, and it feels like a lightning storm in my veins. Fire crackles in the air between us, and for a split second, I can tell he feels it too. There's something different about him this evening. I can sense it when he locks the door behind him and stalks toward me. Maybe it's the rigid set of his shoulders or the tightness in his jaw. The hurricane in his eyes seems more turbulent than this morning, and on instinct, I back up, bumping into the apothecary cabinet.

"Did I tell you to put on a bathrobe?" he asks, his voice low and menacing.

My fingers curl around the soft material, holding onto it as if he could make it implode merely by looking at it.

"It was in the bathroom."

"I want you naked," he growls. "I want you ready. Don't make me say it again, Ella."

I wasn't wrong about his mood. He looms over me, his features a mask of anguish that runs so deep, I can almost picture the divide in his soul. I want to ask him about it. I want to unearth his most intimate secrets and expose the man hiding within the beast, but that's a dangerous want to have.

My eyes move over his face, and the energy between us shifts again. An electric current. A drop in temperature. Storm Thorsen is coming, and I realize I'm not at all prepared for it.

His fingers curl around mine, prying them away from my robe. Deftly, he unties the knot at my waist and peels the material off my shoulders. The robe pools on the floor, and a shiver moves through me as his eyes rake over me with an intensity that feels like a physical caress.

"Do you want to play, *gudinne*?" He cups my face in his large hand, and unconsciously, I lean into his warmth. For that one second, he is so gentle I could almost believe everything is going to be okay. And then he grabs me by the hair and wrenches my head back so I can't look away from him.

"Tell me how much you hate me."

I'm silent. Tense. Confused. I don't know what he wants from me. It feels like a trick until his eyes betray him. He wants me to provoke him. He wants me to make him angry so he can use that emotion to do whatever he wants.

"Does it matter how I feel about you?" I ask softly. "I'm here so you can do what you like with me. This is what we agreed on."

"Say it," he commands, the vein in his neck throbbing. "Tell me how you really feel."

"My emotions are mine." I level my eyes at him. "You can have my body, but not my thoughts."

"I'll have what I want." He wraps his fingers around my throat, squeezing in warning. "Your only purpose is to please me. Now get on your knees."

When I fail to comply, he cages me in against the cabinet and uses his grip on my throat to arch me back until my legs give out, and I crumple before him. When his hand falls away, I drag in a deep breath, massaging the sting he left behind. There's something so depraved in me to enjoy this. I don't want to analyze it too closely, but his brutality is hard-wired to produce a chemical reaction in me. I want more of this violence. This push and pull between us. I want him to exert his sovereign power over me every chance he gets.

"You're learning." He pets my hair with a tenderness I didn't think he was capable of only a moment ago.

When he hauls my face toward his trousers, my cheek rubs against his erection. It's harder than steel, pulsing against my skin, even through the material.

"Kiss it," he murmurs.

My hands fall onto his leather Oxfords, clinging to his feet as I peek up at him. Is it the magnetic pull between us or our agreement that urges me to bring my lips to the caged beast throbbing in his trousers? I can't be sure of anything right now, only that when I follow his command and kiss his royal endowment, he rumbles his approval, and that sound ricochets through me like a bullet.

Slowly, he unzips his trousers, his eyes searching for something inside me. Revulsion. Deceit. Mistrust. Whatever it is, he doesn't find it. The muscles in his forearm flex, and he glares down at me with obvious disappointment.

"You aren't fooling anyone."

"I'm not trying to," I whisper.

His eyes cloud over, and for a long moment, he just watches me as if he's trying to figure me out. Maybe I'm paranoid, but I think I'm fighting a losing battle with Thorsen. Against my better judgment, I'm here. I'm giving him two months of my life to torment me, control me, own me. But still, he is doubtful.

When he reaches down and tugs the tie from the bathrobe out of the loops, a nervous tension blooms in my gut. He grabs my chin and wraps the fabric belt around my head several times, obscuring my eyes. And I have to wonder why. Why doesn't he want me to see him?

The warmth of his fingers slips away once he's finished, and I'm entombed in darkness. But I can still hear him moving around the room. Opening a drawer in the cabinet, and then another. When he returns, he fists a handful of my hair and tugs me upright again, walking me in a different direction until my knees bump against the bed, and I collapse forward. My face falls against the comforter as he pulls my hips back, spreading my legs apart. His hands feel huge on me, and I don't doubt that he could easily break me. He's the most powerful man I've ever seen, and I don't know how my body will sustain him.

He grabs my wrists and secures them behind my back, binding them with what feels like another rope. And then his fingers trace over the scars on my arms, eliciting a trail of goose bumps down my spine.

"It's a shame to see such beautiful skin destroyed," he mutters.

My body tenses beneath him, but he doesn't acknowledge my discomfort. His warmth disappears for a second, and then I hear a bottle opening. When he touches me again, he glides his palm over the curve of my ass, prying my cheeks apart and forcing me to open for him.

"I can smell how much you want me," he hums. "You filthy little liar. Does your hate for me get you off?"

My lips seal shut. That question feels like too much of a minefield to navigate, and I don't want to go there. Regardless, Thorsen doesn't wait for a response. The next thing I feel is something cold and metallic sliding through my arousal before it settles somewhere forbidden.

"What are you doing?" I jerk as he presses the object against my ass.

"I'm going to fuck you." His hand comes to rest on my lower back, holding me still as he moves the object deeper, forcing it past my resistance. "And I'm going to come in you."

I drag in a ragged breath, paralyzed by the invasion. It feels like I'm being stretched wide open, and it seems to go on forever until he finally halts, seating the object inside me.

"Your Highness—"

He twists the metal, and a thousand sparks shoot through my core as my breath hisses between my teeth. It's so intense I feel like I can't breathe. Or move. Or think.

"Don't call me that," he warns. "Don't call me anything. I'm nothing to you."

He drags me back to the floor again. And this time, I can hear his belt, followed by the rustle of clothing as he shoves his trousers down. The object inside me moves every time I clench, and I don't know how to sit, but Thorsen doesn't give me a choice in the matter when he grabs my head and his cock bumps against my lips.

"Suck it." His rough voice commands.

On his order, my lips part as if they have a mind of their own. But I'm still thinking about how I should resist because it feels like I'm falling into a black hole I'll never climb out of. Those thoughts are swiftly carried away when he groans, his hard flesh sliding over my tongue and all the way to the back of my throat. I gag, and he pulls back, but only for a second before he does it all over again. Spit drips out the sides of my mouth and down onto my breasts, and he rubs it into my skin and tugs on my nipple. I gulp around him, the effect vibrating through me and waking something primal I didn't even know existed. Whoever she is, this animal wants more. It must be her that hums against him as he finds his rhythm, casually fucking my face as he manhandles my skull between his hands.

I can't see him, but I can hear all his sounds. His strangled groans, the hitch in his breath, the contractions of his muscles beneath his flesh. His grip on me falters, and he pulls away as if he wants to stop, only to come back for more. I think I must have woken something primal in him too.

"Enough."

His sharp directive slices through the air as he withdraws without warning and steps away. He's breathing hard, and I can feel his eyes burning into me.

"You said you were a virgin," he snarls. "Are you a liar, *gudinne*?"

"No." I tilt my chin up toward him. "I'm not."

"I don't believe you." His voice is an accusation.

"Don't believe me." My legs fall apart, summoning him. "You'll find out anyway."

There's a long pause, and I'm desperate to know what he's thinking. I don't know what to expect from him, and I think that's what scares me the most.

"Stand up," he orders.

I rise on shaky legs, hissing from the sting of the rug burns on my knees as I wait for his next instructions. When he touches me again, it isn't with affection or roughness. It's merely with purpose when he bends me over the bed, hauling my ass to the edge. The sticky arousal between my thighs perfumes the air around us, and Thorsen drags his fingers through it, using it to wet his cock. When he tugs the toy from my ass, I suck in a breath as something else takes its place. Something hard and undeniably male. He presses the head of his cock against the hole, and I wiggle in his grasp, bucking up only for him to shove me back down.

"It won't fit!" I screech, suddenly panicked.

"It will," he insists. "Now be still, or you really aren't going to like it."

How the hell would he know? That fleeting thought disappears as a wave of different sensations floods my body. Adrenaline shoots through my veins as warmth pools in my belly, and it's all too much. It feels as if I'm being torn in half as he digs his thumbs into the curve of my back and shoves his cock deeper. Just when I think I can't take anymore, he keeps going and going, until finally, he bottoms out, and a guttural sound rattles in my chest.

For a moment, he's so still, I freeze too. Even the slightest hitch in my breath makes me feel him. I squeeze my eyes shut and try to focus on relaxing. On breathing. But I'm just so full. He's so huge. And he's *inside* me.

He moves then, just an inch, maybe two. I can't be sure, but it ignites a fire in me. A bite of pain mixed with an aching emptiness for more. I don't know what that more is until his fingers slip between my thighs, massaging my clit.

He murmurs something that sounds like a curse, but I don't know. It isn't English, and it's so low it's difficult to understand him. I want to curse too as he circles his fingers around the bundle of nerves that feel like they were made just for him. He knows exactly how to touch me, how to make me beg for more. I must be insane. That's the only conclusion I can come to as the monster in me urges me back, rocking my body into his cock.

Thorsen grunts, one hand digging into my hip while the other slowly tortures me. It feels like I'm going to explode, and I think I want to.

"You want to be fucked?" he whispers, leaning his body over mine. I can smell him. The spicy, masculine scent of his aftershave, and the sweetness of his breath. It's an intoxicating combination, and I think something must be wrong with me because I shouldn't enjoy any of this.

"Please." The word leaves my lips like a prayer.

A feral sound bleeds from his lips, and he drags his cock from my warmth, only to feed it to me all over again. A shudder moves over me, and I melt into the bed when he does it again and again, building up a rhythm while his fingers play me like an instrument.

"Come, Ella."

I barely hear him over the blood rushing in my ears. Everything has dulled to a pinpoint. I can't see, I can't hear, I can't even tell if I'm breathing as the pressure reaches a breaking point I'm not sure I'll survive. And then without warning, it happens. He slaps my pussy, and I scream as wave after wave rolls through me, gushing against his fingers and soaking him in the evidence of my body's betrayal.

Another unidentifiable curse heaves from his lips as his fingers dig into my flesh, and he thrusts deep, stilling as his cock pulses inside me. Warmth leaks into my body, and I know he came in me, just as he said he would. For a few moments, neither of us moves. He's still lodged inside me when his breath returns to normal, and he slowly relaxes his grip on my hip. But he doesn't pull away. The hard cock I was so terrified of softens within me, and Thorsen's come drips down my thighs.

Slowly, my heart returns to normal too, and the buzzing in my ears drifts away as I come back down to earth, accepting what still seems too surreal to believe.

The prince just fucked me.

In the ass.

17

THORSEN

SOMETHING HAMMERS against my chest when I look down at Ella bent over with legs spread wide, and my dick still lodged into her tight ass. I should have pulled away, but I can't admit to myself that her warmth is too appealing. Without consciously realizing it, my fingers graze her back. Massaging her. Touching her with a gentleness that she should never know. At least not from me.

My thoughts are at war when I stop, forcing myself into action as I remove her blindfold and pull my wet dick from her. I don't owe her anything, and the next logical step would be to leave her here to look after herself. This was our agreement. I wanted nothing more than the relief her body could provide me. A release that has always felt mechanical, up until now.

When I brought her here, I wanted to cave in to my own selfish desires and consider nothing else. No expectations. No questions or doubts about her intentions. No forced conversations and pressures to be something I'm not. I thought it would be easy, but Ella is changing the game. Something nags at me, insisting there should be a balance.

A small amount of give and take would be fair. But nothing about this situation is fair, and I knew that from the start. I took her, I coerced her, and now I'm going to use her. That won't change. So, what difference would it make for me to give her anything other than my darkness?

Ella peeks at me over her shoulder, cheeks flushed and eyes bright with something I'll never possess. But for now, it has to be enough that I can taste it in her. This light. This goodness.

"What am I supposed to call you?" she asks.

"I already told you." I tuck my dick away and zip up my trousers, avoiding her gaze. "You shouldn't call me anything. I'm nothing to you."

"But you are," she insists.

My nostrils flare, and the energy in the room pressurizes as I wait for a lie to pour from her lips. Will she tell me that I'm royalty, and therefore she should address me as such? Or will she be like the others, professing that I mean something to her when I've only ever given her a reason to hate me?

"You're a person," she says. "And you have a name. There will be times I need to address you, and I'd like to know what's acceptable."

"What would be acceptable is if you had listened to me the first time."

Ella doesn't blink. She just analyzes me as though she's trying to understand me, and it makes me uneasy. My first instinct is to extricate myself from the situation. But I shouldn't be running away from her. She should be the one who's afraid of me.

I need to prove a point to her. She's a fool if she thinks she can humanize me. Trying to get inside my head is against the implicit rules, and it's a punishable offense.

"Stay there," I command.

I can feel her watching me as I choose a leather riding crop from the wall. She's quiet and brave until I turn around and come for her again. But one glance at my face has her scrambling for the door.

I give chase, capturing her around the waist and smothering her scream with my hand. When I force her onto the ground, her face scrapes against the carpet as I straddle her and pin her down with my weight. From this position, I have the perfect view of her come-filled ass.

"Why are you doing this?" she cries. "I did what you wanted."

I can't give her an answer for that, and I want her to understand there won't always be answers. Drawing my arm back, I unleash the crop against her left ass cheek, and she sucks in a sharp breath as red blooms across her skin. But she doesn't cry out. She doesn't make a sound or even flinch. Even when I rain down another blow. And another.

Frustration compounds inside me as I smack her harder and faster. When her welted ass fails to produce the results I want, I venture all the way down to her calves, but she refuses to give me so much as a tear.

"Are you really this accustomed to pain?" I demand.

When she denies me an answer, I grab her foot and slap the arch. Finally, she releases a guttural sound, but it isn't enough. She's challenging me, forcing my hand as I slap the soles of her feet until she screams so loud there can be no doubt her nerves are on fire.

"Please," she begs. "Too much! It's too much!"

My chest heaves as I toss the crop aside and look down at her. Nothing has ever been as beautiful as her body with my marks all over it. Right now, I want to fuck her again. But when her face gives way to silent tears, something inside me cracks. She isn't the first woman I've made cry, and she certainly won't be the last, but this is different somehow. Ella's tears are bleeding emotions from me I don't care to identify. She's fragile beneath me. So soft and pure and... *mine*.

My stomach churns violently as I consider how much I'd like that last sentiment to be true. But I can't. I won't. She's nothing to me. Even now, with my come inside her and my marks on her skin, she's just a toy. A pretty caged bird.

"Let's get you cleaned up." My voice is gentler than I expect, and when I ease my weight off her and scoop her up into my arms, she doesn't protest. If anything, she curls into me, leaning her face against my chest, her eyes shuddering closed.

How can she take comfort in such a monster? How can she not realize how dangerous this is for her self-preservation?

When her eyes flutter open, I force myself to look away as I carry her into the bathroom. I set her down on the chaise and focus on what I have to do, one step at a time, so I can't get caught up in the confusing thoughts poisoning my mind. Placing the stopper in the tub, I turn on the water and adjust the temperature, so it's warm but not too hot. Ella will be sore, and for right now, I think I am done torturing her.

When I gather her into my arms again, she blinks away her own emotions, staring off into the distance as I gingerly place her in the tub. It has to hurt, but she doesn't show any evidence of her pain as I ease her body back against the porcelain. She just lies there, numb and closed off. And I think that bothers me more than anything because I'd much rather have her tears.

I try to focus on what I need to do, adding soap and building a lather in my hands. Starting with her legs, I work my way up to her breasts. When my thumbs graze her nipples, they harden for me, and it feeds my urge to touch her everywhere.

I'm not thinking clearly when my fingers move between her thighs, and I start to toy with her again. Ella sighs, closing her eyes as she gives in to me without even realizing it. She's wet and slippery, and it lends a frantic pace to her pleasure. I study her face, her breath, every sweet sound as I finger her and grope her tits with my free hand. Within seconds, she's already coming for me again, spasms rocking through her body, lips falling apart as she hums out her release.

A goddess on fire.

Her breath calms, and I wash her in all the places I missed, sometimes going over the same curves twice. When I come to the scars on her arms, her eyes fly open, and she tries to recoil. My fingers capture her wrist, locking her in my grip as I survey the mangled skin, touching it with a tenderness I didn't know I was capable of.

"What happened, Ella?"

She swallows, and the bathroom is so quiet I can hear her every breath. I wonder if she'll be open, or if she'll try to keep her secrets. Either way, she won't escape me until I've learned everything there is to know about her.

"It's from the fire," she whispers. "I fell into it and ended up badly burned."

Her story reeks of half-truths, but for now, I don't push it.

"Come." I hoist her body up into my arms again, drenching my own clothes in soapy bathwater. "I'll dry you off, and then I'll bring your dinner."

"Thorsen." My mother lights up when she sees me. "Lavinia will be so pleased you're here. She hasn't spoken of anything else all week."

I force a smile for her benefit and sit down beside her. "I'm more interested in spending some time with you first."

Her eyes dim, and she drags her hand across her lap, trying to reach out for me, but it's not working as well today. Soon, it won't work at all, and this is a stark reminder that these moments are fleeting. The problem is I simply don't know how to make the most of them.

"I thought you'd be happy," she says. "Isn't Lavinia the woman you've been looking for?"

When it takes me too long to answer, it only seems to add to her anxiety.

"Oh, dear. Have I gotten things confused again?"

"No, *Mor*." I squeeze her fingers. "You haven't."

The threat my father made still lurks in the back of my mind, and truthfully, I can't bring myself to admit any alternate reality. My mother has always thought so highly of me, even when everyone else turned their backs. She never abandoned me or told me I needed to snap out of it or tried to correct my behaviors with harsh words and a cold heart. She has only ever been warm and considerate, and I can't bear the thought of her discovering how much of a monster I truly am. If she had so much as an inkling of what I've already done to Ella, she wouldn't have the will to live through the week.

"Thorsen." Her hazy eyes roam over my face. "Have I been a bad mother to you?"

"What?" I inhale sharply. "Why would you even ask me that?"

"I just... I don't know." She stares off into the distance, recalling something I'm probably better off not knowing.

"All these years, things have been so tense between you and your father. And you've always been so... angry. I can't help wondering what I might have done differently."

My eyes fall shut on a sigh, and pain lances through my blackened heart. I have to remind myself that it's better she doesn't know. I've always wanted to protect her from the ugly truths hiding in this family, and now more so than ever. But it doesn't change the regret I carry deep in my soul that she wasn't the first person I went to in my time of need.

"F-f-father, may I speak with you?"

He looks up at me from his desk, his face stern. Even at ten years old, I understand that he's a man with many burdens. Too many to count. I don't want to be another. But I'm scared, and I'm tired, and the pain is too much to keep inside anymore.

"What is it, Thor?" he asks. "I'm busy."

My lips freeze, and my body ices over as I wonder if I should just leave. I don't want to make him mad. All I ever seem to do is bother him. But the pain, I feel it every time I move. Every step I take. Every breath I inhale. I've never known such pain, and even now, my eyes are blurry with unshed tears. Father always tells me that men don't cry. I know I can't let those tears fall because it will make me weak. But I also know if I leave here right now, I'll be a different sort of coward.

"I-i-it's about the speech therapist," I blurt. "Ms. Nilsen."

"What about her?" He drops his pen, focusing his attention on me. And for a minute, I think it will be okay. I think he will help me.

"I d-d-don't want to do p-p-private lessons with her anymore," I tell him, harnessing my bravery like every hero I've ever read about has taught me to do.

"And why is that?" His eyebrows pinch together, and the vein in his forehead throbs. Is he angry with me or Ms. Nilsen?

"She d-d-did something to me," I whisper, the shame eating

me from the inside out. "S-s-she does stuff to me. Bad stuff. She t-t-touches me, and it hurts—"

My father's desk rattles as he stands, startling me. I stumble back into the door behind me, and fear steals the breath from my lungs when he rounds the desk, looming over the room like a dark cloud.

"You dare to come in here and lie to my face?" he roars. "Is it not bad enough that I have a fucking retard for a son, and now you want to make up stories because you're too lazy to do what's required of you. You'd be so lucky to have a woman like Ms. Nilsen even look twice at you, you pathetic little fuck."

My mouth dries up, and my body trembles so badly, I can't move or speak or think. I hate myself for this. I should never have come to him. I should have hidden the pain, stuffed it down, and forgot about it. This is what always happens. I freeze when I need to move. The same thing happens with Ms. Nilsen, and I just want it to end. I want everything to end. But it's far from over when my father grabs me by the collar, shaking me.

"I asked you a question." Spittle flies from his lips and hits my face, and all I can focus on is that throbbing vein in his forehead that looks like it's going to explode.

He yanks me up off the floor and drops me face down onto his desk, tugging me back, so my legs hang over the edge. I know what's coming, but I'm paralyzed, and when his palm collides with my ass, a guttural scream erupts from my belly until I no longer sound human.

Through tears, I beg him to stop as shards of pain splinter inside of me, the vibrations amplifying the wreckage Ms. Nilsen left behind this morning. When I close my eyes and try to escape, all I can see is her with the broomstick. It isn't my father anymore. They are one. And I realize now I can't trust anyone. The pain is all I'll ever know.

. . .

"Thor?" My mother's voice pulls me from the memory, and a shiver moves over me as I try to blacken it out, stuff it down, and forget it ever happened. "Are you okay?"

"I'm fine." My voice cracks, and I clear my throat, resolving to assure her that I really am. "I'm sorry. It's been a long week."

I hate that I've only added to her worries, and I need to fix this.

"You aren't a bad mother," I answer her question from before. "You have been the best *Mor* I could have asked for. I'm only sorry I wasn't a better son."

A tear slips from the corner of her eye, and she shakes her head as I dab it away for her. "You and your brother are the best things I've ever done in this life. I couldn't and wouldn't ever want to change a single moment. As long as I know you'll be okay, that's all I want, my love. I want you to be happy. And I think Lavinia will make you happy if you just give her a chance."

Happiness is an illusion, but I understand this is what my mother needs right now. She needs to believe in the fairy tale. The one she never had.

"You don't need to worry about me anymore," I promise her. "Everything is going to be okay. For now, let's just enjoy the time we have together."

18

THORSEN

"THIS IS INCREDIBLE." Lavinia locks me into her sights as she brings a fork full of fish to her lips.

She's been perfectly poised all night, the ideal date. Soft-spoken, well mannered, graceful. I can only wonder what's really lurking beneath the surface. If I had met her under different circumstances, I might have thought she was attractive. She is, in fact, beautiful, and it's obviously her most beloved trait because she checks her appearance in a pocket mirror every chance she gets. But her beauty doesn't appeal to me the way she hopes. And the fact she's a liar only cements my resolve that I'd never respect her as a wife.

"I'm glad you're enjoying it." I discreetly check my watch, counting down the minutes until this evening is over.

Her eyes roam over my plate as I sit back and drink the rest of my *akevitt*. "Aren't you going to finish your dinner?"

"I'm not very hungry." I shove my half-finished meal aside.

"That's too bad." Her voice dips, taking on a raspy quality. "I'm starving."

It isn't difficult to comprehend the meaning behind her

words. But she makes the additional effort of encouraging her affection by reaching out to graze my arm. Unlike Ella, her touch sends a chill through my veins, and I withdraw without a second thought. Lavinia narrows her eyes at me but recovers quickly.

"When you're finished, we can take a walk in the garden." I try to move the agenda my father planned along at a breakneck pace.

Lavinia nods but takes her time, drawing out the meal as long as she can. In that time, I have three more glasses of *akevitt*, and I'm bleary-eyed and unsteady when we finally depart the dining room. She secures her arm in mine without asking, and I'm just drunk enough that I can pretend I don't give a fuck as we step into the garden.

The scent of roses and lavender carry on the breeze, mixing with Lavinia's perfume to create a sickly-sweet smell. The moon alights the path before us, and we walk on in silence, not wandering in any particular direction, and for a second, I manage not to think about anything. Not even the blonde who has been haunting my every waking moment.

"When can I see your estate?" Lavinia asks.

I recall the schedule my father gave me, remembering that it was one of the items I'm supposed to check off. Take Lavinia on a picnic. Another day, the theater. And inevitably, the estate. For a moment, I wonder what she would think of the naked woman hiding in my guest quarters. I wonder how Lavinia would react to the level of depravity she doesn't even understand I'm capable of.

"Perhaps next week."

She pauses, her features tight. "Have I done something to upset you, Your Highness?"

I use the opportunity to shrug her off. "What makes you ask such a question?"

"You seem... disinterested." She pouts. "You've been quiet all evening, and I'm just wondering if there's something I could do to ease your worries, whatever they may be."

"You mean like your pussy?"

Her mouth falls open, and she puts on a good show of pretending to be stunned by my vulgarity.

"Your Highness!" A blush spreads across her cheeks, and I cock my head to the side, examining her.

"That is what you're offering, is it not?"

She glances around as if we might have an audience before a secret smile curves her lips. "If that's what you wish, I would not deny you."

"Would you deny me your ass? Or your mouth?" I ask forcefully. "What about restraints? Or whipping? Or pain in general? I think it's only fair that you understand what you're asking for."

She visibly flinches but attempts to cover it smoothly with a laugh. "I had no idea you were so... devious."

"That's the least of it," I tell her.

I knew within the first five seconds of meeting her that this woman would never submit to a man. Not willingly. But she thought she could outwit me, and I want to see how far she will go in this scheme of hers to catch a prince. What level of depravity will she tolerate in her pursuit?

"You're a strong-willed man." She stares up at me with admiration so fake it nauseates me. "A leader. A prince. The future King of Norway. And I can tell you this, Your Majesty. Nothing would please me more than pleasing you, whatever that entails."

"Your dedication is admirable." I offer her a cold smile. "But for now, I think it's time to say good night."

"Thorsen?" Ella stirs from sleep, my name a prayer on her lips. How familiar she's become already.

I should remind her what I am to her. Nothing. But instead, I drag the blanket down off her body, exposing her naked flesh. What a sight she is to behold. The moonlight from the window bathes every curve with a blue halo. The goddess. The angel.

Her legs fall apart easily beneath my palms, and when I kneel between them, her arousal perfumes the air, sweet like wildflowers. My head dips forward, fingers skating up her rib cage to grope her tits. The breath from my lips teases against her pussy, and she breaks out in goose bumps, unconsciously arching her pelvis toward me in offer.

When my tongue lashes her, she moans, thrashing against the bed as I grip her thighs and force her legs back. She is exposed, wet, and wanton. And I should know better than to give her what she craves, but the *akevitt* has gone to my head, and all I know for certain is I will die right now if I don't taste her.

I bury my face between her thighs and fuck her with my mouth. Ella responds to me the way only she can. She awakens from her slumbering desire, her fingers curling into the bedspread, breath hissing between her teeth. Her spine arcs up like a feline, the softest notes of musical pleasure playing from her lips. I want to listen to this track on repeat.

I don't know what the fuck is wrong with me, but she's getting inside my head. Making me feel things. Making me question everything. And still, I can't stop.

Her breasts heave as the first spasm rocks through her. She cries out and quakes against my mouth, toes curling as her head collapses onto the pillow. The orgasm bleeds every bit of tension from her body, and she's content, but I'm not.

I'm not in my right mind when my lips graze the inside of her thigh, leaving a kiss there before I roll over beside her and stare up at the ceiling. I want to fuck her more than I've ever wanted anything. But things are spinning out of control. I shouldn't be here in her room in the middle of the night. She shouldn't be infecting my thoughts during the day and making the seconds more tolerable. Already, there's a whispering lie promising a future that could never be true.

She could take the darkness away. She could be the antidote for the chaos in my mind.

I can't ever let myself fall into that trap. I'm thinking of new ways to punish her when she rolls onto her side and reaches out for me hesitantly. Her fingers graze my crotch, and there's a protest on my lips, but I'm too weak to give voice to it. When she palms my erection through the trousers, a shudder moves through me, and my eyes fall shut. If I can't see her, I can pretend I'm not defenseless against her enchantment.

The zipper of my trousers comes down, and she cups me through my briefs. Without intending to, I rock up into her palm, silently signaling I need more. Ella doesn't let me down. Her gentle fingers slip past the band of my briefs and curl around my engorged dick like she owns it.

Maybe it's the alcohol in my blood, but not knowing what happens next doesn't make me feel as out of control as it should. I'm not commanding her to do anything. I'm not even watching. I'm just allowing it to happen, and it's terrifying how okay I am with that right now.

She strokes me like she's worshipping me. Like I'm her lover, and she wants nothing more than to please me. But we both know that isn't true. She's pleasing me for the money, just as I'm only letting her for the release. But for a minute, we can ignore those truths. I can let them fall away as she moves her body closer, her arm brushing against mine as she drags her palm up and down my cock until the tension explodes through my balls.

When my release shoots across my shirt, Ella reaches over to clean it up. My fingers lock around her wrist before she can even undo the first button, and my voice is a warning when I issue the command.

"Don't."

Her arm falls away from mine, but she doesn't retreat. She's still beside me as I yank off the shirt and toss it aside, leaving only my bare chest and a vulnerability I don't like. I should move. I should force myself to get up, but right now, my eyes are too heavy, and my body's too relaxed to fight it.

Just a few minutes. A few minutes and then I will go back to my room.

19

ELLA

SUNLIGHT FILTERS in through the window, dancing across Thorsen's cheekbones. Even in his sleep, his unease is palpable. A part of me longs to reach out and trace over the tension in his face, to ease it away, but then I remember the way he recoiled last night when I moved to touch his shirt. It wasn't just another episode of his turbulent mood swings. It was instinct. Something I recognize all too well. I'm more certain of it now than I've ever been. Something happened to him. Something terrible. Thorsen is masquerading behind a cloak of hostility, and I'm desperate to find out why.

It shouldn't matter to me. I'm only here for two months, and not because I came here of my own free will. But there has always been something inside me that wants to fix the broken and mend the hurt in those who can't help themselves. And I feel deeply that Thorsen is someone who hasn't ever been able to help himself. He isn't going to make it easy on me. I know that before he even opens his eyes, and the temperature in the room drops.

He's confused at first, blinking as he takes in his

surroundings. His eyes flare when they land on me, and it feels like my whole body frosts over. Wordlessly, he sits upright, swinging his legs over the bed as he glances toward the door. The door that he left unlocked and open all night.

"You didn't run," he murmurs, almost too low to hear it. "That was a mistake, Ella."

"We have a deal." I sit up too. "Why would I run?"

"Because you should." He turns away.

The echo of approaching footsteps in the hall effectively ends our conversation.

"Thor?"

The face I recognize from the media appears, and I know immediately this is his brother. He was at the ball too, and we almost met on the palace lawn before I slipped away.

I'm scrambling to make myself appropriate, pulling the blanket up over my chest when he focuses on me. His eyes flash with surprise before he turns to Thorsen, who has gone rigid as a staff. At some point in the last second, he extricated himself from the bed. Judging by the expression on his face, I'd venture a guess that his brother is oblivious to our arrangement.

"Well, isn't this a nice little party?" Calder smirks. "You've been holding out on me, brother?"

The muscle in Thorsen's jaw works as he drags his eyes away from me and focuses on his twin. "Calder, this is Ella."

"Ella," Calder repeats as if he's testing it out for himself.

His eyes move over me, and the similarities between him and Thorsen catch me off guard. I never noticed it before in the photos the media prints, but they really do look alike. There's something undeniably intense about Calder too. Between the two of them, they suck all the oxygen from the room.

"Where did you find this one?" Calder asks curiously.

He doesn't recognize me from the palace. Maybe it was the mask, or the gown, or the fact that I never spoke to him. But I can't decide if this new development is good or bad.

"Ella was just about to take a shower," Thorsen says.

Calder looks back and forth between us as if he's trying to figure out something. At the same time, I've never seen Thorsen so unsettled, and I can't understand why.

"I suppose we should let her get to it." Calder smirks.

Leaving his shirt on the floor, Thorsen joins his brother and heads for the door. My eyes drift to the solid expanse of muscles along his back. It's the first glimpse I've had of him like this. Something that would otherwise appear casual seems out of place for Thorsen. I don't get the impression he walks around often without his clothes on. From the rigid set in his spine, I'd venture a guess he doesn't often wake up shirtless beside a woman either. But it would be naïve of me to think he doesn't have sex with them. According to the papers and the few bits and pieces I overheard from Lavinia, he's had multiple sexual partners who have gone to the media afterward, eager to spill the details of their illicit encounters.

I can't imagine what that must be like. And when Thorsen glances at me over his shoulder, I'm beginning to understand why he doesn't feel like he can trust me. He still wants to warn me away because it's safest for him to keep everyone at a distance.

He pauses on the threshold, his eyes drifting to the lock. Calder notices, and he waits, watching his brother with interest. I'm curious, too, holding my breath as he decides how to handle this situation. When he shuts the door, I listen carefully, watching the lock. But it never clicks into place. A strange thrill shoots through me when I consider what that means.

Is he going to allow me to explore the estate?

Recalling his words about the shower, I decide it's best not to test the boundaries just yet. And honestly, after last night's encounter, I could really use a shower. When Thorsen slipped into my room in the late hours of the night, it surprised me. As I squeeze my thighs together, I can still feel his palms on me, spreading me apart, tasting me. I don't know if I'll ever get used to the way he makes me feel, and I can't help but wonder what it will be like when he finally takes my virginity.

Walking into the bathroom, I turn on the tap and check the water, adjusting the temperature until I get it just right. When the spray is to my liking, I step inside and scrub my body and wash my hair while I contemplate the risks of stepping outside of this room.

Does Thorsen want me to? Or is it some kind of a trick?

I'm not any closer to an answer when I towel off my body and brush out my hair. When I get back to the room, I'm surprised to find a silk bathrobe with a brand-new tag on it waiting for me on the bed. As I'm examining it, the door swings open, startling me.

Thorsen fills the frame, wearing a fresh pair of trousers and a button-down shirt. His hair's still wet, and he's freshly shaven, and between us, his aftershave lingers in the air. When his eyes move over my towel wrapped body, his pupils flare.

Is he disappointed? Angry? I can't tell.

"Put on the robe and come down the hall to the kitchen," he says. "You'll be joining Calder and me for breakfast."

The pulsing vein in his neck alerts me to the tension simmering beneath the surface, so I nod. "Okay."

He casually eye fucks me for a few long, lingering moments and then disappears again.

I slip into the robe quickly and loosely braid my hair to pull it away from my face until it dries. When I poke my head out the door and into the hallway, it still feels as though I'm doing something forbidden. But that fear is outweighed by the desire to explore Thorsen's estate.

When my bare foot hits the shiny white tile floor, it echoes off the wall, and I turn my head in each direction, trying to get my bearings. I have two choices of direction, but it's obvious from the distant noise to my right that the kitchen is presumably that way. Still, I find myself pivoting in the opposite direction, curiosity leading the way as I tiptoe farther down the hall.

The first door I come to is on the left, and it's identical to my own. But when I turn the handle and open it, I know without a doubt this isn't just another guest area. The spicy scent of Thorsen hits my nose first, followed by the dark details of the room. While the hallway is light and brightly painted, this room is shrouded in tones of gray with heavy drapes obscuring any outside light pollution from the windows. A melancholy feeling hangs in the air, and I know this is definitely his room.

Glancing over my shoulder, I half expect to see him lurking behind me as I venture farther inside the space. But he isn't there, and I'm free to explore. As far as furnishings go, the room isn't all that different from mine. His bed is bigger, and the closet too. On the right side of the suite, a set of French doors leads to a balcony. Noticeably absent are the plethora of sexual torture devices he must keep contained to my space.

My fingers graze the bed where he usually sleeps before moving on to his nightstand. Pulling open the first drawer, I find nothing of importance. The second drawer yields nothing either, and it confuses me. He lives here full-time, yet it doesn't seem like he lives here at all. I walk into his closet, examining the neat rows of trousers and shirts hanging from the racks. In Thorsen's world, only four colors exist, apparently. Gray, black, blue, and white. On the opposite wall, there's a similar theme amongst his Oxford style shoes, consisting of only black or brown, in varying designs.

As I wander from the closet and into the bathroom, I wonder if this is what his brain is like too. Is he living in a pre-technicolor world where the shades of his mind are so limited he has trouble distinguishing anything with real vibrancy?

The master bathroom is another clue that he's a man who doesn't have a taste for the excessive lifestyle into which he was born. While I don't doubt that his clothes are expensive, I'm beginning to sense a pattern. Thorsen lives for the necessities, evident by the few toiletry items he keeps in his vanity. A shaver, cream, shampoo, soap. In another drawer, I find a manicure kit and some hair gel. It seems like that's about as exciting as it's going to get. Then I open the last drawer on the bottom, which appears to contain towels and handcloths. But when I push them aside, I notice a small black case beneath them. It looks like a shaving bag, but it's thin enough that I'm questioning if there's even anything in there.

When I unzip it, the only item inside is a dark blue glass bottle with a hand-scrawled label. *Nerium Oleander*. I'm not familiar with the name, but as I examine it, something feels off about it. Is this what he used to drug me?

A noise from inside the room startles me, and I quickly shove everything back into the drawer, shutting it as quietly as I can manage before I peek around the corner.

"Oh!" A frightened older woman peers back at me. Her maid's uniform indicates she must be a part of his house-keeping staff.

"Sorry." I offer her a sheepish smile. "I... um, got lost. I was looking for the kitchen. We haven't met yet, but I'm Ella."

"Lisbet." She glances over her shoulder nervously as she points at the hall. "You shouldn't be in here, Ella. The kitchen is down the corridor to the right."

"Sorry," I murmur again, scurrying away quickly.

Out in the hall, my racing heart calms as I place one foot in front of the other, putting as much distance as I can manage between Thorsen's room and myself. I repeat the name of the label on the glass bottle under my breath a few times, committing it to memory so I can look it up later.

As I venture closer to the main area of the house, I notice a difference in the brightness around me. Natural light floods in from the windows, sparkling off every surface inside. When I reach the kitchen, I'm surrounded by more white. The cabinets, the island, the dining table, and chairs... everything is white. It's beautiful but empty. There's no sign of Thorsen or Calder, but there's a set of French doors ahead that lead out onto the terrace. And from where I'm standing, I can hear the gentle lapping of water nearby.

Suddenly, I'm questioning if we're even in a house at all. Is this just a huge yacht? I remember Lavinia mentioning something about the royal family being fond of their yacht. But no, this can't be. I would have felt it moving. And I would have heard the water outside my window if it was right beneath me.

"There you are." Calder pokes his head around the French doors, his eyes roaming over me with a casual interest. "We're eating outside. It's a beautiful day. Come join us."

I follow his lead, squinting into the sunlight as I step onto the terrace. It becomes apparent right away that we aren't on a ship at all, but the house is perched on a hill, overlooking the bay. It's stunning and surreal. A slice of Norwegian paradise.

Thorsen is watching me carefully as I venture toward the table, taking in my new surroundings. I feel off-balance and uncertain. He hasn't dictated the boundaries of my newfound freedom yet, and I suspect that's because of his brother's presence. But that doesn't mean there aren't unwritten rules I still need to abide by.

"Take a seat." Calder pulls out a chair for me, and Thorsen watches our interaction with an intensity that makes my stomach flip.

"Please, help yourself." Calder gestures to the spread on the table, with a heavy variety of meats and cheese and rye bread.

I opt for one of the lighter options, yogurt, and muesli, along with a handful of odd-looking berries I haven't yet been able to identify. Meanwhile, the men fill up on smoked salmon and bread.

"No salmon?" Calder holds the plate out to me in offer, and I shake my head.

"I'm a vegetarian."

Thorsen pauses, glancing at me with an odd expression, and it almost looks as though he's irritated I revealed this information to his brother. He's been serving me meals that include meat, and I've just been leaving it on the tray. Either he hasn't noticed, or he didn't think to ask.

"Ahh, I see." Calder sets the tray aside with a nod. "I can appreciate that."

We eat our breakfast in silence, quietly gazing out over the water. Thorsen's estate includes a private beach as well.

There's a path leading down to it, and I absently wonder if he'll ever allow me to explore that area when Calder interrupts my thoughts.

"My brother was just telling me about your arrangement."

My eyes widen when I look at Thorsen for confirmation. He doesn't give anything away as he continues to chew, his jaw working while he harpoons me with that steely gray gaze.

"What about our arrangement?" I ask cautiously.

Calder leans back against his chair, draping an arm over the side as he turns to meet my eyes. "Thorsen and I don't have any secrets. He tells me everything."

His statement is resolute, but the tension radiating off Thorsen is palpable. I don't think it's as true for him as it is for his brother.

"So, he told you that he kidnapped me?" I challenge, feeling brave for a moment.

Calder arches a brow at me. "Is it really kidnapping if you agreed to stay? I don't think you'd still be here unless you wanted to."

I see. So, they are both fucked up.

Regardless, I can concede that he has a point. Thorsen told me I had a choice. Maybe I just didn't want to accept that as a fact because it was easier to believe I was here against my will. Otherwise, I'm just selling myself for three thousand pounds a day.

The yogurt in front of me suddenly doesn't seem so appealing, and when I push it aside, Thorsen seems to take issue with it. Frustration seeps into his features, but before he can say anything, the same housekeeper from his room appears.

"I'm sorry to interrupt your breakfast, Your Highness."

Lisbet's eyes dart around nervously as she speaks as though she's about to throw herself onto a grenade. "But Hayes has called several times for you this morning, and I've been instructed to tell you that if you don't return his call now, he will be making an appearance himself."

Thorsen shoves his chair back, scraping it over the stone tile, and tosses a napkin onto his plate. He murmurs something in Norwegian, and Calder chuckles under his breath.

"The life of an heir apparent."

Thorsen looks back and forth between the two of us, almost as if he's hesitant to leave, but when Calder glances up at him in question, he doesn't say anything else. I watch him go and then fold my hands in my lap, feeling a little strange when I stop to think that this is my reality. A week ago, I was scrubbing floors on my hands and knees, and now I'm eating breakfast with two royal princes in one of the most incredible estates I've ever seen.

"I was surprised to see you here this morning," Calder says. "Thorsen isn't usually in the habit of bringing women home on his own."

Usually? Does that mean he's done this with other women before? Something prickles inside me as I imagine Thorsen with all the others. How many were there before me? Is this what jealousy feels like?

"It's just a casual arrangement," I answer with a note of bitterness I can't hide.

"Regardless, I don't think I need to tell you that whatever happens in this house stays in this house."

Something has shifted in Calder. I notice it in the tightness around his eyes. But I don't understand what he's trying to say, exactly.

"What do you mean?"

"You won't go to the media," he says. "That's what I mean."

"I would never." I shake my head, a little offended that he'd even think I'd do something like that.

"It wouldn't be the first time a woman has broken that promise." He shrugs.

"Well, I'm not like that." I fold my arms, feeling defensive. "Whatever the other women did has nothing to do with me."

After a tense moment, he nods, seemingly satisfied with my response, and then his lighthearted nature returns.

"Has he had sex with you yet?"

"What?" Heat blooms across my cheeks and an image of Thorsen fucking my ass comes to mind, but I'm not about to divulge that.

"I didn't think so." Calder stares out over the water. "Thor probably hasn't told you this yet, but he likes to share. It's easier for him when I'm there too."

"You mean... the two of you—?"

"We share the same women." His eyes rake over me with a heat that reminds me so much of Thorsen, it confuses me.

"Have you ever tried it before?" he asks. "Being with two men at the same time?"

"No," I choke out, and I'm pretty sure my face is on fire. But if it is, Calder doesn't seem to notice.

"If you want to make him happy, then you should think about it. Thorsen has never been very good at handling women on his own. I'm honestly surprised he took the initiative to bring you here at all."

"So, the two of you do this often, then?" My voice feels strained, and I hope it's not obvious.

"Usually, I bring the women to him." Calder takes a sip of his coffee. "He doesn't do relationships."

I don't know if it's the sudden bite of the breeze or something else that leaves me feeling unsettled and cold, but when Thorsen returns, he seems to notice the shift in the atmosphere too. Calder and I both look at him in the way people often do when they've been caught talking about you. Except I know he couldn't have actually heard anything.

"What was that about?" Calder asks.

"My schedule." Thorsen returns to his seat. "Hayes wanted to make some adjustments this week. I'll have to cancel our plans on Thursday. The king has requested me to accompany the Prince of Brunei to a polo match while he's visiting."

"Ahh... well, in that case, perhaps we can make the most of today." Calder grins.

When the vein in Thorsen's neck twitches, I get the feeling they aren't simply talking about a lazy Sunday lounging around the house.

"Ooof." I exchange the empty shot glass for the water in front of me, guzzling while Calder laughs. Meanwhile, Thorsen is observing me with a lazy sexual possessiveness I feel deep between my thighs. He's lounged on the sofa with a glass of the potent drink they call *akevitt* in his hand and a downright predatory hunger in his eyes.

He's been watching me this way all afternoon as Calder comes up with new ways to entertain us. At first, it was a game of cards he tried to teach me. Then at some point, that evolved into a debate between the two brothers on the rules, which quickly morphed from English to Norwegian. Now

Calder has raided Thorsen's liquor cabinet, opting to play bartender while he offers me samples of their local favorites.

"You don't like it?" Calder pours himself another shot.

"It's... intense." My eyes are still burning, and so is my throat.

"We Norwegians are intense." He smiles at me, and that hunger in his eyes has returned too. I wonder if Thorsen can see it. I wonder if this is what he wants, just like Calder said.

"What do you usually drink then?" Calder asks.

"Nothing, really." I shrug. "I've only ever had one drink before. My friend Charlotte gave me a bottle of champagne on my eighteenth birthday. I didn't care for that much either."

Calder plucks a small baggie from his pocket. "Maybe she's in the mood for something sweeter. What do you think, Thor?"

The muscle in Thorsen's jaw works as our eyes lock, and for a minute, nobody says a thing. I'm holding my breath, wondering what he's going to say. I'm nervous and maybe a little excited too. I've never done anything crazy. And I don't know if it's the liquor warming my belly or Thorsen's predatory gaze that makes me want to do something crazy.

"It's up to Ella," he says finally.

I examine the little pink pill with the smiley face on it. "What is it?"

"Ecstasy." Calder opens the bag and takes out a couple of pills, offering me one. "You just swallow it."

"What does it do?" I rotate it between my fingers.

"It makes you feel happy." He tosses his onto his tongue and chases it with a sip of his drink.

I can't tell what Thorsen wants from me. He said it was my choice, but is it really? Does he expect me to take it? Or does he want me to say no? I really have no idea, and right now, he's so closed off I can't read him.

Taking the gamble, I toss the pill onto my tongue and take a sip of water. It slides down my throat easily, and when I open my eyes again, Thorsen is pouring himself another drink.

"Aren't you going to take one?"

"He doesn't like it," Calder says.

"Oh." That answers my question.

"Let's put on some music while we wait." Calder drags a remote off the coffee table, pressing a few buttons, and the overhead speakers come to life. It's an instrumental track that fills the silence between us as Calder leans back against the sofa and closes his eyes. I follow his lead, my head only a few inches away from Thorsen's thigh.

At some point, the music becomes faster, more frantic. Or maybe that's my racing heart. I don't know how long has passed since I took the pill, but when I wiggle my fingers, I'm already starting to feel the effects of it. My whole body is warm and relaxed, and everything seems so much more profound. The notes of the music, the clash of the drums, the scent of Thorsen's aftershave so close I can almost taste it. I want to lick his skin and taste his salt, and the intensity of that craving builds inside me when Calder's hand settles onto my back. His fingers graze over my shoulders, and it feels like I'm on a roller coaster of sensations as goose bumps break out along my skin.

"Does it feel amazing?" His voice vibrates into my skull, and I nod.

"So amazing."

He brushes my hair aside and massages my shoulders while I reach out for Thorsen. I don't even realize I'm doing it until my fingers tangle with his. And this time, he doesn't stop me. He's a beautiful terror. A hypnotic aura of black and red. I've never wanted anything so much.

Calder's fingers fall away, and he tells me to do what feels good as he gets up and sits beside his brother on the sofa. The only thing I can think about is crawling onto Thorsen's lap, so that's what I do.

"So tense," I murmur as my fingers come up to touch his face. "Let me take it away."

For a second, his eyes fall shut, and he shivers against my fingertips. It feels as if I'm seeing him for the first time in the most vibrant colors. Everything is sharper, edgier. So much detail and beauty in one complicated man.

I grind down against his cock, and I could swear it's the most earth-shattering experience of my life when I drag his fingers between my thighs. I'm wet for him, and I want him to know it. His face is so serious I want to dissolve all his worries away. But I'm getting too close, and Thorsen won't allow that. He turns the tables, brushing his thumb against my clit.

"Holy shit." I hiss under my breath as a feverish thirst blazes through my body.

Whatever I was doing just a second ago is long forgotten when he glides his fingers through my arousal. It feels like he's strumming every nerve as his other hand slips into the robe, groping my breast. Calder watches us with a fixation that makes me feel like I'm going to spontaneously combust. My entire body sings praises for Thor's masterful touch as I curl my fingers into his hair and bury my face in his neck. Dragging in long, deep hits of him, I roll my pelvis against his hand, my orgasm barreling at me with the speed of a freight train.

Too soon, it explodes through me, obliterating any inhibitions I might have had left. Nothing is off-limits when I come back down to earth. I'm warm and sated but desperately eager to ride that roller coaster all over again. My eyes move to Calder, and I remember what he said earlier. They share everything, and right now, they want to share me.

"Are you thinking about what it would be like?" Calder asks. "To have both of us inside you?"

My eyes drift to Thorsen, and something has changed in him. Or maybe it's my imagination. I ask him what he wants, but it occurs to me I only asked him inside my head. His eyes are closed off again, hiding his emotions away. He's here, but he isn't. What does this man want from me? *What do I want from him?*

"I want to make you happy." I breathe the words against his lips. "I know what will make you happy."

I sink into the space between the two men, unknotting my robe, and draping it open, so they both have access to my body. I'm not sure how this works, and I think it shows. But Calder puts me at ease by brushing the silky material off my shoulders, revealing my breasts.

My nipples are tight, and when he brushes over one of them with his fingers, it makes me shiver. Thorsen watches the interaction with dark, brutal eyes as Calder dips his head forward and lashes my nipple with his tongue.

I arch into him and moan, my fingers coming to rest on the bulge in Thorsen's trousers. He's so hard for me, but he isn't moving. Or speaking. Or blinking. And I can't figure out if I'm doing something wrong.

"How do you want me?" I ask him.

Calder is the one to answer, releasing my nipple from his mouth and pivoting my head toward Thorsen's crotch. "Suck his cock. He likes that."

I fumble with the zipper on his trousers as the music pounds in my head. Calder adjusts my body across the sofa, hoisting my ass into the air as his fingers trail over my spine, leaving a path of goose bumps in their wake.

Everything feels so insane. The slightest touch is like an orgasm on steroids. But I want Thorsen's touch more than anything. When I finally get his pants open, I peek up at him as I grab his dick through his briefs. He's as still as a statue. I can't even tell if he's breathing. That's when I notice his fingers, silently tapping against his glass.

Tap. Tap. Tap. Tap.

I recognize it now. The thing he's been doing all night.

"Four," I whisper.

He winces, staring down at me as if I just saw into his very soul. There's a moment between us when nothing else exists, and I think maybe I'm getting through to him. And then Calder's tongue lashes against my pussy, and a strangled sound vibrates in my throat. I lurch forward, groaning right before I face-plant against Thorsen's hard cock. *Concentrate. Concentrate.* I try to remember that as I kiss him through the material, and then let my baser instincts take over, biting at the black cotton fabric.

He sucks in a breath, his fingers tangling in my hair, and rubs my face along his length. But his eyes aren't on me anymore. They are fixated on Calder behind me. He's fucking me with his tongue, digging his fingers into my hips. It's so intense I think I'm going to scream.

But Thorsen. *I want to please Thorsen.*

I yank down his briefs and tuck them under his balls, which has the immediate effect of making his already massive cock even bigger as it juts up from the confines of his trousers.

My tongue darts out to lap up the salty liquid that's already beaded on the tip. It makes me feel drunk or high or both. All I know is I want to lick him like he's my favorite candy, so that's what I do. He reinforces the strangling grip on my hair, and his body becomes more rigid with every passing second.

Calder nips at my clit, and I jolt, moaning as another wave of pleasure crashes over me. Tension is building deep in my core again. I'm going to explode with Calder's face between my thighs and Thorsen's cock buried deep in my throat.

The fun and games are over when Thorsen takes control, forcing my head down his shaft until I gag. He lets me come up for air for a second and then does it all over again. I whine for his roughness, but this isn't his normal dominance at play. He's trying to punish me, and I don't understand. Why is he so fucking pissed?

That's what this is. In the foggy depths of my mind, it occurs to me that he's angry. Not just angry, but livid.

My nails dig into his thighs, and Calder forces my pelvis against his face, sending me off into a kaleidoscopic oblivion with so many colors, they look like fireworks streaking through the night sky.

I can barely draw a breath as I collapse into Thorsen, and he pulls my face off his dick, staring down at me like a man scorned. I reach up to touch his face, apologetic, as Calder unzips his pants behind me.

Something snaps in him then. It all happens so fast I can hardly comprehend it. One minute, I'm lying face down in Thorsen's lap, and the next, he's up on his feet, taking a swing at his brother. Calder staggers back, clutching at his jaw while he stares at his brother with wild, confused eyes.

"Thor?"

"Fuck you," Thorsen roars, eyeing us like we've betrayed him. "Fuck you both."

He stalks down the hall, leaving me with Calder, who

looks like he's been doused in ice-cold water. I know because I feel it too.

"Who are you?" Calder murmurs in disbelief.

We don't say anything else. We can barely look at each other. He tugs his pants back up and zips them closed, and that's the last image I have of him as I chase after Thorsen.

My feet slap against the floor, the sensation vibrating all the way up to my skull. When I reach his door, I fling it open and don't bother to close it behind me. I find him standing at the vanity in the bathroom, staring into the mirror. *He seems so fucking broken.*

Tears splash onto my cheeks before I can contain them. I charge toward him, giving him only a second of warning before I jump into his arms, forcing him to catch me. He stumbles backward, collapsing against the vanity, and I cling to him, squeezing his face between my palms. My lips crash against his, and he freezes, hissing when I tug on his lip, drawing blood.

"Kiss me," I beg. "I know you want to taste me too."

He tries to resist, but I'm a wild animal that can't be controlled. I claw at his shirt, his pants, everywhere I can reach, desperate to feel his flesh on my flesh.

"I want you," I chant. "I only want you."

His resistance snaps, and he cups my ass beneath his forearm, hauling me off to his bed and dropping me onto it. His fingers come up to the buttons on his shirt, and in his frustration to get them open, he pulls the fabric apart with his hands, sending buttons scattering everywhere.

He's unzipping his pants again while I'm spreading my legs for him. Thorsen tugs his dick free and doesn't bother to take off the rest of his clothes. With his pants hanging from his hips, he comes for me, hot and dark and god-like in my pounding, frantic eyes.

He mounts me, spreading my legs as wide as they will go to accommodate his massive body. His cock is an angry beast against my hip when he reaches down and grabs my face. His eyes wild with thunder, I can see his chaos reflected back at me. But he won't let his mind have a voice, even when he desperately wants to.

My palm comes up to rest on his cheek, and for a moment, it tempers the war inside him.

"Only yours," I whisper the lyrics playing on repeat inside of my head.

He growls his approval, dipping his head to claim my lips as his cock bumps against me. I want him so badly. I want to feel him inside me, the place where no man has ever been. The temple just for him. I want him to fuck me until his body gives out.

I drag my nails over his shoulders, and he shudders. Reaching down between us, he adjusts his swollen cock, slipping the head inside me inch by inch. It's slow and excruciatingly hot. If there's pain, it's washed away by the lightning storm in my veins. His is a high that a chemical can't give me. A force of nature true to his namesake. He is the god of thunder. And when he finds refuge deep in my body, and I'm stretched around his throbbing masculinity, something settles into my bones that I never would have anticipated.

Completeness. A balm to the lonely existence I lived before him. He isn't just inside my body. He's in my mind. My blood. My beating heart. And when I look up into his beautiful, tormented eyes, I don't know how I'm ever going to survive him.

I place my hand on his heart, and Thorsen rolls his hips inside me, his head falling back, lips parting. At this moment, I'm certain he's the most divine illusion that ever existed. I want to remember him this way forever. The man who took my virtue and stirred the flame inside my soul. I want it branded into him too. This moment forever imprinted in his mind as the holiest experience he's ever had.

My body melts for him, pulling him closer, fingers digging into his ass as he thrusts into me. He sinks his teeth into my breast, taking ownership of me as he brands my skin with his mark. My lips hum against his throat, inhaling the addictive scent of his sweat and spice. I want to rub my body all over his flesh, bathing myself in this man for eternity.

The seconds seem to stretch on forever. He's the machine to my mortality. I'm raw, swollen, and used up in the best possible way when he finally lets me come again. The orgasm is even more insane than the last two, ripping through my body like shrapnel and splintering me apart. When I open my eyes again, I'm gifted with the sight of Thorsen coming unraveled. His muscles flexing, body tensing, throat working as he buries himself inside me with a grunt. His dick pulses in me, come spurting into my womb until I'm so full, it starts to leak out between my thighs.

The beautiful god collapses onto his forearms, caging me in against the bed. For a long beat, he stays there, catching his breath as his dick softens inside me. And somewhere in the span of a few minutes, the vibrations in my skull start to fade away, reality threatening the edges of my vision.

I'm coming down, and right now, more than anything, I want him to tell me it's going to be okay. I want him to take me in his arms and hold me. But Thorsen doesn't do either of those things. He rolls beside me instead, glancing at me like I'm the enemy before he tosses his forearm over his face and sighs.

A tear leaks from my eye, and I mourn the loss of my ignorance. I'm full of his life force, but my soul is empty. For better or worse, I'm starting to feel something for this troubled man. What those feelings are, I don't yet know or understand. But they are there, lingering beneath the surface. And I'm beginning to wonder if I'll ever remember a time that existed before or after him when he's through with me.

When I study the profile of his face, the lines and curves that make up the most complicated man I've ever met, only one thing's for certain. He's going to destroy me.

20

THORSEN

"THORSEN." Dr. Blom shuts the office door behind him and takes a seat across from my desk.

Plucking a piece of the stern from my pile, I examine it, trying to determine the best way to maneuver it into the designated space.

"I see you have another one," he notes. "How many is that now?"

"Ten."

Ten of the same model ships. None that have lasted more than a week. I don't think it's so much about the end result anymore but rather a distraction from these meetings. If I could get away with hauling the ship in all its varying pieces to the rest of my meetings throughout the week, I would.

"I spoke with Calder yesterday," Dr. Blom informs me. "He told me what happened between you."

Discarding the piece I'm not quite certain about, I opt to search through the pile for something else. Something more familiar.

"Would you like to share your thoughts?" he prods.

"Not particularly."

For a minute, the sound of the clock is the only noise in the room. But I know Dr. Blom isn't finished. Not even close.

"He said you hit him."

My fingers freeze, seemingly immobile, as the image of shock on my brother's face returns to my mind. I've never hit him. Even when we were young, and he would piss me off, I never once thought about really hurting him. But when I saw him trying to take Ella from me, I wanted to murder him. A part of me wants to believe it was all a dream. That's the only way I can rationalize it.

"I didn't mean to." My brows pinch together. "It just happened."

"Because there was a misunderstanding?" Dr. Blom answers. "He thought it was business as usual with this new woman. That you two would do what you've always done. But that bothered you, and you didn't tell him so."

I tug at the collar of my shirt and wonder what Ella's doing right now. I left her in my bed yesterday, and she slept there all night. This morning, I gave Lisbet instructions to bring her breakfast, and I left the door open for her. She's free to roam the house now, but that lingering question is still there. Will she try to leave me?

"Do you like this girl, Thorsen?" Dr. Blom invades my thoughts. "Is that why you felt compelled to hurt your brother?"

"No." I stare at the blurry pile of pieces in front of me. "I don't feel anything."

"It's okay if you do," he says. "I understand how these new feelings could be frightening for you. I don't think you've allowed yourself to like anyone in a very long time."

My attention wanes, and I forget where I'm supposed to place the piece between my fingers. I check the instructions again, but the words are just fuzzy shapes. Dr. Blom is wrong. I don't feel anything for Ella. She's only here because I'm paying the sanctuary. If I wasn't, she'd already be gone.

"Calder says you let her touch you."

Heat creeps up my neck as I glance at him. "She was high."

"But you weren't." He arches a brow at me. "You don't normally let women touch you like that. Not unless you're in control."

"I was still in control," I lie.

There was nothing controlled about my thoughts or feelings when Ella crawled into my lap and touched me that way. Like she couldn't breathe without me. Like she would die right there if I didn't let her feel me. I've never allowed a woman to touch me so freely. But it felt... *good*. And for a second, I could pretend that it was real. That it was the most authentic experience I'd ever had. Until Calder touched her too. *Until she came for him too.*

"Can you tell me about Ella?" Dr. Blom asks.

I glare at him. I don't want to tell him about Ella. Ella is mine and no one else's. But I can't say that because it doesn't make any sense, even to me. She isn't a part of my plan. I only have limited time with her. Two months of peace, and then I'll let her go. Pressure throbs in my temples, and I start talking because I don't want to focus on that.

"She likes animals. She takes care of them."

"So, she's kind," he remarks.

"She's fucked up." I meet his gaze. "Like me. That's why she's here. That's why she's with me."

He sighs, shaking his head. "Do you think someone couldn't care about you unless they are broken too?"

"She is broken," I insist. "She cares too much about other things. About other people. She shouldn't."

"Do you mean she shouldn't care about you?"

"She doesn't," I growl, tossing the piece of plastic in my hand aside. "We're just using each other."

"Yet your father has you dating another woman back at the palace." He frowns as if this is problematic. "Someone he wants you to marry."

"She doesn't matter."

"Do you think it would do any good to have an earnest conversation with your father then?"

I stare at him, blank.

"Right." He shrugs. "Then perhaps you should consider your options. Would you care to revisit the topic of renouncing your right to the throne?"

"That isn't necessary."

"Why?" He studies me with a cautious intensity.

Because I'll never make it to the throne. But I can't tell him that. I can't tell anyone what my plans are.

"It's my duty," I answer coldly. "And nothing can get in the way of that."

"You look beautiful, *Mor.*"

"Thank you, Thorsen." She smiles up at me from her wheelchair. "I hope you don't mind me joining you for cocktails this evening. I just felt so good today, and I thought I should seize the moment."

"I never mind anything you do." I sit down beside her. "You know that."

Lavinia offers us a forced smile. "You two are so sweet together."

"He's very special." My mother nods. "He's always been so different. When he was a boy, he used to bring me flowers from the garden. It would drive the gardener's mad. And he had the cutest stutter. It took him years of speech therapy to overcome that."

My lungs burn, and I can feel the color draining from my face as I reach over and touch my mother's arm. She's staring off into the distance, her eyes glazed, and when she returns her attention to me, her expression falls.

"Oh, dear, I forgot. I wasn't supposed to tell anyone about that, was I?"

"It's okay." My voice is tight. "Let's just talk about something else."

She thinks she's embarrassed me, and when her eyes fill with shame, I feel like even more of an asshole.

"It's all right, *Mor*."

"I'm afraid I've spoiled the evening, haven't I?" Her body sags into the wheelchair. "You two should go on your date now. I'm getting very tired."

"Yes, we really should get going," Lavinia chimes in.

"Let me walk you back to your room." I stand, and Lavinia moves to follow before I narrow my eyes at her. "I'll return shortly."

Her lips flatten as I leave her standing there, spinning my mother's chair around and pointing her in the direction of her room. She's pensive as I wheel her down the hallway, and I don't know how to fix this awfulness between us either.

In her room, I help her into her bed, and she glances up at me with more love than I've ever deserved. "I'm sorry I mentioned your stutter. I didn't mean to upset you."

I take a seat beside her. "You didn't upset me."

"Don't lie to me," she scolds. "My brain might be rotting away, but don't you dare lie to me."

"It isn't about the stutter." I sigh.

"Then what?" Concern colors her eyes.

For a second, I consider what it would feel like to confess the truth I've been carrying for all these years. The truth I should have gone to her with in the first place. But even as a grown man, there is still that question. *Would she believe me?*

Regardless, it would be selfish to confess such darkness to her now. It could only ever make her feel helpless in an already helpless situation. What I really want to say to her is that she's given me the courage to do what I've always wanted. When she's gone, I can go too.

"It's nothing," I assure her. "I just don't like people to know about the therapy."

"You have nothing to be ashamed of." She shakes her head. "But I won't bring it up again. In fact, I'll make a note of it, so I don't forget. Now, could you do me a favor?"

"What?"

"Go enjoy your night with Lavinia."

I choke down all the reasons I can't and nod. "I will."

21

ELLA

AFTER WAKING up alone in Thorsen's bed this morning, I wandered the house under the guise of exploring. But really, I wanted to see where he was and what he was doing. I only made it to the second level before Lisbet spotted me and firmly turned me around. She ushered me away from the closed door behind her, and it occurred to me that Thorsen must have been inside.

Had he told her to send me away, or was she just trying to look out for me? She seems so skittish, and I get the sense that she's nervous around Thorsen. But now that I think about it, who isn't? He comes off as cold and calloused, and I truly think that's what he wants people to believe. But I know otherwise. I've seen glimpses of the man beneath. The man who ravaged me so passionately last night, the images will be forever burned into my mind.

There is a fire in Thorsen Lykken. He just wants everyone to believe it's burned out.

As afternoon fades to evening, and Lisbet seems to disappear, I use the opportunity to resume my exploration. My goal is to find a computer or a phone, so I can contact

Charlotte and do a google search for the name on Thorsen's mysterious blue bottle. But as it turns out, there doesn't seem to be a landline anywhere that I can see. Or a computer for that matter. At least not on the first level.

When I return to the second level, the house is so quiet it makes me a little nervous. If Thorsen catches me sneaking around like this, he'll probably be furious. But he's been gone for hours now, and I have to admit I'm a little curious about where he might be. Is it possible that he has someone else stashed away, and he visits her too?

I dismiss the notion as ridiculous and turn the doorknob that the housekeeper ushered me away from earlier. It isn't locked, and when I step inside, I'm surprised to find an office. It's darker, like his bedroom, and there's a partially built model ship sitting on the wood desk. When I walk around and sit down in his chair, I can imagine him here, carefully examining the pieces as he puts them together. I lean back and take in the space, noting the details of Thor's world. I have to admit that I'm hungry for this information. This intimate knowledge of a man who seems like such a mystery to so many.

His office has a few bookshelves, but most of the titles are in Norwegian, so I can't be certain of what he likes to read. On the opposite wall, there are a couple of photos. One of him and his brother, and another of a woman who I know is his mother. She's a beautiful woman, and I can see a lot of Calder in her. But Thorsen has darker features, which I presume he's inherited from his father.

Apart from a plant and a filing cabinet, there's nothing of much importance here. But I get the feeling he spends a lot of time in this room. This feels like his space.

To my disappointment, his desk drawers don't seem to contain a lot other than the necessities. Pens, pencils, paperclips, staples. But in the middle drawer, I find a leather binder, and when I open it up, I think it's a tablet, but it's really just an electronic calendar. After fiddling with the buttons on the screen, I manage to translate the words into English. Suddenly, I find myself enrapt in the details, reading through a day in the life of a prince. Instead of starting with today, I click back a few pages, skimming through the meetings and tea appointments and sporting events he's required to attend. There are so many, it's difficult to keep track of, and I can't even imagine how he goes from one thing to the next. But the thing that surprises me most is all the charitable endeavors he seems to participate in. Every week, there are at least three days dedicated to supporting his chosen charities. It's so at odds with what the media says about him, and I have to wonder if they know this side, or if they simply choose to ignore it.

On the schedule for today, there's a note that he has a meeting with Dr. Blom in the morning. And I recognize that name as one that appeared the week before too. Why would Thorsen need to see a doctor every week? It seems strange, but there aren't any explanations typed in the boxes. Every week, it's the same time. Nothing changes.

But it's his agenda for this evening that has me really curious. It has the name *Eugen Onegin* typed out with Oslo Opera House below it. What would Thorsen be doing at the opera? And the more haunting question is... who is he with?

Absently, I click through the rest of the days in the coming weeks, looking for clues. But there aren't any names, other than those of the public figures he meets with on a regular basis. Still, I keep clicking, all the way into next month until I see one square that stops me cold.

Return Ella.

That's all it says. As if I'm just another item on his to-do list. But should I have expected anything else? This was the deal we made, right? So why does my throat feel so raw when I swallow? And why does it hurt worse than I ever could have imagined thinking of going back home to the only life I've ever known. Narcissa will probably turn me away before I can even step foot in the door.

Hopelessness threatens to swallow me whole as I click to the next week in the schedule, not really paying attention to the blank spaces until I see one dated a week after our time comes to an end.

Aokigahara Forest?

Another oddity. Is he planning to go on holiday?

"What are you doing?"

My head snaps up at the sound of Thorsen's voice, and the air in my lungs seems to evaporate as I meet his stormy gaze. He's dressed in a smart black suit with a bowtie, and his hair is styled in that artfully messy way that makes him look like he just fucked someone's brains out. I just don't want to believe that's true.

"How many of us are there?" I ask.

"What?" He stalks into the room, towering over the desk as he removes the leather case from my grasp and slams it shut.

"How many other women do you do this with?" My voice wavers, betraying the emotions I still can't quite admit. "Do you have other women stashed at different houses? You go see them, and then you come back here to me?"

He stares at me, his expression blank as if he's trying to determine something for himself. "What does it matter?"

"It matters." I yank the robe he gave me around my body as I stand, my sudden insecurity threatening to expose me. I'm on the verge of tears, and I don't even know why. But I gave myself to him. I gave him my body and maybe a piece of my soul too. And now he's standing here, emotionally bankrupt, asking me why it matters.

"Are you having sex with other women?" I demand.

"What would you say if I told you I was?" His face is a mixture of curiosity and irritation, and I can't tell if he's trying to provoke me, or if he just thinks I'm insane.

"I'd say I was leaving." I swallow.

Shadows dance beneath his eyes as he circles the desk, and I stumble back in the opposite direction. I don't even know why I do it, but it's just instinct that makes me run. Out of the office, down the stairs, and toward the kitchen. I can hear his footsteps behind me, quick and hard. He doesn't have to run to keep up. His legs are long, and the predator inside him is confident. He will catch me, and he will devour me.

I make it as far as the terrace doors before he grabs me from behind and hoists me into his arms. He stalks down the hall to my room and tosses me onto the bed inside. I crawl toward the opposite edge, and he grabs me by the ankle, yanking me back. He pins me against the mattress with the weight of his body, and reaches beneath me, yanking the fabric of my robe apart. I squirm against him when he shoves his fingers between my thighs and grinds his hard cock against my ass.

"You're not leaving me, Ella," he growls into my ear. "We had a deal."

"I'm not sharing you with someone else." The words tumble from my lips before I can filter them, and Thorsen freezes behind me.

His touch is surprisingly gentle when he brushes the hair back away from my face. When he turns me in his arms to face him and presses his hips between my legs, I can't escape the intensity in his eyes.

"You don't have to," he murmurs so quietly, I'm not even sure I heard him correctly.

In the next breath, his lips are on mine. Kissing me. Tasting me. Fueling this craving for him that I can no longer deny. He fumbles with the zipper on his pants and removes his cock while he blazes a trail of hot kisses down over my throat, and eventually, my nipples.

When he sucks my breast between his teeth, my hands find refuge in the dark, silky strands of his hair. I'm sore, but I want him. No, I need him inside me again. When I drag my fingers down over his shoulders, he bumps the head of his cock against me.

I suck in a breath, shivering as he begins to push his thick, hard flesh inside me. He's so fucking big, everywhere. His hands, his dick, his gladiator body. He could crush me. Smother me. Choke me. But right now, he isn't Thorsen, the dark prince. He's Thorsen, the gentle lover, kissing my face as he waits for my body to give way to him. I can't even pretend there's any other option as I melt beneath his touch. How little it takes for him to bend me to his will.

"*Min gudinne.*" His breath tickles my ear.

Using his palms to spread my thighs farther apart, he adjusts his body snugly into the space made just for him. He feeds his cock into me with a torturous slowness, his lips clashing with mine. And this is where we begin and end. He moves in me, rolling his hips, thrusting as his suit scrapes over my nipples. He's poetry in motion, and each angle never fails to capture my attention all over again. He fucks me the way I imagine every woman must want to be fucked. It's soft, and then rough, all-consuming, fire and passion.

I cling to him desperately, praying it never ends as his teeth scrape over my throat, my collarbone, the most sensitive places on my body. He sucks at my skin, tasting me as he thrusts deep into me, spiraling out of control.

"Come for me." His hand moves between my thighs, and in a matter of seconds, he's setting off an explosion.

The aftershocks are still crashing through me when he buries his cock with a growl, releasing himself inside me again. His fingertips come up to kiss my face reverently, and when his eyes meet mine, something changes between us. The earth stops moving, and everything becomes quiet and still. Does he realize it too? *Does he know he just made love to me?*

When I reach up to touch his face, his eyes fall shut. For one blissful moment, he gives in to me, leaning against my palm, breath ragged. How long has he been starving for this affection? How long has he gone without?

"Thorsen," I whisper.

He opens his eyes again, and in a split second, everything changes. The shutters come down, and whatever softness I saw in him has been exiled to the darkest pit of his soul.

"What do you think you're doing?" He grabs my hand and pulls my fingers away.

I blink, startled by the raw anger in his voice.

"I want to touch you," I croak. "I like to touch you."

"You want to trick me," he accuses.

A million different emotions flash through his eyes in the span of a second. Fear, mistrust, doubt, confusion.

"It's not a trick." My voice wavers. "Not everything is a threat. Least of all me."

His nostrils flare, and whatever trust I was hoping to gain obliterates when he pulls his cock out of me. Within seconds, he's dragging me across the room and back to the cross. He intentionally turns me against the wood, so I can't see him, and I realize as he's restraining my hands and feet that this is his defense mechanism. He's never allowed anyone to get close to him. He has to be in control. He has to have dysfunction. Is that why he's shared every other woman with Calder?

"Who hurt you?" I demand.

Thorsen freezes, his hands on my ankle, and for a second, I think he might even answer me. But then he cinches the cuff tight, strapping me in for whatever punishment he thinks I deserve for getting under his skin.

His footsteps pad to the wall with all the devices of pain and torture, and I crane my neck to find him selecting a paddle. When his eyes meet mine again, they are so empty it scares me.

"Nobody can hurt me, Ella," he says as he comes to a halt behind me. "Least of all you."

He whips the paddle against my ass, forcing my body into the wooden frame as I suck in a sharp breath. There isn't even time to think about it as he slaps me three more times, and I quickly notice a pattern developing. Slap. Slap. Slap. Slap. Always sets of four. Even when he's sadistic, he's ritualistic.

He isn't going easy on me, and this isn't like the crop. The wood bites into my skin with every extension of his rigid arm and warmth blooms across my backside as blood rushes to the surface. It's intense, and the vibrations of the paddle so close to my sex leave me with an empty ache to have his cock all over again, even as his come drips down my thighs. The sickness inside me finds comfort in the pain as I resolve not to let him prove his point. He can't hurt me either. Throughout all of it, I don't make a single noise, even when he slaps me harder, and I think that's what pisses him off the most.

"You think you are so clever." His fingers pinch at the raw skin, groping my ass cheek as he discards the paddle. "Let's play a game, Ella. We'll see how clever you really are."

He disappears again, rummaging through the cabinet against the wall until he finds what he needs. My beating heart slows for just a second as I catch my breath and strengthen my resolve. It doesn't matter what he comes at me with. There's nothing he can do to truly hurt me. I want to tell him so. But then I hear the familiar flick of a lighter, and all my bravery goes up in flames.

"Thorsen?" I crane my neck, frantic, but he won't look at me.

His eyes are on the candle. And I'm not strong anymore. My body thrashes against the restraints as I begin to murmur my protests.

"Please not that," I whisper. "Anything else. Anything else. Just not that."

I don't know what he's going to do, but in my mind, the only scenario playing on repeat is that flame igniting my flesh. White-hot pain. Singed nerves. The burning smell. It all comes back to me, consuming my thoughts and stealing my breath.

I squeeze my eyes shut, chanting the same thing over and over again. Please. But Thorsen isn't listening, or if he is, he isn't responding. And I realize I was so wrong. He does have the power to hurt me because he knows my fear, and he's hell-bent on exploiting it.

"Thorsen, please—"

Heat licks along my back, burning a path all the way down to my ass, and I release a blood-curdling scream as I arch into the frame, desperate to get away. Another path ignites, this time over my thigh before yet another trickles down my arm. And that's when the true terror takes over.

I can feel it happening before I'm truly cognizant of it. The dimming noise around me. The explosive rhythm of my heart. And finally, the elephant on my chest, squeezing the air from my lungs.

My vision narrows to a pinpoint, and I try to reach for my throat as the panic attack consumes me, only to find that I'm still strapped to the cross. Darkness threatens, and I sway before my feet collapse, and my face collides with the wooden frame. The last thing I hear in my conscious state is Thorsen's startled voice.

"Ella?"

22

THORSEN

"Ella."

My fingers slip on the buckle around her restraint, and I swear under my breath as I yank one ankle free, then the next. My hands are trembling. My throat feels hot. I don't understand what's happening to me as I fight to get her wrists free.

Heat licks along my throat as she touches me between my legs, raking her nails over my penis. She tells me it feels so good, and how lucky I am that she's teaching me how to be a man. Acid coats my tongue, and I try to choke it back, but I can't. When I vomit, she curses at me, reaching for the broomstick she keeps next to her desk.

"P-p-please, no." I shake my head, frantic.

She tells me this is the only way to cure me before she turns me around and shoves me over the desk. Tears leak from the corners of my eyes, and pain splinters the length of my spine as she shoves the broom handle inside me. I retch again, but nothing comes up this time.

She twists the handle and then pulls it back out, lashing me across my back. The thunderous crack echoes off the walls, and my vision blurs as I sway to the left. Before I can fall, she shoves me back onto the chair and climbs on top of me, forcing my head back as she lifts her skirt. My head collapses back against the chair, and she forces me inside of her.

"That's good," she praises as I squeeze my eyes shut and wait for it to be over. "You like this very much, Thorsen."

"Ella." I scoop her limp body into my arms and brush my fingers over her face. "Wake up, *min gudinne.*"

She stirs, confused, and then terrified as she glances down at her arm. When I wipe the red wax away, she crumples into herself, breaking down into full-body sobs. I did this to her. I'm an emotional terrorist, and I think I just fucking broke her.

I drag her up against my chest and sweep the hair away from her face, kissing the tears on her cheeks as I try to find the words to comfort her.

"It's just wax." My voice is rough and raw. "Just wax, Ella. You're okay."

But I know she isn't okay. I didn't really burn her, but she thought I was. I knew exactly what I was doing when I manipulated her fears in my moment of weakness. All because I was too much of a coward to admit she fucking terrifies me. I wanted to punish her for making me feel this way. She was just supposed to be a toy. Someone to use and control and release the pressure at a boiling point inside me. But Ella is fucking everything up. The way she looks at me, touches me, and even worse... the fact that she refuses to hate me no matter what I do to her. It's all too much.

I want to tell her she should go. Things are already confusing between us, and time will only complicate matters. But the thought of her walking out now isn't something I can accept. She promised me two months. When they're up, I have to leave her. I have to do the only thing that's ever made sense.

"It isn't okay." Ella shakes her head against me, even as she clings to my suit. "You terrify me, Thorsen. You are so fucking broken, and I don't know if I can survive you."

"I know." My eyes fall shut, and my grip on her tightens. "And I can't promise that you will."

Her body shakes as she continues to cry, and at some point, I realize that I'm rubbing her arm. It feels at odds with all the unwritten rules I have about women, but even as I consider that, I can't stop. I don't want to.

"There needs to be some kind of boundary," she says finally, her voice weak, but resolved. "If I tell you something is too much, then you need to accept that. Don't push me past my breaking point again, Thorsen."

I want to promise her I won't, but I know myself better than that. Whatever this thing is between us, it's too volatile for my own good. She sets me off in a way nobody else ever has. My emotions are amplified to the point of being so intense I can't deal with them. For twenty years, I have only known numbness, but I fear that Ella is bringing me back to life.

"I need to have control." My lips brush against the shell of her ear, and she shivers. "It's the only way."

"So have your control," she whispers against me. "But don't provoke my fears because you're upset."

My fingers blaze a path over the lines of her face, and she's so soft, it surprises me that she can be hard too. It isn't common for women to challenge me this way, and it makes me question everything about Ella's motives.

"Is it really worth it?"

"What?" She blinks up at me.

"The money." My voice feels brittle. "Is it worth two months in hell with me?"

She frowns, and she's quiet for so long, it only compounds my frustration. I don't like her silence. I want her thoughts. I want them all in their rawest, most unfiltered form.

"I want you to save the sanctuary." She toys with the hemline of my suit. "That's all I've wanted for months. But I don't want to think of our arrangement that way either. I don't just want you to see me as the person you're paying to be here. Because that isn't how I think of you."

Her words settle over us, heavy with too many landmines to navigate.

"It must be so exhausting to feel everything so deeply," I mutter.

"It's my curse." She rests her head against my shoulder with a familiarity that makes me nervous. "But I know you feel things too, Thorsen. Even if you can't admit it."

"We aren't talking about me."

"Why do you do it?" she pushes. "Why do you want everyone to think you're so heartless? I know that isn't true."

"You don't know anything," I bite out.

"I know there's a lot more to you than people give you credit for. I saw your schedule. All the work you do for charities and your country. You are capable of doing good, and you do good every week, you just don't want people to know it."

"It's my duty. There's nothing more to it."

"You have no idea how much power you have." She shakes her head in frustration. "All the things you could change. The lives you've already changed."

"Ella." My voice is a warning. "This isn't up for discussion."

Her lips flatten, and she falls quiet, but I have a feeling this isn't the last I'll be hearing about this from her. It's better if she just accepts things as they are. When she looks at the world and sees possibilities, I need her to understand there aren't any in me. I'm a parched desert where nothing can grow, and she could rain down her light on me every day, but that won't change anything. I'm certain of that.

"Let's get you cleaned up." I carry her into the bathroom, repeating the process of filling the tub and testing the water before I set her down inside it.

When I reach for the soap, she stills my arm, wrapping her delicate fingers around my wrist as she looks up at me with the bluest eyes I've ever seen. "I want to wash you."

The word no is already perched on my tongue. "Ella—"

"Please?" she begs. "Just this one time. I'll be quick."

Before I can even answer her, she's sliding her hands inside my jacket and pushing it down over my shoulders. I shouldn't let her have her way, but I'm curious to see what benefit she possibly thinks she could gain by washing my body.

Her fingers deftly move over the buttons of my shirt next, tugging the hem from the waistband of my trousers. I do the rest of the work and discard the clothing onto the bathroom floor. When I'm standing before her naked, my cock at eye level, it occurs to me again how small she is. Yet, she isn't afraid of me. Even after I paddled her ass and tormented her with the wax. Her courage has returned, not wavering for a second in the face of the monster as she summons him to join her.

I step inside the tub, and she shifts her body to the front, leaving the back for me. Water sloshes against the sides and over the edges when I sit down, resting my back against the smooth porcelain. Ella perches her body weight onto her knees as she wedges her frame between my spread thighs. I've never done this with anyone, and I'm hyperaware of her as she explores my body with her eyes. She's a hungry little goddess, and I've never felt more like prey.

Ella squeezes some soap into her hands and works them into a lather, starting in on my feet first. A tremor moves through me as she massages the insoles, her small fingers working magic that I never knew existed. There's a chemical reaction in my brain, a shot of dopamine on steroids. My eyes fall shut, and a heaviness settles into my bones as she touches me with a sincerity that I want to believe is real. Even after I tortured her, she only has good to give me. Good that I don't deserve.

"Does that feel okay?" she asks hesitantly.

I grunt in response, not bothering to open my eyes, and I can almost feel her smile as she watches me. A few more seconds. That's all I'm going to give her. But then she moves up my legs, massaging my calves as she goes. I never knew there was so much tension there. But as it turns out, there's tension everywhere, and Ella finds it. I don't even know how long it goes on for. She bathes me. Rubs me. Takes care of me. And I let her because I'm under her spell. She sees things in me that nobody else ever has, and it plagues me.

Four.

Her whispered observation when she was on the ecstasy comes back to me as she washes my body in strokes of the same number. I should tell her to stop. I should warn her I know exactly what she's trying to do. But it feels too good. Nothing has ever felt this good.

Ella's fingers crawl through the hair on my head, pressing into my skull as she straddles me, her pussy rubbing against my cock. I'm hard for her again, but I don't want to move. I want to stay in this dream forever, where nothing can ever rob us of this moment.

She tilts my head back, and I open my heavy, drugged eyes to meet hers. So pretty. So blue. She clasps my face between her palms and rocks her body against me as her lips find mine. I kiss her back, lazy and possessive as my fingers curl into her hips.

At some point, she slides my dick inside her, bathing me in her warmth. It feels like heaven, and I can't figure out what's so special about her. Why haven't any of the others ever felt like this?

Ella seems to read my mind, forcing my head back against the tub, so I have a direct view of her as she rolls her body along the length of my cock. She reaches down for my hands, tangling her fingers with mine before she lifts them over my head and pins them to the tile behind me. Her eyes are dark and hot, wild with lust as she fucks me. She isn't trying to control me; she's trying to possess me. And I let her because I realize at this moment, I'm defenseless against her.

I could easily overtake her. Flip her over and hammer into her from behind. But I don't want to. I want to watch this fire goddess awaken me. I want to watch her give me pleasure like I've never known.

She bites her lip to stifle a groan, and in the process, she loses her grip on my wrists. When she collapses into me, I tug her nipple with my teeth, and she squeezes my dick with her body. The first spasm leaves her gasping for breath, and I wrap my arms around her, holding her hostage as I drive into her from below.

Water splashes everywhere and Ella's hands slide down the edge of the tub as she cries out over and over again. When she starts to kiss my throat, sucking at my skin and torturing me with her teeth, it's all over for me. She rocks her hips against me, owning every convulsion of my cock as I unleash inside her. We fall into each other, breathless, and don't resurface again for several minutes. When I do, I'm aware of the fact that my arms are still wrapped around her and my cock limp but tucked away in the sanctuary of her body.

What are you doing to me?

I want to ask her, but I can't bring myself to admit that anything is different. Instead, I reach for the soap and follow through with the mechanical actions of washing her body. But there's nothing mechanical about it when she shudders and closes her eyes, leaning her face against my chest with a contented sigh. She could live right here, and I could die right here.

"Tell me what really happened." My voice is rough when my fingers move over the scars on her arms.

When Ella opens her eyes again, they are tormented, and I don't know what to expect. She could lie to me again. She could dismiss the question, which is what I usually do. Or she could tell me the truth. One way or another, I'm determined to get it out of her, but as it turns out, I don't have to.

"My mother died when I was young," she says softly. "And when I was nine, my father decided to remarry. He moved us to London to live with my new stepmother and her daughters. But we weren't there for long at all when he died too."

"How?" I ask.

"We were robbed while we waited for the train." She lowers her lashes, avoiding my gaze. "He was trying to protect me. They wanted all of our jewelry, and we'd given them everything except for the necklace I was wearing. It was my mother's, and I know he was just trying to keep it for me. But the men attacked him, and one of them stabbed him. He died so fast... there was nothing we could do."

When I swallow, it feels like there are nails in my throat. The image of a young Ella watching helplessly as her father dies of such violence before her is almost unfathomable. Except I know that it isn't. Evil is everywhere in this world. You merely have to open your eyes to see it.

"Did they hurt you too?" I croak.

"No." She shakes her head. "They ran. The police found them eventually, and they were charged, but it didn't change the facts. My father was gone, and I was left with a woman who hated me."

"Your stepmother?"

She nods. "She's always blamed me for that day, and if I'm being honest, I blame me too. They've spent my entire life punishing me for it, and I just let them because I thought it's what I probably deserved."

Her confession is so raw it leaves me speechless. How could she ever think so little of herself? And how could fate be so cruel as to take away everything from her at such a young age?

"Anyway, over the years, there have been incidents," she continues. "Mostly with my stepmother. But my stepsisters too. One of them is worse than the other. She's spoiled rotten, and when things don't go her way, she lashes out. That's what happened one night when I refused to do her homework. She pushed me into the fire and then told her mother I fell. I never said otherwise because I had a feeling she would just do something even worse."

She finishes her story with a deafening silence, and I don't know what to say. There have never been words to comfort me, and I suppose in that way, I am emotionally crippled. I have no words for Ella, either. But in my own fucked-up way, I want her to know I'm sorry. I'm sorry for what she's been through already, and I'm sorry that she ever crossed my path. Because more than anything, she needs someone to save her, and that isn't me.

I brush the wet hair back over her shoulders and cup the back of her skull, kissing her with a brutality that betrays the things I keep saying I don't want. She accepts them. Every messy second of my unspoken lies and pretty words. And when I'm done promising her things in my head that I can never say out loud, I towel her off and carry her naked body back to my bed.

23

ELLA

I'M NOT EXACTLY sure what time it is when Thorsen leaves me. I only know that it's late when he returns, the bed dipping as he sits on the other side, examining something in his hand. In the glow of the lamplight, I can make out a blue bottle. It's like the bottle I found stashed in his bathroom drawer.

"What is that?" I ask sleepily.

He straightens his spine, turning to study me. "It's a sleeping elixir."

"Is that what you gave me? At the sanctuary?"

He screws the lid back on and shakes his head, setting the bottle onto the nightstand. The muscles in his body seem restless, and I'm beginning to understand that he doesn't get a lot of sleep. But I wish he trusted me enough to tell me what keeps him up at night.

He kicks off his shoes and lies back on the opposite side of the bed, not bothering to remove the rest of his clothes. We're an arm's length apart, but it may as well be separate continents, and I'm not willing to accept that.

When he leans over and turns off the light, I scoot closer,

inch by inch, until the side of my body bumps against his. He stiffens, and I don't dare breathe until, eventually, he starts to relax again. We don't say another word to each other. But when I close my eyes, feeling his warmth against me, I am content.

Something stirs me from my sleep, and when I open my eyes, I find Thorsen trying to extricate himself from my body. Somehow, during the night, we ended up with our arms and legs tangled together while my face found a home on his chest.

When our gazes collide, I'm sure I've never seen him so flustered. He's confused and only slightly annoyed. But he pauses for a second, and then shakes off his thoughts, whatever they are, before removing his body from mine.

The bed is cold without him, and I feel a strange sense of loss as he turns and walks toward the bathroom. I'm not really sure what to do with myself, so I wait there while he showers, enjoying the luxuries of his bed and the faint ghost of his scent that still lingers.

When he reappears again, he's freshly shaved and dressed and back to his typical unyielding self.

"Lisbet will make you a vegetarian breakfast this morning," he says. "I have to go out."

"Okay."

He heads for the door, but I call out to him, and he turns back around.

"Can I have my phone?"

"Why?" His eyebrows pinch together. This is an issue for him. He still doesn't trust that I won't go to the media and tell them all wild stories about their not so beloved prince.

"I want to call Charlotte," I say. "And Olivia too. I want to see how the animals are doing."

He hesitates, and I'm fairly certain he's just going to say no. But he surprises me when he nods stiffly. The resignation in his eyes tells me he fully expects I'm going to betray him somehow. Now I'm even more eager to prove that I won't.

"I'll leave it on the kitchen table for you," he says.

"Thank you." I smile at him, and he shifts uncomfortably.

"There are clothes waiting for you in your bedroom," he tells me. "Should you want them."

I don't get a chance to thank him because as soon as he utters the words, he disappears around the corner, his footsteps echoing down the corridor.

Clothes and a phone? Is it possible that I'm actually getting somewhere with Thorsen? I don't want to get my hopes up, so I try not to think too much about it as I roll off the edge of the bed and force myself upright.

On the nightstand, Thorsen's glass bottle remains, and out of curiosity, I pick it up to examine it. It's identical to the other bottle, except this one has a different label. It's a sleep elixir.

When I open the nightstand drawer on his side of the bed, there are several more just like it tucked away in there. Determined to find out exactly what they are, I grab the bottle from the top and then head to his bathroom, rummaging around to remove the other one stashed there too. With both of them in my hand, I make my way back to my room and seek out a space to hide them.

That's when I notice the closet door propped open, and just as Thorsen said, there are clothes hanging from the racks. I peek inside, and an overwhelming tide of anxiety washes over me when I realize just how many there are. Not only does it look like he bought half the city's clothing supply but expensive labels at that. It's way too much, and that isn't even the worst of it. There are shoes and handbags too, which seems odd because it's not like we're going anywhere together, right?

Shoving those thoughts aside, I grab a messenger bag and drop the two bottles into a zippered compartment. Then I move on to pick out my clothes for the day. After twenty minutes of hesitation, I settle on a basic white blouse and skinny jeans, deciding the rest is too complicated to navigate. I've spent years in my thrift shop clothing, and I'm almost afraid to touch some of the nicer items. It comes back to me not deserving things like this, and I can only imagine what Narcissa would say if she saw me now.

After showering and braiding my hair, I wander into the kitchen to find Lisbet has already set out an assortment of items on the table.

"Is it okay to eat in here?" she asks with a curious gleam in her eyes as she studies me. "Or do you prefer outside?"

"In here is fine." I offer a smile. "You've already set the table."

"It's no trouble to change it," she says quickly.

"I'm happy to eat inside," I insist.

After a minute of hesitation, she nods and then points out the array of food she's gathered. Fruit, yogurt, cereals, and bread.

"Thank you very much, Lisbet." I give her an awkward little bow because I'm honestly not sure how I'm supposed to address her. Nobody has ever waited on me like this before, and I feel a little guilty that she has to. "This looks amazing."

"Let me know if I can get you anything else," she says,

the tightness in her features loosening up a bit. "His Royal Highness left a phone for you as well. Just there."

I pick up the familiar cell phone and take a seat. Lisbet disappears, and I bring the screen to life, noting that it's fully charged. I wonder if Thorsen has been through my phone, but then again, it only makes sense that he has. He knew about Charlotte, obviously from my list of contacts, which really only consists of her and Olivia.

While breakfast looks delicious and my stomach is already rumbling, I'm anxious to get my phone calls in while Thorsen's still in a giving mood. Who knows what the weather will be like when he returns today?

The first person I call is Olivia, and she answers on the second ring.

"Ella?" I can practically see her smile through the speaker. "Is that you?"

"Yes, it's me." I smile back even though she can't see me.

"Oh, my God. What on earth is going on? I've been getting deposits every day. Is that really from you?"

I pause for a moment, considering the best way to answer this question. "Yes, I'm... working for someone," I explain. "And it's a two-month contract, so you should see plenty more where that came from."

"Ella, I can't even begin to thank you. I don't know what to say."

"I don't want you to say anything." I reach for a slice of bread and add it to my plate. "I just want to make sure the animals are taken care of. That's all."

"Well, thanks to you, they have food in their bellies," she says. "And if things continue at this rate, I should be able to pay off the vet bills in a week."

"That's great news." I sigh in relief. "You'll be able to keep things going then?"

"If this continues, then yes," she answers cautiously. "But I have to ask, Ella. What kind of job are you doing where you're earning this much money every day?"

I break off a corner of the bread and crumble it between my fingers. I don't want to lie to Olivia, but I can't exactly tell her the truth either.

"I can't say much about it. Only that I'm working for a wealthy man, who's been very generous."

There's a pause on the other end of the line, and Olivia's voice is filled with obvious concern when she speaks again. "Is it legal?"

"Yes." I swallow.

"Are you keeping any money for yourself?" she asks.

"I really don't need very much."

"Ella," she scolds. "You have to keep something for yourself."

"The only thing I want is Alfred," I tell her. "Please just take care of him for me until I can see him again."

"He's not going anywhere," she assures me. "He misses you very much."

"Thank you, Olivia. I should let you go. I have to call Charlotte too while I can."

"Okay," she agrees. "Check in as soon as you can. You know I worry about you."

"I'll be in touch."

"Oh, Ella." She stops me before I hang up. "Can you at least tell me the name of the ship you're working on? Just in case I don't hear from you, or if there's an emergency?"

My eyes dart around the room, seeking out inspiration for a ship name when it hits me. "God of Thunder."

"Huh," she murmurs. "What an unusual name."

"I'll talk to you later, okay?"

"Okay, darling. Take care of yourself."

After I hang up, I video call Charlotte and explain things all over again. But she's not quite so easy to convince. She can smell a fishy story from a mile away, and she makes me promise to keep in touch with her weekly, no matter what. Guilt eats at me when she tells me how worried she's been. But what's even more concerning is that she went to the house to check on me, only to discover that Narcissa and the girls are gone.

They couldn't possibly be out looking for me, could they?

I dismiss the idea as ridiculous, and as soon as I hang up with Charlotte, I try to call the manor. But true to Charlotte's word, the phone just rings and goes to voicemail. It doesn't make any sense, and the more I think about it, the more confused I get.

Narcissa doesn't have any other family to speak of, so where would they go? It's a question that disturbs me all the way through breakfast. But given that I don't have any answers, I decide to put it aside for the time being and focus on what I need to do while I still have my phone.

Pulling up an incognito browser, I type *Nerium Oleander* into the search engine and wait for the results to pop up. After reading through the first few paragraphs, I conclude that it's a flowering shrub, which only adds to my confusion. Why would Thorsen have this in a bottle? Is it some kind of a liquid concentrate? And what is he planning to do with it?

After searching through a few more articles, the answer sends a shiver down my spine. The oleander plant is known for its cardiotoxicity, and I suspect the concentration in that blue bottle is likely fatal. I don't even know how to begin processing that information.

The first initial thought I have is that he must intend to use it on someone, but I quickly dismiss that as a crazy notion. Thorsen drugged me to bring me here, but there's no way he would actually poison me. Or anyone else for that matter. But the alternative is something too dark to consider.

And then I recall that note in his calendar after he sends me home. Aokigahara Forest. When I first saw it, I thought he was going on a holiday. But what if it isn't? What if it's something so sinister, my mind can't even admit the possibility?

"Thor?"

The phone in my hand clatters onto the table as I discover Calder standing in the entryway, and we both freeze.

"I was looking for Thor," he says, his eyes darting away.

"He isn't here." I close out the browser on my phone and turn off the screen. "He said he had to go out this morning."

Calder frowns. "There wasn't anything on his schedule."

"I'm sorry. I don't know where he went."

We're both quiet, and I think he's just going to leave, which would probably be best. It's more than awkward between us now, and from the awful look on his face, I'm guessing Thorsen still hasn't spoken to him yet.

"You're the girl from the ball in London," he says finally. "Aren't you?"

"Yes," I admit.

He walks around the table, opting to take a seat at the far end, away from me. "I should have known."

"I should have told you when you didn't recognize me," I say. "Or asked Thorsen what he wanted that night. I just assumed..."

"You assumed his brother was giving you reliable information." Calder shakes his head. "I swear, I never would have done anything if I'd known he felt that way. He's never wanted anyone for himself. It just... it caught me off guard. I thought I was helping him with you."

"I think he has it pretty well handled."

"I get that now," he says. "But he still hasn't spoken to me. I've been calling and texting. We've never gone this long without talking."

"I'm so sorry." I focus on my plate, hating that the entire situation went down the way it did. "I never wanted to hurt him either."

"It wouldn't be the first time he's heard that," Calder remarks.

"If you want to accuse me of something, go ahead and say it," I challenge him. "So far, I've done nothing to hurt him. My phone is right here, and you don't see any media reports on him yet, do you?"

He studies me, trying to determine if I'm trustworthy, and then sighs. "Trust me when I say I'm not trying to be an asshole, but you have to understand how many people have taken advantage of him before. A lot of people seem trustworthy, but that doesn't necessarily mean anything."

"I get it." My tone softens. "I've seen the papers. And I know Thorsen isn't the man they portray him to be."

"You're probably the first woman to say that who actually means it." Calder smiles. "I can see why he likes you."

"I do mean it. I wouldn't say it if I didn't. But I also know that Thorsen is damaged. And sometimes, I don't think he'll ever see his way out of that despair."

Calder stares down at his folded hands. "I probably shouldn't tell you this, but it's public knowledge anyway. He had a girlfriend once, six years ago. She was his first."

Jealousy sprouts up inside me, and I find myself leaning forward, desperate to hear every word about this woman. "What happened?"

"She was playing him," he answers. "It was the first woman he trusted after... well, after some really horrible things happened. I didn't think he'd ever trust anybody. But he met Anja, and he thought she was someone who might be different."

"And then she betrayed him?" I whisper.

"She was feeding information to the media and raking in paychecks." The pain in his voice is visceral, and I can tell it wasn't just Thorsen who got hurt by this situation. Calder cares so deeply about his brother that he feels his hurt too.

"That's awful." I blink back tears. "I had no idea."

"It wrecked him," Calder says. "He wouldn't want you to know that, but I think it's important you do. When he tries to push you away, it's because he's scared. But the fact that he brought you here means something. He sees something in you, and I want you to swear to me you'll never hurt him like that, Ella."

"I won't," I swear, abandoning the defensiveness I felt just a few moments before. "I know it probably sounds crazy, but... I care about him."

"It isn't crazy." He shrugs. "Thorsen is easy to love. He just hates himself."

I'm tempted to ask him about the bottle of poison, but I don't want to worry him unnecessarily. Not yet, at least.

"Our mother is dying," Calder tells me quietly. "He probably hasn't mentioned that either."

"No." My throat pinches. "He hasn't."

"Brain cancer," he says. "It's a tumor. The doctors say it won't be long until she's gone."

"I'm so sorry." The words heave from my lungs.

"Thorsen is close to her, and I'm worried about him. He's going to need you, Ella. You can help him through it. I believe that's why he brought you here. He knows what's coming, and he needs someone to get him through it."

"Of course, I will." I nod. "I'll be there for him, no matter what."

"He's going to push you away. He'll push all of us away. But maybe you can get through to him."

"I won't let him do that," I insist. "I won't let that happen."

It's an admirable notion, but from the anguish on Calder's face, I can tell it's not going to be that easy. He's been down this road with Thorsen before. Something horrible happened in his past, and he's still fighting those demons every day.

"Has he ever... tried to hurt himself?"

Calder snaps his attention back to me, and I know before he even says anything that I'm right. "Why would you ask me that?"

"I just—"

"What the hell do you think you're doing?"

Thorsen's voice catches us both off guard, and we turn toward him with matching expressions of guilt. I'm horrified when I see the same sense of betrayal and hurt burning in his eyes.

"Thor." Calder pushes his chair back and stands up. "I need to speak with you."

"Why are you here?" His eyes dart between us. "Why are you with Ella?"

"He was looking for you," I tell him. "That's all."

But I know that isn't all. He looks like he's about to blow a gasket, and he's already assuming the worst even though it isn't logical.

"Get out." Thorsen glares at his brother.

Calder sighs, lingering for a minute before he decides

that it's best not to provoke him. He offers me an apologetic glance and then disappears, leaving me alone with the thundering god. I hold my breath, waiting for whatever comes next, but as it turns out, he only has one thing to say.

"Get down on your knees."

24

THORSEN

ELLA CRAWLS TOWARD ME, her fingers gripping the cold tile floor as her eyes shine with regret. She doesn't understand the meaning of the word. Not yet.

When her knees bump against my shoes, she reaches up with trembling hands and unzips my trousers without being asked. Much to my irritation, it only takes her fingers brushing over the bulge in my briefs to make me painfully hard for her.

"Nothing happened, Thor," she says with such familiarity, it only adds to my ire. "We were just talking."

"Please me." I tangle my fingers in her hair and force her head back. "That's what you're here for. Or have you forgotten?"

She tries to nod, but my grip is too tight, and I can't relent. Because in my mind, I'm still questioning it. Ella tries to put me at ease by dragging out my cock and sucking it into her mouth. My eyes fall shut, and I give into her for just a second. But it isn't tempering my frustrations.

I want to fuck her until she's completely wrecked, her skin swollen and flushed and smelling of me. That only bothers me more. There's no room for this hunger inside me. But the more I taste her, feel her, possess her, the more I want. It's like a drug, and she's making me question my sanity.

I yank her head back, and my dick falls out of her mouth. She looks up at me in confusion, but I have nothing to say as I pull her up from the floor and drag her back to the kitchen table. There's a good chance Lisbet is still around, but I really don't give a fuck right now.

Bending Ella over, I unzip her jeans and drag them down over her hips, revealing her glistening pink pussy waiting to be destroyed by me. When I slide my fingers through her arousal, I can't stifle the groan in my throat.

"Is this for me?"

"Only you." She breathes the words so righteously against the table.

I slap her pussy, and she yelps right before I shove my dick balls deep inside her with contentment I'll likely never know again. Fuck her for making me feel this way.

I glare down at her, rubbing her hair over her face so she can't watch me. My fingers curl into her hips, and I fuck her into the table, using her like a doll as I think about nothing else but getting myself off. She's quiet as a saint, biting her lip and trying to be good as she lets me take her like an animal. I smack her ass a few times, branding the creamy skin with my handprints, and still, she doesn't make a peep. When that fails me, I lean my body over hers, yanking her blouse apart and pulling it down until her shoulders are bare. She tries to look back at me again, and I pin her head to the table with my palm. When my teeth sink into her shoulder, she finally gives me what I want. A scream that sounds like music to my fucking ears as my dick surges inside her, stuffing her full of my come.

"Mine," I snarl, belatedly realizing I said that out loud.

Ella trembles in my grasp, squeezing my dick inside her to milk me dry. I think she likes being full of my come. I think she likes it so much I could imagine what it would feel like to impregnate her.

That thought stops me dead in my tracks. I pull my wet dick out of her and leave her there, hanging on the edge of the table. Messy and filthy and mine. That word keeps reverberating in my mind, and I need to make it stop. My eyes move over her, and I'm trying to figure out what to do next when Calder calls out for me again.

He rounds the corner from the main hall, and when his eyes land on Ella, he quickly averts his gaze.

"Calder," I growl.

"It's *Mor*," he chokes out. "You need to come now."

"She's had several seizures," Astrid explains. "This isn't uncommon."

"When?" My eyes move over the frail woman lying in my mother's bed. It doesn't look like her. Her gaze is so unfocused she hasn't even noticed us.

"Throughout the night," Astrid answers.

"Why wasn't I informed immediately?"

She fiddles with the IV bag attached to my mother. "That's not up to me."

"Where the hell is the king?" I demand.

Calder's lips set into a grim line, a sure sign that he's hiding something.

"What is it?"

"Let's step outside." He tries to usher me away from our mother. "We can discuss it there."

I hesitate, but Astrid is quick to give me her reassurance. "She needs to rest. If she becomes cognizant again, I'll let your father know immediately."

"If?" I choke out.

She offers me a pitiful expression that's meant to be sympathetic, I'm sure, but it does me little good. That woman is our mother, and we were supposed to have more time.

"Things can change rapidly with this disease," Astrid says. "Timeframes are only estimations. In my experience, it's not atypical for something like this to occur out of the blue. It's not generally a slow transition."

"Thor." Calder reaches out for me, but I shrug him off.

I knew this was going to happen, but I'm not ready for it yet. And I'm terrified that I'll never have another coherent conversation with her. When I walk around the bed and take her hand in mine, she doesn't even seem to notice. Her eyes are focused on the ceiling, unmoving, until they fall shut and remain that way.

"She's exhausted and medicated," Astrid tells me. "I think after some rest, you will have a better visit."

I don't want to leave her, but I know she's right. She needs to rest, and I need to speak with Calder about why our father can't be fucked to come visit his dying wife.

After we both give her a kiss on the cheek, Calder and I step out into the hall. He drags a hand through his hair, restless energy burning in his eyes.

"First, I want to apologize about Ella," he says quickly, holding his hand up before I can argue. "I didn't realize, Thor. I thought I was helping you, but I can see now that I wasn't. And I need you to know it will never happen again. She's yours. I get that. I'll never come between you two, and I hope you can find it in your heart to forgive me."

When I don't respond, he reluctantly moves the conversation along. "As far as our father is concerned, there's something I've noticed, but I didn't want to upset you."

"What is it?"

His attention drifts down the hall, and he hesitates for a second before gesturing for me to follow. "Maybe it's better if I just show you."

He leads the way to our father's suite, and I follow wordlessly at his side, trying to process the warring emotions in my mind. There are too many to identify, and I feel too much. All I want to do is get drunk. I know it won't solve anything, but at least I wouldn't feel like this.

"Is he here?" I ask as Calder turns the knob on the king's door.

He shakes his head, and I follow him inside. The room is just as I remember it even though I haven't found an occasion to enter this suite since I lived at the palace many years ago. Everything is still decorated the way my mother preferred it, in shades of white and gold. But in place of my mother's things, someone else's belongings have infiltrated. It takes me a minute to notice all of them. The dressing gown draped over the chair. A pair of black heels. A gold necklace on the bedside table.

"What is this?" My heart kicks against my ribs in protest.

"They're Narcissa's." Calder glares at the offending items. "It appears the two of them have become quite close."

I feel like I've been punched in the gut. I don't want to believe that he would do this to our mother. Not while she's dying. But my denial doesn't make it any less true.

"No." I grab the necklace the nightstand and hurl it at the wall. "I will not stand for this!"

"Thor." Calder tries to hold me back as I head for the

door. "Think about what you're doing. He'll ban you from the palace. You won't be able to see *Mor* again."

What he's saying makes sense, but I'm not done yet. My fist sails into the wall, leaving a gaping hole as a gift to my father when he returns.

"Feel better?" Calder asks.

"No."

"I don't like it either," he says. "And I don't trust any of them. But we have to be smart about this."

"Where are the women now?" I clip out.

"I don't know. Father called me this morning to tell me about *Mor*, and he said nothing else other than he wouldn't be here. He had a luncheon to attend."

"Of course, he did."

"What are you going to do?" Calder calls after me as I stalk down the hall.

I leave him to follow as I open the door to my father's office, moving around the desk and grabbing the remote for the monitors on the wall. Calder shuts the door behind us, watching as I flip through the rooms of the palace. It takes several minutes, but I finally locate the women in the east drawing room. They are having afternoon tea, but from the looks of it, none of them are happy.

I adjust the volume, and Calder and I listen intently to their conversation.

"Quit being so dramatic, Lavinia," Narcissa chastises her daughter. "It isn't my fault you've done a poor job of winning over the prince."

"I need more time," she hisses. "You can't just barge in and take over."

"You're just pitching a fit because she's going to be queen and not you," Magnolia sneers.

"Girls." Narcissa lowers her voice. "What does it matter?

We need to keep the big picture in mind. One way or another, we'll be living in the palace. Either by my hand, or Lavinia's, if she can ever get the prince to change his mind."

Magnolia snickers and Lavinia's face mottles with red as she stands up, tossing her napkin onto the table. "This isn't over."

She storms away, and Narcissa merely shrugs as she and Magnolia resume their tea. I mute the screen again and flip it back to the main channel.

"The queen isn't even in the grave yet, and Narcissa thinks she's going to replace her," Calder fumes.

"*Mor* isn't safe here." I pace the length of the room. "We need to do something."

"He'll never let her go," Calder says. "And she won't want to leave either. She has no idea what's going on just down the hall."

I know he's right, but I don't want to accept that. We can't just leave her here while this is happening right under her nose.

"We can work in shifts," Calder suggests. "I'll look after her for part of the day, and you part, and we can call Aunt Runa to come. Now that the time is close, she'll want to be with her anyway."

"Father won't turn her away," I agree. "And he'll have to keep his dick in his pants while she's here."

"I'll make the call now." Calder fishes his phone from his pocket. "You have a date with Lavinia this evening, right?"

I cringe at the mention of it. "Yes."

"Don't cancel. You'll just provoke Father if you do. And don't mention anything about Narcissa yet," he advises me. "Right now, they think they have the upper hand, and it's best to keep it that way while we devise a plan."

"I'll come back this evening to stay with *Mor*."

"Just come in the morning," he says. "You have Ella at your house. There's nothing keeping me at home. I'll watch over her today, and aunt will probably be here by morning."

"Okay."

"Thor," Calder calls after me as I turn to go. When I glance back at him, his expression is grim. "We're going to get through this."

25

THORSEN

"DINNER ON A YACHT," Lavinia croons as she takes her seat. "How romantic."

"My father planned it."

Her eyes flash, and it seems my temperament is finally getting on her last nerve.

"Ah, yes, your poor father," she says. "I can only imagine what this situation with your mother is doing to his heart."

The steward comes to pour our drinks, but my eyes don't move from her face. "His heart?"

"Oh, yes." She brings a hand to her lips, playing coy, but it feels like she's taunting me. "I suppose I shouldn't have said anything. I didn't upset you by mentioning it, did I? It's just that he told us about his own health struggles, and I assumed you already knew."

The steward tries to leave after pouring me a couple of fingers of *akevitt*, and I gesture him back, snagging the bottle from his hand. "You can leave it here."

Lavinia smiles as the steward disappears, letting out a contented little sigh as she traces the tines of her fork with a long, red nail. "So, tell me, Thorsen, how are you feeling about your mother? Would you care to talk about it?"

"How do you feel about your mother?" I dissect the lines of her face, noting how hard they are compared to Ella's. She may well be sculpted from ice.

Unsurprisingly, she doesn't answer my question, but as the evening wears on, I can't help feeling that she's still trying to provoke me. One inane question follows another, and she doesn't back down, even when I stop answering her. It's around this time, I realize I've had far too much *akevitt*, and by the time we leave, every word she utters is a challenge to my foul mood.

It isn't until we're on the gangway that the pieces begin to fall into place. The first snap of a flashbulb blinds me, followed by a torrent of others.

"Prince Thorsen, is it true that you're engaged to this woman?" one of the paparazzi shouts.

"Yes, it is." She grabs my arm and flashes a ring I hadn't even noticed she was wearing. But it's unmistakable now. That ring belongs to my mother.

"What the fuck are you doing?" I hiss into her ear as the photographers continue to snap photos and bombard us with questions.

Lavinia doesn't waver for even a second as she turns my face back to the cameras while she leans into me. I yank her away from the scene just as Han, the head of my security detail, rushes to join us.

"I'm sorry, Your Highness. We weren't aware you were leaving."

"Take us to the car," I demand.

He leads the way while the mob trails us. Once we're secured in the back of the car, I speak to the driver in Norwegian, requesting some privacy. He nods and closes the partition between us, and when I turn to Lavinia, she looks like she just won the fucking lottery.

"What the fuck did you just do?" I wrap my fingers around her throat, tempted to squeeze the life out of her. Her hands come up to mind, nails digging into my flesh as she glares at me.

"I wouldn't do that if I were you," she threatens. "You wouldn't want the media to hear all about how you beat your future wife, would you?"

"You'll never be my wife." I shove her back, and a venomous haze clouds over her eyes.

"On the contrary, I think I will. You see, Thorsen, there's a benefit to being at the palace. You could only imagine all the things I overhear. Conversations between your parents. The pillow talk between your father and my mother. There are so many details I've become privy to. Details I'm sure you wouldn't want getting out."

I know I shouldn't, but I take the bait. "Such as?"

"Such as your psychological problems and your little visits with a certain Dr. Blom. Does that ring a bell?"

I can feel the blood draining from my face as she closes in on me like an insect trapped in her web. She couldn't know. There's no way my father would bring it up after all these years. I don't want to believe it, but Lavinia isn't even close to done.

"It's funny, you know." She holds her hand out to examine the ring on her finger with a smile only a psychopath could wear. "The way your father tells it, you came crying to him about a woman teaching you how to be a man. He said you should be so lucky to have a hot woman like that. Did you have any idea that for a good ten years, he didn't think you could even figure out how to use your dick?

Until that girlfriend of yours came along. What was her name again? Anja something or other?"

"Fuck you." I drag the bottle of *akevitt* from my jacket and take four drinks.

"I don't really care about your problems." She leans back into the seat with an easiness that betrays how confident she is that she's won. "I just want the title. You don't have to fuck me. You don't even have to like me. You just have to marry me, or else I'm going to blab to the whole fucking world. And when I'm finished, your reputation will forever be cemented as the most fucked-up man in Norway."

"You think you've got it all figured out." I take another swig from the bottle as the driver pulls to a stop at the entrance of the palace.

"You'll cave." Lavinia lifts her chin. "It's just a matter of time."

She reaches for the door, and I lurch over her, snatching her hand.

"What the hell are you doing?" she screeches.

"Give me my mother's ring," I bellow into her face. "Or so help me, I will break every one of your goddamn fingers to get it off."

Her bravery fractures, and she looks at the driver, but he's following my orders, ignoring us until I alert him otherwise.

"There's nobody to save you here." I slide the ring off her bony finger and pocket it. "Perhaps you should consider that before you start making plans to walk down the aisle."

"I will ruin you!" she shouts in my face. "You have no idea what I'm capable of."

"And you have no idea what I'm capable of." I open the door and shove her out. "But test me again, and you'll find out."

My sweet little fire-breathing goddess is asleep in my bed when I get home. When I pull back the covers, she stirs, blinking up at me with sleepy eyes. And then she smiles, ruining everything.

I came here to punish her. The entire way home, visions of me beating her ass red were the only thing tempering the rage in my soul. I wanted to hate fuck her and torment her and make all the blackness go away. But now, she's so content to be in my presence that I can't bring myself to do it. This isn't what I brought her here for. She isn't supposed to look at me that way, and I'm not supposed to feel... *like this*.

I'm intoxicated, but it isn't the alcohol in my veins that's left me so off-balance. Heat crawls up my spine, threatening to choke off my airway. How dare she do this to me? How dare she make me feel?

"Thorsen?" she whispers. "Are you coming to bed?"

Are you coming to bed?

Does she really think she's domesticated me? And worse yet, why haven't I told her no? Why haven't I told her she should be in her own room, in her own bed?

"Go back to sleep," I growl, stumbling for the door. "And leave me the hell alone."

26

ELLA

SOMETHING IS WRONG. I can feel it in my bones.

Calder's words from earlier come back to mind. *He's going to push you away. He'll push everyone away.*

I can't let that happen. I'm too deep in it already, swimming in feelings more expansive than an ocean. Maybe that makes me sick in the head, but there are only two options right now. Let Thorsen's demons win, proving that he's alone in this world, or show him that no matter what he does, there will always be someone who cares, whether he likes it or not.

I drag my tired body up from the bed, wrapping the silk robe around me and knotting it at the waist. The first place I check is his office, but he isn't there. When that fails me, I wander around the house like a ghost, haunted by the fear in my heart.

Nerium Oleander.

I know the bottles are still in my bag because I pulled them out this afternoon while he was away. But there's still a sense of desperation clawing at me as I search the house, turning up nothing. *Where is he?*

The mantra plays on repeat in my mind while I stand in the middle of the kitchen and close my eyes, listening for a sound. Any sound. But all I hear is the lapping of water against the shore outside.

Outside.

I head for the terrace, opening the French doors, and when I find him sitting there bathed in the moonlight, I don't think I've ever been so relieved. He looks just as tormented as I feel, his profile staring up at the star-littered sky.

Wordlessly, I crawl onto his lap and grip his face between my hands, finding the confirmation I need in his hazy eyes. He's drunk and emotional. But when I bring his head to rest against my beating heart, he doesn't protest.

"Thor." I kiss his forehead and comb through his hair with my fingers. "I'm not going anywhere."

His fingers curl into my robe, holding me hostage as I comfort him the only way I know how. Touching him softly, I kiss his face with a reverence I truly feel. Even in his darkest moments or his cruelest, he leaves me spellbound, and I don't think he has any idea. But I want him to.

"*Min Gud*," I murmur into his ear, using the phrase I learned on Google today. If I am his goddess, then he is most certainly my god.

"Ella." He holds me in a bruising grip. "Don't ever leave me."

"Don't make me," I whisper.

He reaches up to cup the back of my skull, forcing my lips to his. He tastes of *akevitt* and fire, and I'm feverish, working to undo his pants while he parts my robe and shoves the material aside. A frenetic, desperate hunger swirls between us as we come together, and I sink down onto his cock. Thorsen groans into my neck, and I force his head back, so he has to look at me.

When our eyes collide, there's no other way to describe it. It's a clash of thunder. *A coup de foudre.* Electricity crackles in the air between us, and my heart soars. It's intimate, and it's raw and more powerful than any reckoning Mother Nature herself could stir up.

He moves me. He shatters my world. And I understand it at that moment, clearer than the stars in the sky above us. Somewhere along the line, I fell in love with this beautifully broken man. It's liberating and terrifying, and I think I know deep in my soul this is a suicide mission. He'll never be able to love me back.

Can he see it in my eyes? Can he understand what I'm experiencing as we become one on the terrace under the Norwegian sky?

"I feel you." I place his hand over my heart. "In here."

When he freezes, I cover his lips with my fingers and shake my head. "Don't believe it. Don't even acknowledge it. I just had to say it before it poisons me from the inside out."

He watches me with an intensity that makes my racing heart smolder as I rock into him, easing his head back and falling into the only comfortable rhythm we know. Blood pulsing, hearts pounding, flesh on flesh. We live for these stolen moments. Whether it's punishment or passion, this is our therapy. The seconds turn into minutes, our eyes locked on each other, neither one of us brave enough to look away.

He comes for me, and I keep fucking him until I shatter around him too. When I finally collapse against his shoulder, I'm too exhausted to move, and Thorsen doesn't ask me to. I wrap my arms around him, and he holds me back, and we stay there like that for so long our limbs go numb, and the cool air prickles our exposed skin.

"Aokigahara Forest," I whisper into his neck. "Tell me you'll never go there."

His body turns to steel beneath mine. "How do you know that name?"

"It was in your calendar." I close my eyes and shudder. "And today, I looked it up. I know what that place is. I know what people do there."

His fingers dig into my jaw, and he leans closer, inhaling me as he closes his eyes. "You could never understand."

"So make me."

He stills, the sound of his breath the only thing between us. It feels like we crossed an invisible barrier tonight, but I don't know what to expect. He could shut me out, and a part of me is already bracing for that, but he chooses not to.

"My brain is like a radio constantly trying to find the right channel," he says. "An ad commercial, lyrics, static. It never ends. But I can make it stop."

"No." I squeeze his face and force him to listen to me. "I won't let you."

"You don't know me as well as you think you do, *gudinne*. You see something in me that doesn't exist."

"Then let me in," I beg. "Trust me enough to tell me something real. Give me a chance to prove that I won't betray you."

"Something real?" His throat works. "What does the fire-breathing goddess want to know?"

I tap my fingers against his chest, working up the courage to say the thing that might provoke him the most. But he's just drunk enough, and tired enough, and well fucked enough that I think he might finally tell me.

"Who hurt you?"

A cold laugh reverberates from his cavernous chest, and he shakes his head, eyes empty. "Nobody, Ella. I was lucky."

"Lucky how?" I ask.

"Lucky enough to have a woman teach me the ways of being a man. Her lessons were thorough, and it turns out you can cure a speech impediment with savagery."

My stomach churns as I start to make sense of his words, and my lips are so dry, I have to lick them before I can form words again. "How old were you?"

"Ten."

I barely hear him. He's drifting away, falling asleep, and I can't let him go.

"Thor." I smooth my fingers along his pinched brows, and he opens his eyes again. When he sees the despair in mine, he shifts beneath me, his muscles tightening.

"I was joking."

"No, you weren't." My voice shakes, and the floodgates of my emotions crash open before I can contain them. The image of him as a child, abused in that way, cuts me so deep it feels as if I'll bleed to death right here. A trail of tears begins to fall down my cheeks, my heart splintering as I grieve for him.

I'm wrecked, and I can't hide it. Thorsen doesn't know what to do, and that's painstakingly obvious when he tries to comfort me. His palm comes to rest on my lower back, and it only makes it worse because I should be comforting him.

"I lied," he says again. "It isn't true."

"It is true." I touch his beautiful face. "I heard you. I've been listening all along, so don't deny it. Not to me."

He buries his face in my neck and nods against me, and for the longest time, we just sit there, wrapped up in each other. His confession feels significant because he opened up to me, and I don't think Thorsen has opened up to anyone in a very long time. But the war isn't over, and in many ways, I sense it's just beginning.

"Let's go to bed," he murmurs, rising to his feet as I cling to his body.

He pulls up his pants and covers me with my robe, and then carries me through the house to his bedroom. After he drapes my body onto the center of the bed, he kicks off his shoes and crawls in behind me, tucking me against him.

"Just for tonight," he whispers into my hair.

"Tonight," I whisper back. *And every day for the rest of our lives, if I have anything to say about it.*

27

THORSEN

"How is she?" I ask.

Calder takes a sip of his coffee and nods upstairs. "She's awake now and well aware of her surroundings. She asked about you twenty minutes ago."

"You should go get some sleep," I tell him.

"I'll stay a while longer if that's okay with you."

I nod, and we walk together to our mother's suite. I'm not sure what to expect, but when we enter, she's propped up in her bed, and it appears she's rebounded dramatically from yesterday.

"Thorsen," she rasps. "There you are."

I take a seat beside her, and Calder pulls another chair from across the room to join us.

"How are you feeling?" I examine her with blurry eyes.

"Better today," she says. "These medications make me so loopy it's difficult to know what's going on anymore. I told Astrid I didn't want to take anything until you came today."

"You should take your meds. I'm not going anywhere for a while."

"Did you clear your schedule?" She frowns.

"Yes." Much to my secretary's annoyance. I don't doubt the king will have something to say about it as well.

"Aunt Runa is on the way," Calder informs us. "She'll be here this afternoon."

A bleak acceptance passes over our mother's face. She's aware that we're assembling the troops for a reason.

"You boys have always been so protective of me," she whispers. "Are you afraid for me, my dear sons? Is that why you're standing guard at my bedside?"

Calder and I glance at each other, and Mother laughs.

"It's okay. I may have brain cancer, but I'm not brain dead. Not yet, anyway. I know what's going on here."

"You do?" Calder stiffens beside me.

"Your father has always been a restless man. He doesn't have the patience to deal with something like this. He's found comfort where he can, I suppose, as he has many times over the years. I've made peace with that."

"We didn't think you knew," Calder says quietly.

"I know more than you give me credit for." She smiles, but it fades when she looks at me. "There are only a few things that have eluded me over the years."

The door to the suite slams open, startling all of us, and when I turn, my father is standing on the threshold, his expression furious.

"Thorsen!" he roars. "What have you done this time?"

"Why don't you tell me." I sigh.

He spills into the room with Lavinia, Magnolia, and Narcissa hot on his heels. When I lay eyes on Lavinia, my stomach sours. She has a bruised face that certainly wasn't there when I left her last night, but I suspect I already know where this is going.

"Did you get drunk and rough her up last night?" the king demands.

"It's okay, Your Highness." Lavinia smirks at me before she bows her head. "He was having a difficult time, and things just got out of control in the bedroom."

Calder jumps up to defend me, but my mother cuts him off.

"Thorsen?"

When I see the alarm on her face, tiredness seeps into my bones, and I just know I can't fucking lie to her anymore. I can't play the villain in this scenario even if that's what would be best.

"It isn't true, *Mor*."

"Bullshit." My father stomps toward me, shaking his finger while the vein in his forehead throbs. "I should cast you out of this family! I should have sent you away as a child. You have always been trouble. You worthless, pathetic excuse of a man. You aren't fit to be king!"

"Then take your crown and shove it up your ass." I hurl my chair back and step toward him in challenge. "I don't fucking want it. Give it to Calder."

"I don't want it either." My brother joins me at my side. "Let the family name die with us."

"I will ruin you for this!" My father comes at me, drawing his arm back at the same time my mother screams at him to stop. I wait for the blow, but Calder strikes first, surprising all of us when he knocks the king on his ass with a single punch.

Before I can blink, he's launching himself at our father with an untapped rage I never knew existed in him. I'm frozen, watching it all unfold as Calder pummels Elias Lykken in the face over and over again.

"You never protected him!" he snarls. "This is all your fault!"

"Calder." I haul him off our battered father, and he

shoves me away. When Elias stumbles to his feet, he's breathless and shocked as his eyes move between the two of us.

"What do you mean, Calder?" my mother demands. "What do you mean he never protected him?"

Calder's eyes have taken on a life of their own. All these years, he's carried my secret, and I never knew how much of a burden it was until now.

"It's time, Thor," he says. "If you don't want to hear it, I suggest you leave the room. But either way, I'm telling her now. She deserves to know the truth."

My protest dies on my lips when I look at my mother. She's clinging to every word desperately, and Calder has just confirmed what she always suspected. Something happened, and she won't rest now until she knows the truth.

I turn away and head for the door, pushing past my father and Lavinia. When I stumble down the hall to the kitchen, I consider raiding the liquor, but I can't imagine that will benefit the situation. Instead, I find a quiet seat in the drawing room, where I kick back and stare up at the ceiling.

For a moment, I find myself wishing that Ella was here, but then I regret that. I don't want her to witness all this ugliness. I only want her to know me separately from my father, so he can never taint her vision of who she thinks I am. Because even when I'm cruel to her, she still looks at me like I'm her hero.

I close my eyes and allow the quiet to consume me, but inside, my head is loud again. Those dark thoughts get stuck on repeat. *A knife in the kitchen. A roof on the palace. I could just get in the car and leave, see what happens.*

"Thorsen." Dr. Blom's voice startles me, and when I open my eyes, I'm met by the sight of him and Calder together.

"I thought it would be best to have Dr. Blom help us navigate this one," Calder says quietly. "He's ready to go with you. *Mor* wants to see you."

My eyes move over the man in the wire-framed glasses. For years, he has tried to help me, and for years, I have pushed him away. I could never figure out why he kept showing up, seemingly with a genuine interest in my life and my well-being. I've only ever been a miserable bastard to him. But right now, something becomes so painfully obvious I'm ashamed that I never allowed myself to notice it before.

He cares about me. He truly wants the best for me. That sentiment is right there in his misty eyes. He's withholding that emotion for my benefit because he knows this is going to be hard for me. Perhaps one of the hardest days of my life.

"I'll tell your mother anything you want me to," he says. "If you give me permission to speak freely about our sessions. I think this is the right thing to do. I think you'll be surprised how much of a burden this secret has been."

"Okay."

Both of them are surprised, but when I rise from the chair, they edge toward the door, preparing for me to change my mind any second. There's no point in fighting it now. Calder has already told her the worst of it. I can tell by his blotchy red eyes.

We walk in silence to my mother's suite, and there's no sign of my father in sight.

"He left with Narcissa." Calder reads my thoughts. "I doubt they'll be back for a while."

Nodding, I steady myself as Dr. Blom opens the door to my mother's room and gestures us inside. She's in her chair again, and I don't know how she's even managing to stay upright as weak as she is right now.

"You should be in bed." I come to kneel before her.

"Oh, Thorsen." She reaches out for me with a trembling arm, pulling me close as she lets out a heart-wrenching sob. "I've failed you. My god, I have failed you."

"No." I look up at her. "You never did anything wrong."

"I should have known." A river of tears flows down her cheeks. "I should have pushed more for answers."

"I wouldn't have told you," I insist. "It wouldn't have mattered what you did."

"All these years, you were so angry, and I never understood what happened." Her body shakes beneath the weight of her grief. "Why couldn't you come to me?"

"I didn't want to upset you."

"Upset me?" Her voice fractures. "Thorsen, I'm your mother. It was my job to protect you."

"I'm sorry." I bow my head, trying to quiet the raging storm in my mind.

"You went to your father?" she questions. "And he didn't believe you?"

When I don't reply, Dr. Blom steps in.

"May I?" He gestures to the empty seat beside us, and I nod.

"Your Highness—"

"Please, just call me Frida."

"Frida," he agrees. "It isn't uncommon for children to keep the abuse secret in these circumstances. Thorsen went to someone he thought of as his protector, and he was punished for it. In Thorsen's mind, it only compounded his shame. I think it would be very difficult for anyone to trust that someone would believe or help him after such a betrayal of trust. Perhaps this would explain why he didn't feel he could tell anyone else."

"Calder said he mocked you." My mother's fist curls in

her lap, and I don't think I've ever seen her so angry. "Is that true?"

"You know what he's like," I say. "I don't want to talk about it anymore."

Her face crumples, and her tears multiply, making me feel like an asshole all over again.

"I'm not upset with you, Thor," she assures me as Calder hands her some tissues. "I just... I would give anything to change this. To go back and fix it for you."

"But you can't. It was a long time ago."

"Is this why?" she croaks. "Is this why you tried to hurt yourself before?"

When I don't answer, Dr. Blom intervenes. "Would you like me to tell her, Thorsen?"

"Please," she begs me. "I need to know."

My shoulders are stiff, but I force myself to nod and then try to tune out the conversation that follows. It doesn't work.

"Thorsen has never opened up to you about his diagnosis because he didn't want to worry you. But I think maybe it will help you to understand. He has a peculiar form of OCD. It causes him to have intrusive thoughts about self-harm on a frequent basis."

My mother brings an unsteady hand to her mouth, stifling a sob. "You mean... you still... have these thoughts every day?"

"They can feel uncontrollable," Dr. Blom answers. "But they are manageable if the patient is willing. Thorsen has a prescription that can often be helpful if he were taking it."

I scowl at him, feeling betrayed by his keen observation.

"I've noticed a shift since your mother's diagnosis," he says. "You haven't been doing the work. You've been telling me what I want to hear. And I suspect that you are making plans."

Calder glares at me, and my mother breaks into hysterics again. Dr. Blom manages to calm her down with some reassuring words, but it doesn't change the fact that she knows now.

"My oleander concentrate," she whispers. "You took it, didn't you?"

When I don't respond, she nods as if she's starting to understand.

"Your father told me I was imagining things, but I knew it had gone missing."

"Where is it?" Calder demands.

"It doesn't matter," my mother says. "Because Thor is going to dispose of it, and he's going to make me a promise."

I stand and turn away, fighting the urge to pace. Dr. Blom watches me as my mother makes her decree.

"Promise me you're not going anywhere, my darling. No matter what, even on your hardest days, you will keep fighting. Can you do that for me? Can you give me your word?"

When I say nothing, she goes on.

"I won't have any peace until I know you're okay. I can't leave you here like this. Please, sweetheart."

My eyes pinch shut, and I wish I could start this day all over again. I wish that Calder never told her. But it isn't just her. It's Ella too. The guilt is eating at me. They both threw a wrench into my plan, and everything is all fucked up, and I don't know what else there is to say. If I make her this promise, I'm breaking the one I made to myself. But I don't see any other alternative.

"I can only promise to try."

"You will," she says without a doubt. "And don't you worry about your father, I will deal with him. As for Lavinia—"

My attention snaps back to her.

"I made a mistake," she says. "That has become painfully obvious. And I am making it clear right now that I don't want you to marry that girl, Thorsen. Promise me you won't."

Calder chuckles, and despite the gravity of the situation, even I can find some humor in that too.

"I won't marry her," I promise.

"All I want for you, my son, is to follow your heart. Wherever that may lead you."

Calder pins me with his gaze, adding, "I think you already know where that is."

28

ELLA

"Thorsen?"

My eyes roam over the shadow lingering above the bed, but the room is so dark, it's impossible to make out his features. I'm on the verge of fear when he pulls off the blankets and flips on the bedside lamp. He looks haunted in the soft orange glow, and it's obvious that whatever happened tonight, he's been through hell.

"Is your mother okay?" I sit up and reach out to touch him, but he pushes me back onto the bed.

As he stands there, eyes on fire, I'm not quite certain whether I should run or beg for mercy. But when he reaches out for my face, his touch is full of reverence.

"I just want to look at you," he murmurs. "Sometimes, I think I only imagined you in my head."

"You didn't." I lean into him. "I'm here."

He unbuttons his shirt, slowly removing it and dropping it onto the floor before he moves on to his trousers. His briefs are still on when he mounts me, his hands coming to rest on my head. He falls onto me, kissing me with more passion than he's ever shown.

He drags his hands up my body, pulling my silk night-gown with them. I arch into him, and Thorsen groans, finding his way inside me. My body is his church. His place of worship. And he's feeling especially devout tonight. We come together with a manic craving that will never be sated. I need to hear it from him too. I need to know I'm not the only one who is homesick for this place when we aren't together. Beyond all reason, I am in love with him. Can he ever find a way to love my broken parts too?

He kisses me everywhere. Tastes my skin and inhales me. He fucks me one second and makes love to me the next. And somewhere between darkness and dawn, we both find our release, and he collapses into me, struggling to hold his own body weight from the sheer exhaustion of his day. When he rolls over, he brings me with him, so we are side by side, facing each other. Our legs and hands and breath still tangled.

I curl my fingers over his beating heart. The words are silent, but he reads them in my eyes.

I feel you.

Thorsen reaches for my hand, bringing the palm to his lips so he can kiss it. Then he places his palm over my own heart. A promise in the darkness, with words too vulnerable to say. And for a few blissful minutes, as we drift off to sleep like that, it feels like everything is finally going to be okay.

Thorsen

"Thorsen."

Something nudges my arm, and I groan.

"Your phone," Ella murmurs. "Calder keeps calling you. He's called three times already."

I open my eyes and meet hers. She's halfway propped up but still trapped in my arms as she points at the nightstand.

A few seconds of silence pass before the phone starts ringing again, and when I pick it up, a sickening feeling swirls in my gut.

"Calder?"

"You need to get to the palace," he says. "Now."

My pulse thrashes in my ears as I drive through the palace gates, the tires crunching over gravel before the car comes to a stop. Outside, a team of medical workers is assembled, and one vehicle, in particular, catches my eye. It's the coroner.

My body feels as if it's made of lead as I trudge toward the entrance. Calder is already waiting for me there, his expression grave.

"Where is she?" I try to push past him. "Where is she?"

"She's fine." He holds me back and forces me to look at him. "*Mor* is fine."

"She's fine?" My lungs inflate with the first full breath I've taken since he called me thirty minutes ago. "Then what's wrong?"

"It's Father," he says.

"Father?" I repeat. "What about him?"

His eyes are empty, completely devoid of emotion when he delivers the news. "He's dead, Thor."

The earth beneath me sways, and I stumble back a step. Calder reaches out for me, steadying me with his hand.

"Dead?" I wheeze.

"His heart," he says bitterly. "They think it just gave out on him in his sleep."

What he's telling me seems too surreal. Too convenient. That miserable bastard couldn't just be gone. Not that easily. He was supposed to be around for years, making all of our lives hell.

"Is he still here?" I ask.

Calder nods. "He's upstairs in his bed."

I push past him, and he falls in step beside me. "Thor, I don't think this is a good idea."

"I need to see it for myself."

Calder struggles to keep up with my stride as I stalk through the palace, up the stairs and down the hall to his suite. When we reach the doorway, a few paramedics are inside, loading his pale, lifeless body onto a gurney.

The first thing that hits me is how utterly discontent he looks, even in death. And the second is a wave of grief so profound, it nearly brings me to my knees. But I can't understand why. I hated him. I've always hated him.

"It's okay to feel something," Calder says quietly. "At the end of the day, he was still our father."

"He never liked me." I blink, trying to dispel the blurriness in my eyes. "It shouldn't matter."

Calder falls quiet beside me, and there's nothing left to say as we watch the paramedics wheel him toward us. They offer their condolences and ask us if we'd like some time to say our goodbyes.

"No." I turn away. "I need to check on *Mor*."

"She's asleep." Calder follows me out into the hall. "It's been a difficult morning. I think it's best we don't disturb her right now."

"I just need to see her." I stay the path. "I won't wake her."

In Mother's room, we find her asleep, just as he said she was. Aunt Runa is at her bedside, and she greets us both with hugs and condolences as we join her. For lack of a better plan, I sink down into one of the chairs, and Calder takes another. For a long while, we just sit there, lost in our own thoughts.

"Do you really believe his heart just gave out?" I ask nobody in particular.

Aunt Runa regards me curiously. "It was only a matter of time, was it not?"

"The doctors said he had years left."

She takes a sip of her tea and shrugs. "Doctors don't know everything."

"Do you suspect it was something else?" Calder frowns.

Lavinia's offhanded remark about his heart comes to mind, but it seems like a stretch to connect those dots. Would she really take things that far? And if not her, perhaps the woman who was sleeping in his bed every night.

"Where are Narcissa and her daughters?" I ask.

Runa checks to make sure my mother is sleeping and lowers her voice to a whisper. "They made quite the spectacle this morning, carrying on with no respect or decorum. Narcissa broke into a fit of hysterics, and there was little choice in the matter. I had them forcibly removed by security and put up in a hotel until Hayes can make their travel arrangements home."

A knock on the door disturbs us, and Hayes pokes his head inside with an apologetic expression. "I'm so sorry, Your Highness. But would you mind if we have a word?"

I drag myself out of the chair and follow him into the hall, with Calder not far behind.

"What is it?" I ask.

"I understand this must be a terribly difficult time for you," he says. "But your father's secretary and I have spoken, and we believe it's imperative we start briefing you on your duties right away so we can handle the press before the story leaks."

"My duties?" The words ring hollow when they leave my throat.

"Yes, sir. As of this morning, you are the King of Norway."

"Thor." Calder steps beside me. "You don't have to do this right now."

"But he will." My mother's feeble voice speaks from behind us.

"Should you be out of bed?" Calder remarks as Aunt Runa pushes her into the hall.

"I'm fine," she answers stubbornly, her eyes moving to me. "Thorsen, I know the past couple of days have been difficult, but the time has come. This is what you were born for."

"What I was born for?" I laugh humorlessly. "The whole country despises me."

"They just don't know you," she insists. "You've hidden yourself well, but now is the time to let them see you for who you are, and they will love you as we all love you."

I know what she's doing. She doesn't have to tell me why she's pushing this. She thinks this turn of events will force me in a different direction and give me a purpose.

"Give it a chance," she pleads. "That's all I ask."

Hayes speeds along the process by throwing another match on the bonfire.

"Your Highness, we don't have much time. I'm afraid it's very likely Narcissa will speak out to the media. We need to stay ahead of it. It's your job now to control the narrative."

"How long do we have?" I sigh, wishing that plague of a woman and her family would just disappear.

He checks his watch. "As of right now, a little under forty minutes."

Once we secured the official press release, Hayes ushered me off to a meeting with the council that extended into the late hours of the night. After everything that's happened, I refuse to let Narcissa humiliate my mother as her final parting shot. That nagging thought is what drives me down the hall to my father's office.

Now that I have the keys, I can access his files. When I sit down at the desk and unlock his drawers, it doesn't take me long to find what I'm looking for. Alongside the dossiers of the many people in our lives, there's a folder for Narcissa and her daughters.

I flip the files onto the desk and open them, scanning through the mundane details of their lives. School records, dates of birth, job histories, relations. It's at this particular juncture that something catches my eye, and I'm half-convinced I must be delusional from exhaustion because this can't be right. But no matter how many times I blink, the name in the file doesn't change. Listed under Narcissa's relatives is a stepdaughter she never mentioned by the name of Ella Bellerose Laurent.

My head spins, and I feel like I'm going to be ill as that information settles into my consciousness. I can't accept it. There's no way Ella could ever be related to her. I don't want to believe it. But the more time I spend flipping through the pages, the more obvious it becomes that it's horrifyingly true. There are pictures of her inside this folder. A family photograph from when her father was still alive, along with a solitary identification photo. The blue eyes staring back at me are unmistakable. That same woman is inside my home. In my bed. And even worse, she's in my head.

I can't deny the link between them, and my paranoia is festering like cancer inside me. She never told me who her family was. She never mentioned Lavinia or Narcissa by name, and now, there's only one conclusion I can draw. Has she been playing me too? Was it all an elaborate scheme between them? They came to the ball to hunt a prince, and I was the only one foolish enough to take the bait. She spoon-fed me a story that was far too convenient in its desperation. Nobody is that selfless. Nobody would make the agreement she made with me unless there was something in it for her.

I feel you.

When I close my eyes, I can still see her whispering those words under the moonlight. They felt so genuine. But now it feels like a betrayal of the worst kind.

Heat licks at my throat, and the moisture on my lips evaporates, scorching my mouth with a bitterness I can't swallow. She tricked me. She lied to me. I was right not to trust her. But she bested me with a performance more cunning than all the others. And now she's going to pay.

29

ELLA

SOMETHING CRASHES, jolting me from my sleep. When I bolt upright, my first thought is that it's a storm. And it turns out I'm right. It's a storm I know intimately, and his name is Thorsen.

Glass shatters against the floor as his footsteps reverberate off the walls like gunshots. The artwork in the hall doesn't sound like it survived, and every instinct inside me is screaming at me to run. I'm halfway off the bed when the door crashes open, and the god of thunder himself steps through it.

"Thorsen?" A cold chill moves up my spine. "What's wrong?"

He comes for me, dark and scary, his eyes ablaze as his fingers wrap around my throat. "Who are you?"

"What?" My eyes move over his face, trying to get a read on the situation. Has he been drinking again?

"Who the fuck are you?" he bellows. "Tell me the truth!"

"You know me," I whisper.

"I don't fucking know you." He releases me as though I burned him and stares at me with such hatred, it cuts me to the bone. But I'm determined to get to the bottom of this. Something happened. I just need to figure out what it is so we can tackle it together.

"Please tell me what's going on," I beg.

He grabs my phone from the nightstand, flipping through apps like he's searching for my dirty little secret. I'm paralyzed with uncertainty, and I imagine this is how it must feel for a mouse to watch a cat. I've never seen him like this. So angry. So scorned. His eyes flash like he's found something, but I know that isn't possible. I have nothing to hide.

He drops the phone back onto the nightstand and walks into his bathroom, pulling open drawers and tossing the contents out onto the floor. When he appears in the doorway again, his neck is throbbing like I've never seen it before.

"Where is it?" he asks.

"Where is what?"

"The oleander!"

I suck in a breath and shake my head. "I'm not telling you."

"This isn't a game," he snarls. "What part of that don't you understand?"

When he comes for me again, I scramble across the bed, but I'm not quick enough. He gets me by the ankle and hauls me back, pinning me with his body weight as he squeezes my face between his fingers.

"Where is it?"

"I threw it in the bay," I lie.

His throat works from the force of his fury, and I don't know how to fix this.

"Did something happen to your mother?" I whisper. "Is that what this is?"

"Don't talk about my mother."

He yanks me up from the bed, and I thrash in his arms as he carries me down the hall to my room. The room I haven't stayed in since he allowed me into his.

"Thor, please." Tears streak my cheeks as he throws me onto the bed and grabs some restraints from the wall. "Punish me if you need to, but don't shut me out. Talk to me. Tell me what's going on."

He forces my ankle into a restraint and attaches it to the bedpost.

"Did you enjoy it?" he asks, repeating the process on the other ankle. "Did you enjoy it when I fucked you, or was that all a lie too?"

"Nothing was a lie." I reach for him when he leans across me, and he shoves my hand away.

"I'm not yours to touch."

His words feel like a punch in the gut, and I'm still trying to recover when he deals his next blow.

"Tomorrow, you can go back to your pathetic little farm and live in the barn for all I care."

"Thorsen, please—"

"I'm not Thorsen anymore." He secures the last of my restraints, leaving me bound across the bed. "I'm the King of Norway, and you were only ever a fuck toy."

I'm the King of Norway. The King of Norway. The King of Norway.

All night, those words have plagued my mind. I keep thinking I must be wrong, but there's only one conclusion that makes sense. Thorsen's father is dead, and he has ascended to the throne.

Grief. That's what this is. There's no other explanation.

The clock on the mantel ticks away, one minute bleeding into the next until the hours seem like an endless abyss I'll never escape. He hasn't come for me. Even the next morning, when light floods in from the windows, he still doesn't come for me.

At some point, Lisbet opens the door, and when she finds me bound to the bed, her face pales, and she scurries away, muttering something in Norwegian. I call after her, but she doesn't come back. More minutes pass. And then hours. Until I can no longer hold my bladder.

I told myself I could endure anything he threw at me, but the longer he leaves me here, the more I question it. Everything seems hopeless as the sun outside rises high in the sky. Where is he? When will he come for me so we can talk this through? Because that's what we do. We fight, and he works out his issues, and then everything is okay. It's always okay. But today it's not. Because when the door opens, and I finally breathe a sigh of relief, it's only to be replaced by dread when I see the face staring back at me.

"Lavinia?" I jerk against my restraints on instinct, but it does me little good.

"Oh my fucking God." Her mouth falls open, her evil eyes raking over me with a hatred so profound, it sears my flesh all over again. "So, this is what he's been hiding all this time?" She laughs as if it's totally implausible. "You've got to be kidding me."

"What are you doing here?" I demand.

"No, Cinderella." She slams the door behind her. "What the hell are you doing in my fiancé's house?"

"Fiancé?"

My heart stills, and time seems to slow as a callous smile curves her lips. "Oh, didn't he tell you that?"

"You're lying. That isn't true."

"Oh, but it is." She comes to sit beside me on the bed, flaying me alive with her eyes.

"No," I insist. "He's been here with me. I don't know how you found me, but what you're saying is impossible."

"My God, you are daft." She glares at me. "Where do you think he goes every day? Where do you think he's been when he isn't around? He's with me, you stupid cow."

An image of Thorsen's calendar comes to mind, and I think back on the night of the opera. I remember the argument we had when he came home in his suit, and I asked him if he was having sex with someone else. He told me I didn't have to share him. Was he lying to me?

My stomach revolts, and I feel like I'm going to be violently ill as Lavinia pulls up an article on her phone and shoves it in my face. It's a photo of them. Thorsen and Lavinia in front of his family's yacht. She's flashing a huge rock on her finger, and the headline says it all.

Prince Thorsen Engaged to Mysterious British Beauty.

"What's the matter, Cinderella?" Lavinia taunts me. "Cat got your tongue?"

"Go away!" I scream at her. "Just leave me the hell alone!"

"In your dreams." She stuffs the phone back into her pocket and stands up. "If you think you're going to ruin everything I've worked this hard for, you have another thing coming."

She glances around the room, her eyes widening in delight when they land on Thorsen's wall of torture.

"Lavinia, no." I fight against the restraints, but it's too late. She's already walking toward them, wearing that same glazed expression on her face from when she pushed me into the fire.

"You don't mean anything to him, you know." Her fingers

trail over a flogger before moving onto a paddle. She picks it up, assesses it, and then sets it aside. "You're just a toy. He would never do these things with me."

"Let me go." I squeeze my eyes shut. "I'll leave. You'll never have to see me again."

"No, I don't think so."

When I open my eyes again, she's eyeing the leather plaited whip hung on the wall, and my blood runs cold as she reaches for it. "You need to be taught a lesson."

"Think about what you're doing." I squirm, glancing at the door. *Is Thorsen here? Does he know she's here?*

Lavinia plucks a gag from the cabinet, examines it, and then comes for me. I thrash against the restraints and let out a bloodcurdling scream, praying that Lisbet can hear me wherever she is. Lavinia lunges for me, seizing me by the hair while she forces the gag into my mouth. I try to fight her, but it's pointless. Without the use of my limbs, she has all the control, and it only takes her a matter of seconds to secure the band around my head.

When she finishes, she leans back to inspect her handi-work, and I try to reason with her around the gag, but it's impossible. Everything comes out so muffled, even if Lisbet were standing right outside the door, she wouldn't hear me.

"I'm going to make you so ugly Thorsen will never want to look at you again."

Lavinia snaps the whip in her hand, practicing. It's small enough for her to control and deadly enough to destroy what's left of me. There's nothing I can do but watch as she gets a feel for it. Nothing can save me now. Not even my god of thunder.

Tears streak down my face as she extends her wrist, lashing me with the first blow. The pain plows into me, blis-tering my nerves and forcing a scream from the depth of my belly. There isn't time for so much as a breath before she snaps it, again and again, raining down misery so acute, I'm convinced this is how I'm going to die.

The leather snake cuts into my flesh, leaving behind welts and trails of blood as it splits the skin. I'm struggling for breath, choking on my gag, and completely helpless in the face of her evil. She's burning me alive all over again, and when I close my eyes, that's all I can see. Fire touches every part of me. This death is the slowest, most agonizing way I could go. And soon, I will be nothing but ash.

By the mercy of fate, my pupils shrink to a pinpoint, and the room closes in, threatening to disappear. I'm floating away to another time and space. A place where pain doesn't exist anymore. I give in to it, and eventually, the blackness consumes me.

30

THORSEN

"I HAVE TO GO, HAYES." I wedge the phone against my shoulder as I unlock the front door. "I'll be back at the palace in an hour."

"Don't forget your meeting at three," he clips out, sounding as distracted as I feel. "For funeral arrangements."

"I haven't forgotten." I pinch the bridge of my nose as I enter the house and drop my keys onto the table. "I'll see you shortly."

He disconnects the call, and I pocket my phone, glancing at the time. It's already noon. When I left this morning at six, I didn't expect to be gone this long, and guilt has been eating away at me all day. Ella is still strapped to the bed in the guest quarters, and I have yet to figure out what I want to do with her.

Last night, I was convinced I had no choice but to send her away. But all morning, while I met with various members of parliament, I considered every other alternative that meant she would stay. Each option was more ridiculous than the last. I could tie her up. Keep her locked in the guest room forever. Gag her so she couldn't ever speak, and never make me believe her lies again.

But were they really lies? I had swung wildly from one certainty to the next. Of course, she was lying. Why wouldn't she be? That's all I'd ever known. But I'd convinced myself she was different. I'd let my guard down, only to be blind-sided again.

As I approach her room, my decision still isn't any clearer. The house is quiet, and Lisbet is on her afternoon break. But something feels off when I reach the door to Ella's room and notice it's cracked. I distinctly remember shutting it last night. But did I lock it?

I push it open, and half expect Ella to come flying at me with another lamp. But the room is silent and still. When I round the corner, and the bed comes into view, the whole world just fucking stops.

"Ella?" I try to blink away the sight before me. The bloody, beaten body of the woman I love.

Love.

I love her. The profound realization hits me like a brick to the head as I stumble forward, heart hammering against my rib cage. She's so still, and I'm fucking terrified that I'm already too late. Her dead eyes are focused on the ceiling, and it takes me a minute to convince myself she even blinked.

When I get to her, I don't know what to do. The sight is too horrific for words. It looks like she's been slashed with a knife, her skin flayed open all over her body.

"*Gudinne,*" I choke out as I collapse onto the bed, crawling toward her. "Who did this to you?"

She doesn't try to speak around the gag in her mouth, even after I remove it. She won't even look at me as I force my trembling hands to release her restraints. It's a painstakingly slow process because her wrists and ankles are just as raw and bloody as the rest of her. My sweet goddess fought for her life. She fought so hard it brings tears to my eyes as I try to figure out how the fuck I'm going to help her. I'm afraid to touch her, move her, but all I want to do is hold her.

"Ella." My fingers ghost over her chin, tilting her gaze toward me. She blinks but doesn't acknowledge me. "Tell me what happened. Please."

Nothing. She stares through me, eyes blank.

I reach for my phone and struggle through my contacts, seeking out the name of my personal doctor. He answers without delay, and I issue my instructions to him with a clogged throat.

"Are you okay, Thorsen?" he asks before I hang up the phone.

"Just come quickly."

Another beat passes, and I take Ella's hand in mine. It's all I can do for her right now. I've never felt so fucking helpless in my entire life. The seconds drag by, and then long minutes until finally, Dr. Hansen alerts me he's outside. I tell him the door is open and meet him in the hall.

"Are you okay?" he asks again.

"No." I nearly fucking lose it. "I'm not. But this isn't about me."

He follows me down the hall and into Ella's room, and when he sees her, the color drains from his face.

"Oh, Thorsen. This is bad."

After carefully relocating Ella to the clean sheets on my bed, it takes Dr. Hansen and his two-nurse team three long hours to clean her up and dress her wounds. She had multiple lacerations that required stitches, including the one on her face. Throughout the entire process, I felt the doctor watching me as he asked her what happened. But she refused to engage with him either.

"She is traumatized," he tells me in the hall. "I have already called for Dr. Blom. He's on his way. But there is a good chance she may not speak at all for a while. She needs to rest."

"What can I do for her?"

"Right now, you just need to give it time. My nurse will stay here and report to me on her progress. Dr. Blom and I will also speak once he's assessed her, and we can decide how best to proceed."

I nod, but my heart has never felt so heavy.

"You have no idea who could have done this?" he asks wearily, and I can see the unspoken question in his eyes. He means to say, did I have anything to do with this.

"I don't know." I repress the urge to break something. All afternoon, I have asked myself that very question. And until I know for certain, my rage is trapped inside me, waiting for a target. "My security is going over the perimeter cameras now."

There are no cameras inside the estate because I never wanted them. A decision I've come to regret after today.

"Call me if you have any more concerns," Dr. Hansen instructs me. "Otherwise, I will be back tomorrow to check on her."

I tell him to let himself out, but it isn't long before Dr. Blom appears, and I have to let him in. When he sees Ella, he immediately turns to me.

"Thorsen—"

"I didn't do this," I growl.

He surveys me for signs of deception and then sighs. "I'm sorry, but you know I have to ask."

"She won't speak." My eyes move over Ella, tormented by the expression on her face. I can't be sure she's even in there anymore. Not until she talks to me. "I don't know how to fix this."

"Who is she?" Dr. Blom asks curiously.

"I met her at the ball in London. It's the same woman you asked me about before."

I leave out the part about me kidnapping her, though I don't doubt Ella will probably tell him herself anyway. I just don't want to lose her.

"Give me some time with her," Dr. Blom says. "I'll let you know when I'm finished."

I hesitate, and he observes me closely. He knows it isn't like me to be so protective, but things are different with Ella. I know that now, and I don't care if he knows it too. But before we can get to that, the head of security knocks on my door, interrupting us.

"Your Highness, if you have a moment, there's something I'd like to show you."

"Go, Thorsen." Dr. Blom gestures for the door. "Right now, this is how you can help."

After taking one last look at Ella, I reluctantly join my security team as they bring up the camera footage on a laptop in my office.

"We haven't been able to identify the individual," Han notes, "but we caught several images. Perhaps you might recognize them?"

My eyes focus on the screen as the person in the footage walks to the front door. Whoever it is, they're wearing a baggy blue hoodie, sunglasses, and black jeans. They also seem to be aware of the fact that there's a camera above them because they keep their head down the entire time.

"Is it a man?" I squint at the screen.

"It could be," Han answers. "Or a woman of medium height. It's difficult to tell with the clothing. But watch this."

The video continues, and the person on the screen unlocks the door with a set of keys.

"What the fuck?" I mutter.

How is that even possible? There are only three other people who have keys to my home. Calder, my mother, and Lisbet.

"Your brother and mother were both at the palace," Han answers my unspoken thoughts. "Calder has his keys, and he's looking for your mother's as we speak. As for Lisbet, she left around eleven for her break. But we called to confirm she was at a café during this time. She's on her way over now."

"Play it again," I order.

Han plays the footage several times before I stop him, and in my gut, I have the same inkling I had when I discovered the news of my father. Is it too much of a stretch to imagine that Lavinia divulged the information about his heart for a reason? Was that a threat I simply missed? And is it possible she would truly hurt Ella to such an extent?

"The fire," I whisper.

"What, sir?" Han asks.

"She said her stepsister pushed her into the fire." My fingers dig into my forehead as it comes back to me. The answers were right there all along. Ella told me about her family, her history with Narcissa and her sisters, but I conveniently chose to forget that when I was on my warpath last night, accusing her of a heinous and ridiculous betrayal.

"Mother fuck!"

I launch the ship on my desk across the room, and Han flinches. But that isn't enough. So I punch the desk four times until my knuckles splinter and bleed.

"Your Highness?" Han looks at me like I've lost my mind.

"This is all my fault," I tell him. "I didn't listen to her."

He doesn't know what I'm talking about, so he has no recourse but to watch me come unglued. I want to murder Lavinia with my bare fucking hands. I want to squeeze the life from her throat and send her straight to hell. It had to be her. There is no other alternative.

"Where are Narcissa and her daughters staying?" I ask Han.

"They left this afternoon." He pulls out his phone and checks the calendar. "Twenty minutes ago. They are on the plane as we speak."

My attention drifts to the figure on the screen, and the longer I study it, the more convinced I become. Ella told me her sister was a psychopath. The evidence is undeniable. Lavinia could have easily stolen my mother's keys just as she stole her ring. The security at my estate has never been as tight as the palace because that was the way I preferred it. I didn't want to feel as if I was living in a prison, but now I wish I had. I wish I had spent my entire life behind bars if only so this afternoon never happened.

"Do you suspect they have something to do with it?" Han asks.

I consider my answer carefully, aware that I'm on a precipice. There are two ways to handle this situation. The royal way, and my way. And I won't let this rest until Lavinia pays in blood.

"No." I turn on my heel and head for the door. "I don't think they had anything to do with it. Let me know if you find anything else."

"Did she say anything to you?"

Dr. Blom shakes his head as I follow him down the hall. "No. I'm afraid not."

"What can we do?"

"Give her time," he suggests.

"You're the doctor." I glare at him. "You should be able to fix her."

"Thorsen, you know it isn't that simple."

I drag a hand through my hair and glance back at the room.

"You really like this girl, don't you?"

His question catches me off guard, and in my fucked-up state of mind, I'm unable to hide my visceral reaction.

"I love her."

Dr. Blom stares at me for a beat, clearly rattled by my confession. "You love her?"

"Yes."

"Is the feeling mutual?" he asks.

"It was." I dip my head uncertainly. "But I don't know anymore."

After last night, and the events of today, it's probable Ella won't ever want to speak to me again. And that's what terrifies me the most.

"This isn't your fault," Dr. Blom placates me.

"It is," I argue. "I restrained her to the bed. Whoever did this to her did so freely because of me."

His eyebrows pinch together, and the concern on his face only convinces me that I'm fucked. Ella will hate me. She'll never recover from this.

"Let's take it one day at a time." Dr. Blom pulls a bottle of my pills from his shirt pocket and rattles them. "The first

step is taking care of yourself, so you can take care of Ella
when she's ready."

My fingers are numb when I reach for the bottle I've
avoided for so long. After I stopped taking my pills, I fell in
love with the darkness of my thoughts, and I swore I'd never
need them again. But my love for Ella is no comparison.
She's the dancing flame in my perpetual night. Her love and
warmth and purity have guided me to a different place. A
place where possibility exists if I don't ruin it for both of us.

Twisting the lid, I dump one of the pills into my hand
and stare at it for far too long. Dr. Blom is right. The first
step to proving I'm worthy of her is facing our future with a
clear mind.

I toss it into my mouth and swallow.

For Ella.

31

ELLA

An entire week passes before I can move without the agonizing reminder of Lavinia's undiluted rage. After that, it's another full week of me getting on my feet again. Cleaning myself. Dressing myself. Feeding myself. These small accomplishments are a welcome relief after having a full-time nurse perform the most basic functions for me.

Thorsen comes and goes, his exhaustion palpable, but he's always hopeful I will speak. Every day, he waits for me to say something, but I can't. Not to him.

Even though I'm quiet, my thoughts are loud. I'm wondering where Lavinia is now, and why he isn't with her. These questions are all I can think of much of the time because holding onto my anger is the only way to stay sane.

Every night, I break down in silent tears when Thorsen comes to lay beside me in his bed. He's always close yet far away. He's afraid to touch me. It's the only reason I've found the strength to resist falling back into this self-destructive pattern with him. I can't allow myself to find comfort in his presence, or his scent, or his warmth when he inches close enough to be felt. I love him, but he shattered me. And for the first time in many years, I realize that I deserve better. I gave him everything, and if he isn't willing to do the same, then I can't change that. I'm tired of punishing myself for things I can't control, and I refuse to be his second best. There's only one thing I can do, and my mind is already made up.

"Ella?" he murmurs beside me in the darkness. "Are you still awake?"

I squeeze my eyes shut, forcing my breath to even out in the hopes he won't try to comfort me again. It would be so easy to get pulled back into his orbit, and I hate him for that. I hate him for bringing me here and making me fall in love with him just so he could wreck me.

"I know you're awake," he says, his voice tormented. "Please talk to me. I don't know how much more of this I can take."

His words strike a chord of fear in my heart, and it's the one thought I can't handle. When I'm gone, will Thorsen try to execute his plan? Will he try to hurt himself? I want to believe he wouldn't do that. Not now. I've seen a change in him since I've been here. He's steadier. More determined. And he's taken on his role of king with a commitment I want him to see through.

Today, when I blurted out my observations to Dr. Blom, he seemed to agree. We've been visiting for the past couple of weeks after he promised not to divulge anything that's said between us. He's been kind, and he's done his best to reassure me, but he told me that ultimately, Thorsen's future is up to him. He must be the one to decide what he wants in this life. He's the only one who can fight his demons. None of us can do it for him, no matter how much we love him.

I know he's right. And this is why I have to leave.

When I confessed my desire to Dr. Blom, he said he would help me, if that's what I truly wanted. Even though the guilt is all-consuming, I believe it's the right decision. It's the hardest decision I've ever made for myself.

"Ella," Thor whispers again, his fingers brushing against my arm.

The shock of his unexpected touch startles me, and the painful sound of grief gets caught in my throat.

"What is it, *gudinne*?" He leans up and turns on the lamp, studying my tear-streaked face. "You've been crying?"

He looks so utterly broken, and I can't understand it. How can he feel this way about me when he broke me too?

"Please say something," he begs. "Tell me what I can do to make this right."

"Nothing." My voice feels rusty when I finally answer him. "There's nothing you can do to make this right."

"No." He leans over me, dipping his forehead to mine. "I will fix this. Just tell me how. I need to know how."

"I was wrong." Another tear spills from the corner of my eye. "I thought I could withstand anything you threw my way, but I can't. I can't survive you."

"Don't talk like that." He silences me with his lips.

I let him kiss me, allowing myself to feel him for the last time. It would be so easy to get swept up in his intoxicating power all over again. He is the embodiment of addiction for me. But I can't keep fighting for something if I'm the only one fighting for it.

"I just want you to be happy," I whisper against him.

Whether it's with or without me.

"Ella—"

"I'm very tired." I close my eyes and roll away from him. "I need to sleep now."

Thorsen slips out of bed early in the morning, just as he has done every day for the past two weeks. Usually, in these early hours, I can hear him conducting business on the phone while he paces the hall. He doesn't like to leave, but inevitably, his duties call him away for the better part of the afternoons. It's a difficult concept to grasp that things have changed so much in such a short period. He's the king now, and he should be at the palace, living his life, taking control of the situation there. Yet every night, he's here with me.

We haven't spoken about his father's death, and a part of me feels guilty for that. I couldn't be mentally present at a time when he really needed me. But I'm emotionally bankrupt right now, or at least, that's how it feels. I think the part that hurts the most is what he told me himself. I was never anything more than a toy to him. Now, he's engaged to Lavinia, and even if I could help him, there's not room for me in this picture.

It's that sentiment that coaxes me from the bed after he leaves this morning. I'm functioning on autopilot when I pack a few outfits from the closet in my guest suite, stuffing them into one of Thorsen's backpacks. When I'm done with that, I grab the purse I had on me when he brought me here and the messenger bag with the two blue bottles.

As I look around the room where it all began, it feels like my chest is caving in on me. I don't think I'll ever get over him, and as hurt as I am, it still takes all my courage to walk away. I shed one last tear for my loss. A loss so huge I'm not certain I'll ever recover.

From my bag, I retrieve the letter I wrote yesterday, explaining my actions. It's messy and raw, with lines scratched out where I tried to wish him well with Lavinia. As it turned out, everything I wrote was a lie. I couldn't understand why he did this. And I couldn't tell him I forgave him because he never apologized in the first place. In the end, the only thing I could say was that I wanted to walk away. Perhaps the biggest lie of all.

With an unsteady hand, I leave the letter for him on the bed and step out onto his balcony, tossing my things over the railing. I don't want to draw any attention by walking past Lisbet with my things. But fortunately for me, she never seems to be all that concerned about what I'm doing anyway. When I get to the kitchen, she's at the counter doing some food prep.

"Good morning." She averts her gaze after she hears me come in. A part of me wonders if she feels guilty for leaving me in the bed when I begged her for help, but it doesn't matter now. I can't change what happened, and as awful as it was, I believe it happened for a reason.

"Would you like some breakfast?" she asks.

"No, thank you. I'm not hungry right now."

She nods and goes back to her work, and I step out onto the terrace, closing the door behind me. Following the dirt path, I head for the slope beneath Thorsen's balcony. Once I've collected my things, I take one last mental picture of the house that started to feel like a home. My eyes swim with unshed tears, but I promised myself I wasn't going to cry anymore. So, I turn away and lift my chin and head for the beach.

After Dr. Blom gave me some money, which I reluctantly accepted, he made a casual observation. Thorsen has a rowboat he sometimes uses to cross the bay to the other side of the city. I didn't ask him for any more details, but I suspected it was his way of telling me I had an out if I wanted one. He didn't want to hurt Thorsen, but he didn't want me to feel as though I had no options either. It was a difficult decision for him, I could tell, but I'm grateful when I find the rowboat easily.

It turns out to be a small vessel, just big enough for me and my things. After a few moments of struggling to get it into the water, and soaking myself in the process, I climb aboard and sit down.

The only experience I have rowing a boat was with my father when I was a child, but I get the hang of it quickly. Two sore arms and one hour later, I reach the other side. There's a boat landing I use to depart, and from there, it's a five-minute walk to the bus station. Every second that passes makes me more anxious Thorsen will discover I'm gone. Will Lisbet alert him when I don't come back from outside? Will she even notice?

After the incident, his security has been busy installing cameras around the interior of the estate. But I don't know how often he checks them or how much of a head start I'll have. All I can do is focus on one breath to the next as I follow the route I carefully mapped out over the past few days. Thirty minutes and two bus changes later, I'm at the ferry terminal, purchasing my ticket. But it isn't until I'm out on the open sea when I can finally breathe again.

The journey back to London is uneventful, but long, taking nearly two days by ferry and train. By the time I finally step foot back onto the familiar streets of Cranbrook, it feels like everything has changed. But I think it's just me.

I don't really have a plan after this, but I know what I want to do. After I get off the train, I walk to Olivia's. She isn't home when I arrive, and Alfred must be in the house, so I visit with the horses and then find a comfortable spot to rest in the barn until she comes back.

I want to call Charlotte, but I had to leave my phone behind. Thorsen could track it or use it as a way to contact me, and I'm just not strong enough for that yet.

Lying back in the hay, I stare up at the weathered wood roof and consider what my life will be like now. I already know I can't go back to Narcissa's. That isn't even a question. Too much has changed, and I'm a different person now. When I close my eyes and try to dream of the future, it feels empty and hollow, but I manage to find some peace, at least long enough to slip off to sleep.

Something tickles my foot, and my eyes fly open. A pungent odor lingers in the air around me, and when I look down, my shirt is soaked through. I thought I forgot where I was, but I didn't. I'm still here, in Olivia's barn, but it isn't Olivia standing over me.

"Lavinia." I curse her name as I force myself upright, meeting her gaze. "What the hell are you doing?"

My eyes flick over the scattered contents of my bag on the ground, and it's obvious she's been rifling through my things. How long has she been there? How long was I completely vulnerable to her before I even realized there was a predator right in front of me? By now, I know her well enough to understand she came here for a reason. The haunting question is why.

"You healed up nicely." She smirks. "But I suppose that scar on your face has been a lovely reminder of me."

"Why are you here?" I stumble to my feet as adrenaline floods my veins.

"Do you think I didn't know you would come back here?" She rolls her eyes. "This pathetic little farm is all you have. I thought it would be fitting for you to watch it go up in flames."

Her eyes dart to the white bottle lying on the ground, and it takes me a second to understand that it's lighter fluid.

"You're fucking psychotic!" I stare past her, trying to figure out my options as my pulse begins to race. But the only way out is to go through her. She's got me trapped, and judging by the smell around me, this whole barn will go up in seconds if she ignites it.

"What else could you possibly want from me?" I ask. "I left Thorsen alone. You got what you wanted."

"What I want is to watch you die," she hisses. "You ruined everything, and now you're going to pay for it."

My eyes bounce around the barn in search of a weapon. Something I can knock her out with. But there's nothing remotely close to me. It feels like another hopeless situation until it doesn't. Until I realize that I am so done with Lavinia terrorizing me. A decade's worth of repressed hostility boils to the surface, settling into my curled fists. Only one of us is getting out of here alive today, and this time, it's going to be me.

"I'll give you a choice." Lavinia pulls a lighter from her pocket and slowly drags her nail over the ridges of the ignition switch. She wants to draw out her torture and make me squirm. But I'm not the same helpless girl who was strapped to the bed in Norway.

"If you do that, you'll never get out of here alive," I promise her. "I'll make sure of it, even if it's the last thing I do."

Her head falls back in laughter, and she breaks into a fit of hysterics over the idea that I could ever fight back. For as long as I've known her, I've let her have the upper hand. I've tortured myself over my father's death, and I fought in vain to prove myself worthy of their love. But there is no love left in my heart for any of them, and Lavinia has pushed me for the last time.

Using the moment of her distraction, I launch myself at her and tackle her to the ground. Her head bounces off the earth with a sickening thud, and the impact stuns her long enough for me to pry the lighter from her fingers and toss it aside.

For a split second, I have the advantage, and I don't waste it. I've never been in a fight to the death before, but that's exactly what it feels like when I punch her in the face as brutally as I can manage. Her head whips to the side, and I draw my arm back again, landing another blow. Red blooms across her skin as blood trickles from her lip, and it feels so goddamn good. But my victory is short-lived.

Lavinia screams like a demon spawn from hell as she wraps her icy fingers around my throat, choking off my air supply. On instinct, my hands come up to hers, trying to pull them away, but the strength she's drawn from her rage feels superhuman.

When I fail to pry her fingers away, I fling my fist at her face again. But my body is already suffering from the lack of oxygen. I'm weak and sluggish, and panic is taking the place of rational thought when I try to crawl away from her. Her arms are locked around me like steel bars, caging me in. I kick and thrash and use everything in my power to fight back, but every passing second only seems to seal my fate.

I can't breathe. She's choking the life from me. Without air, I don't have the strength to fend her off, but I still have my hands, and I know what matters to her most. Digging my nails into her forehead, I scrape them down her face, leaving trails of blood behind as she screams like she's being murdered. Her hands fall away from my throat, and I gulp in air as she touches her face in horror.

There isn't time to catch my breath. I've just damaged what's most precious to her, and she's not going to stop now until I'm dead. I scramble off her, crawling toward the lighter, but no sooner do I have my fingers wrapped around it than she comes for me again.

She shoves my face into the dirt and yanks me back by my hair, trying to pry the lighter from my grasp. I elbow her in the gut, and she grunts, doubling over on top of me. Throwing the lighter as far as I can from her reach, I turn to face her, and within seconds, we're wrestling in the dirt again. Between the punches and slaps and head thrashing, my energy is waning. Whatever hope I may have had for walking out of here today is slowly dissipating. My entire body feels like jelly, and I can hardly control my limbs anymore.

When Lavinia rolls me onto my back again and wraps her hands around my throat once more, there's only one thing I can think to do. As I struggle to hold on to my consciousness, I bring my hands to her face and dig my thumbs into her eyes with every ounce of strength I have left. She shrieks, and I nearly choke as she falls back, dragging her trembling hands to her bloody eyes.

"You fucking bitch!" she screams. "You're going to die for this!"

I try to crawl away, but it's too late. When she pins me on my back again, she presses her knees into my elbows and drags something from her pocket. A familiar blue bottle. She twists the lid off the oleander extract and tosses it aside as she tries to focus with her swollen eyes. I turn my head to the side, but my strength has abandoned me. I'm fading fast, and the only comfort I have as she wrenches my head back is that at least I've probably scarred her for life.

She tells me she's won when she brings the bottle to my lips and forces it between my teeth. As the liquid pours over my tongue and gurgles in my throat, I'm left to wonder if she will still set me ablaze when she leaves. It's the last fleeting conscious thought I have.

32

THORSEN

THE BEAT of my heart echoes through the silence of the bedroom I shared with Ella, but now it just feels like a coffin. Cold, suffocating, and achingly empty.

It's been two days since I've last seen her. When I came home to an empty house, it nearly fucking destroyed me. Within the hour, I had gathered every resource at my disposal. I had the royal guards scouring the streets of Oslo while I personally checked the airports and train stations even though it didn't make sense. Ella doesn't have any money. And now she doesn't even have a phone since she left hers behind.

I flew to London that night anyway. But there were no passenger tickets with her name on them, and she never showed up at the sanctuary or the manor. Her friends haven't heard from her either. Neither the guards nor my security has found anything useful. The last glimpse I have is her climbing into a rowboat to leave me behind.

They tell me she could be on the ferry, but even that doesn't seem reasonable. She would need money for that too. I don't know where she could be, and the longer I sit here wondering, the more destructive I become.

The halls are already littered with the evidence of my frustrations. Holes in the walls. Shattered picture frames. Lisbeth disappeared soon after I interrogated her and brought her to tears, and she hasn't returned since.

Everyone is looking at me like I've gone insane, and I suppose I have. But what do they expect? She left me. And all that remains is her letter of lies.

Dr. Blom was quick to remind me that the way I deal with this challenge will pave the path for my future. I was quick to push him away with angry words and accusations that I suspect are at least somewhat true. In my gut, I know he must have helped Ella. She must have told him she wanted to escape me, and I think more than anything, that's what cuts the deepest.

I've considered every possibility of what the future looks like from here, but no matter what lens I use, it seems impossibly grim. Without her by my side, I could only ever be the cold king everyone expects. Living a life of isolation with the ghost of her memory. Would I do what I always said I would? The dark ending my thoughts have insisted on for many years? No, I don't think so. The forest that used to comfort me in my dreams seems cold and stark since I've known Ella's warmth.

The only solution that makes sense is to take her back by force. I could make her love me again. But first, I have to find her. And I don't know how to do that when every lead seems to fail me.

When I don't find the answers in a bottle of *akevitt*, I close my eyes and try to sleep, but it never comes. There is no peace when I don't know if she's safe and warm. She had to know when she left, this would happen. She had to know what she was doing. She ripped my heart out and took it with her. I can't accept that.

Every second of every hour, I can only think of her. The agony doesn't go away, and it's entirely different than what I've known before. It's emptiness. A void of blackness I'll never crawl out of.

I throw my feet over the edge of the bed and yank open the nightstand drawer. There are six bottles of my mother's sleep elixir inside. One would be enough to knock me out if I really wanted it. But as I twist the cap in my hands, my eyes drift to Ella's letter again. Discarding the bottle, I read the lines for the hundredth time, staring at the scratched-out ink, trying to imagine what she said beneath it.

When that fails me, I pick up my phone and check with Han to see if he has any news. But he tells me there isn't, assuring me he will alert me as soon as he finds something. I text her friend Charlotte again too, but she doesn't respond. It's late in London, and I doubt I'll hear from her until morning.

I take to pacing the halls, and when I tire of that, I walk out onto the terrace and stare out at the bay. But no matter how many times I look for her, she isn't there.

I'm not entirely sure what my motivations are when I summon my driver, who delivers me to the palace at my request. I take to walking the halls there too before I end up at the door to my mother's herbal room. When I step inside and find the shelves full of elixirs, I recall the promise I made to my mother. But what about the promise Ella made to me? *I'm not going anywhere, Thorsen.*

I scoop up a handful of bottles from the shelf and examine them. Perhaps the medication is dulling my senses, or perhaps Dr. Blom was right. This was always a compulsion. An ideation to solve all my problems, but it was only ever a fantasy.

"Thor?"

My mother startles me, and I immediately feel guilty when I find her in the doorway, watching me.

"What are you doing out of bed?" I ask.

"Your Aunt Runa heard you come in." She eyes the bottles in my hand. "I asked her to wheel me down here."

"She shouldn't have woken you."

"I wasn't asleep," she says, and I can tell by the pinched expression on her face that she's in pain. But still, she's here.

"I wasn't really going to do it," I tell her.

"I know." She uses her one good arm to wheel herself farther into the room.

"How do you know?"

She offers me a soft smile. "You wouldn't do that to me."

I nod and set the bottles aside, and suddenly, I just feel so fucking tired. I'm tired of this charade. Tired of this darkness in my head. Tired of disappointing everyone because that's what they expect of me.

"I know things have been difficult for you the past two weeks," my mother says. "Your father's death was hard on you, but I've seen a change in you that I've long suspected. The crushing weight of his expectations is gone, and I think that's terrifying for you because you've never known what it's like to be free."

I can't comprehend how it's possible she can still be so perceptive as she's wasting away. There have been moments over the past few months when she would get confused about the simplest things, but right now, her mind is as clear as I've ever known it to be.

"Am I right?" she asks.

"Yes," I concede. "You're always right."

She sighs, and I've never seen her so relieved. "I worried for some time that perhaps I did the wrong thing. I didn't want you to blame yourself."

"What do you mean?"

Shadows dance across her face as she dips her head. "You had questions about your father's death. Suspicions. And you were right, Thor."

"Lavinia?" The name feels like poison on my tongue.

"No." She lifts her chin to meet my gaze. "It was me."

For a full minute, I'm not convinced I even heard her correctly. Her confession has stolen all the oxygen from the room, and it's too impossible to be true. She has always been the kindest person I know. But the resolve in her eyes can't be discounted, and I know she isn't confused. Not about this.

"You poisoned him?"

She nods with a finality that indicates she's made peace with her decision. "It will never be detected."

"Why?" I study her, trying to understand.

"It was the only thing that made sense." Her voice hardens. "He failed my son, and I could never forgive him for that. I wouldn't leave you here with him, Thor. I couldn't. This was the last thing I could do to protect you, and I would do it again."

When I don't respond, her voice fractures, and it fractures me too.

"Please understand, I have no fear of the consequences of my actions. I only fear that you will never forgive me."

"I forgive you." I memorize the lines of her face, so I'll never forget. "I had no love in my heart for him. I realize that now. It was only ever the desire to be loved."

"Oh, Thorsen." She brings a trembling hand to her lips, holding back her pain. "I'm so sorry he was incapable of seeing how lucky we were to have a son like you."

"I don't mean to upset you."

"Don't apologize," she says. "I want you to tell me the truth, always. Even if it hurts me. Especially when it hurts. Promise me you will from now on."

"I promise."

Through the tears in her eyes, I can see light again. "Now, can we move forward?"

I lean in and kiss her on the cheek before I turn her toward the door, so I can take her back to her room.

"There's something I have to do first."

Charlotte hasn't answered my texts or calls, and I'm beginning to wonder how much of a friend she can really be to Ella. Olivia has been silent too, and my irritation only compounds as the plane taxis in from the runway.

Han called me this morning to alert me he finally had something. A port document stating Ella got off the ferry in London early this morning. As soon as the jet was ready, I was on it. But her friends' sudden silence leaves me with more questions than answers. Now that I'm in London, something feels off, and I can't identify the reason for this lingering tightness in my chest. It isn't until I take my phone off airplane mode that a slew of notifications floods in.

There are three missed calls from Olivia and two from Charlotte, along with a handful of texts requesting I call either of them. The tone is unmistakably urgent, and I can't seem to dial Charlotte fast enough.

"Hello?" She sniffles on the other end of the line.

"It's me," I tell her. "Where is she?"

"Ella's in the hospital!" she cries out.

My heart slows to a crawl, and the phone nearly slips from my grasp. "What?"

"She took something. Olivia found her at the sanctuary, and there was a bottle of Nerium oleander beside her."

My vision swims, and I feel my body swaying as the plane comes to a halt. This can't be real. I'm shaking my head, but the words aren't coming, and when I finally force them out, I don't recognize my own voice.

"Ella wouldn't do that."

"She did!" Charlotte sobs on the other end of the line.

I drag in a breath and try to focus on what I need to do. What is the next logical step? Because right now, I'm too fucking numb to string a sentence together.

"What hospital?" I choke out.

"Hawkhurst," Charlotte answers.

"How long has it been?"

"I don't know." Her voice rises. "Olivia found her thirty minutes ago. We don't know how long it was before that."

"I'm on my way."

I hang up the phone without waiting for a response and meet the driver as I exit the plane, giving him instructions to take me to Hawkhurst right away. When I'm in the car, I dial my mother's nurse. After a brief argument with her about waking my mother, she puts her on the line.

"Thorsen?" she asks sleepily. "Is everything okay?"

"The antidote." My words are stilted, barely audible. "What is the antidote for the oleander?"

"Thorsen, no—" She releases a sorrowful sob.

"It isn't for me, but I need to know right now. Please, *Mor*... there isn't time."

"Charcoal would be the first option," she responds with jarring breaths between words. "Then intravenous magnesium, possibly atropine. But those have their own risks, particularly if the heart is affected. It depends on the dosage. The entire bottle, it's highly unlikely any of those things will help. Who took the oleander?"

"I'll explain later," I apologize. "I have to go. Just... don't worry about me."

I disconnect the call and text the information to Charlotte while asking the driver how far away we are. He tells me we are still forty minutes out, and I don't think I've ever felt so fucking useless. When I dial Charlotte again, she answers breathlessly.

"They've already given her charcoal," she says. "And I told the doctor what you said, but they won't give us any other information."

"I'll be there as soon as I can."

"Are you really her boss?" Charlotte asks, seemingly confused. "How do you know so much about the oleander?"

I stare out the window, wishing what I was about to say wasn't true. "She got it from me."

The other end of the line falls silent, and I don't doubt that her friend is already convicting me and sentencing me to death. But none of her thoughts could be any worse than what I'm already thinking myself. I fucked up, and I hate myself for it. But more than that, I'm terrified for Ella.

"Please keep me updated. I'll be there shortly."

"Okay," Charlotte answers woodenly.

We disconnect the call, and the next thirty-five minutes pass with torturous slowness. When the driver finally pulls up to the curb at the hospital, I'm already halfway out the door before the car even comes to a stop.

Inside, I follow the signs for the emergency department, and it isn't long until I find Charlotte and Olivia waiting in the hall with nervous expressions on their faces.

"Where is she?" I demand. "I need to see her now."

Charlotte's jaw drops, and she stares at me in stunned silence before she reacts. "Oh, my God. Thorsen, as in Thorsen Lykken, the latest crowned King of Norway? That's who I've been talking to? You were who Ella was working for?"

I glance around, looking for someone who can give me information.

"They came out five minutes ago and said she's awake," Olivia informs me. "They'll come back to update us soon."

"Awake?" I repeat in disbelief. How is that possible?

In a daze, I move toward the nurses' station, and the woman behind the desk is scribbling something onto a notepad, not bothering to look up. "What can I do for you?"

"I need to see Ella Laurent, immediately. Show me where she is."

"The doctor will be out soon enough to give you an update—"

"He's the King of Norway." Charlotte comes up beside me and hisses over the desk. "You better do what he says."

The nurse lifts her chin, recognition dawning in her eyes, and she blinks several times before she seems to recover from her shock.

"Oh my God." She discards her pen and stands up immediately. "I'm so sorry, Your Highness. I didn't realize."

"Take me to Ella," I clip out. "I need to see her right now."

She nods and walks around the desk, gesturing for us to follow her. Charlotte trails beside me, and Olivia joins us on the way down the hall. It feels like the longest walk of my life before the nurse finally pulls a curtain aside, and I see her.

She's propped up on the bed with pillows behind her,

struggling to keep her eyes open as the doctor asks her questions. When he sees us, his eyes narrow in on me.

"You aren't allowed back here right now."

"I'm not leaving." I glare at him as I stalk toward Ella.

"He's the King of Norway," the nurse whispers.

The doctor's eyebrows shoot into his hairline, and a moment later, he's shaking his head in resignation. He knows better than to make a scene. This may not be my country, but I could royally fuck his whole world up with a few simple phone calls.

I take my rightful place at Ella's bedside, and when her cloudy eyes find mine, she reaches out to touch me as if I'm not real.

"Thorsen?"

I take her hand and guide it to my chest, and it has the immediate effect of relaxing my entire body.

"*Gudinne*, what happened to you?"

She's battered and bruised, and it looks like she's been through hell all over again. But when she reads the agony in my eyes, she reacts as only Ella could, trying to comfort me even as she's returning from the brink of death. She squeezes my hand, her warmth a balm to the raw wound that feels like a caged beast inside me. She's awake, and she's alive, but how? I still don't understand.

"I didn't take the oleander," she tells me. "I dumped it out after I took it from you and replaced it with oil from your kitchen before I swapped the labels with the sleep elixir."

The suffocating weight on my chest evaporates, and I kiss her hand a thousand times, thanking every god in the universe that fate hasn't ripped her away. My fire-breathing goddess is still here. She still lives on.

"Why would you do that, Ella?" Charlotte asks as she

comes to stand at the foot of her bed. "Why would you take the sleeping elixir? You gave us all a heart attack today. We thought—" Her voice splinters, emotion choking her ability to speak as Olivia tries to comfort her.

"I'm sorry." Ella dips her head, and I can tell she's hiding something. "I never meant for any of this to happen, and I want to explain everything. But can we talk about this later?"

"You can talk about it when you're ready," Olivia assures her.

"Okay." Ella nods, her eyes heavy.

"She needs to rest," the doctor tells us. "We're moving her to a room for observation tonight."

"I'm staying with her," I inform him.

He sighs, but when Ella doesn't argue, he gives up.

"Should we stay too?" Charlotte asks.

"Please don't put yourselves out," Ella says. "I can call you tomorrow morning when I'm feeling better."

Both women reluctantly hug her and say their goodbyes before the doctor insists again on Ella's rest. Once they've gone, the nurse wheels Ella up to a hospital room while I follow at her side. It takes another twenty minutes for them to check her vitals and give her a new IV bag, and by that time, she's fast asleep again.

The weight of the day leaves me exhausted too, and when I collapse into the bedside chair, my head finds a home on her lap as my eyes fall shut. At some point, her fingers curl into my hair, and her presence lulls me into a peaceful sleep beside her.

33

THORSEN

THE DOCTOR COMES to check on Ella one more time, asking her for more details of what happened today. When she gives him a vague response, he warns her that he could keep her on a hold at the hospital until she's assessed and deemed mentally fit to leave on her own.

"That isn't necessary," I challenge him. "She has a psychiatrist back home in Norway. You can speak to him, and he will tell you himself."

"Thorsen." Ella touches my hand, trying to calm me. "It's okay. The doctor's just doing his job, and I understand. But I can assure you, Dr. Hobbs, it was just an honest mistake."

"Please do explain." He arches a brow at her.

Ella proceeds to give him a bullshit story about how she hasn't been sleeping well, and she was locked out of her home, so she went to the farm. She tells him she often napped there, and she took the entire bottle of the sleeping aid, thinking it was a single dosage.

"I see." The doctor studies her. "And what about your injuries? Or the lighter fluid? How do you explain that?"

At the mention of lighter fluid, my stomach revolts with a sickening realization.

"I can't remember how that happened," Ella lies. "I think I was confused, maybe. I could have fallen in the barn. It's hard to say."

Dr. Hobbs isn't buying her story, but he writes down one final note in her chart and sighs. "I'll need to speak with your doctor back in Norway before I make any decisions."

"I'll give you his contact information." I reach for the pad and pen on the table and scribble Dr. Blom's name and phone number.

Dr. Hobbs takes the information and heads for the door. "I'll be back to check on you in the morning."

Once he's gone, I shut the door behind him and turn to Ella. The softness in her eyes betrays her nerves.

"Tell me what really happened, Ella. No lies."

"You first." She glares up at me. "Why are you even here? Why aren't you with Lavinia?"

"Lavinia?" I grimace. "Why would I be with—"

Suddenly, it occurs to me that Lavinia must have told Ella about our so-called engagement. It's something so simple, but it never crossed my mind because Lavinia was barely a blip in my consciousness until I learned of Ella's connection to her.

"I saw the papers." Ella's lip wobbles, and she looks away. "I know you're engaged to her. You can tell me the truth. Please don't lie to me anymore."

"*Min gudinne.*" I turn her face back to mine. "Is that what you thought? Do you really believe I'd ever marry her?"

"What else am I supposed to think?" She swipes a few stray tears from the corners of her eyes. "You were with her. She had a ring on her finger. I saw the photo."

"But you don't know the story." I shake my head, frustrated that I never dealt with this when I should have.

"Are you telling me it isn't true?"

"Of course, it's not true."

"I need more than that," she says. "Make me understand."

I fall into the seat beside her with a sigh.

"When I came looking for you after the ball, I enlisted my secretary's help. He reported this information back to my parents, and they believed Lavinia was the woman I'd been trying to find. They invited Narcissa and both of your sisters to stay at the palace for one month. My father was determined to see me marry her because I had already turned down two of his previous choices. He ordered me to spend three days a week with her, and I did it because he would have denied me access to my mother if I hadn't."

"But you did go out on dates with her?" Bitterness colors Ella's tone, and it has the unfortunate effect of reminding me I have a cock I'd like to bury balls deep inside her right now.

"I went out with her because I had to," I say. "Those dates meant nothing to me, and the entire time I was with her, all I could think about was coming home to you."

"You told me I was nothing to you," Ella whispers.

"I know." I reach for her hand and tangle my fingers with hers, desperate to feel her warmth. "I lied to you because I was angry, and I wasn't thinking straight. I'll never forgive myself for that, Ella. I'm sorry I hurt you. I'm sorry for all of it. I put you through so much, and you stayed with me. You never let me push you away. You're the only woman I want, and I can't let you go. Even if you hate me. I'll find a way to make you care again."

"I want to believe that." She lowers her lashes. "You have

no idea how much I want to believe it. But how can I be sure you aren't planning a wedding to Lavinia like she says?"

"Because she made the entire scheme up," I growl. "She stole my mother's ring from her room and told the media exactly where we'd be. I had no idea what she was doing until she blurted it out herself. Believe me when I tell you I hold no affection for any of your so-called family. While Lavinia was desperately trying to win herself a title, your stepmother was carrying on an affair with my father."

Ella cringes, and I can tell this isn't the first time she's been embarrassed by their behavior.

"But you hid me from your family," she argues. "You could have told them, and you didn't. Were you ashamed of me?"

"Ashamed of you?" My voice hollows out. "No, *gudinne*. I could never be ashamed of you."

"Then why?" she persists. "Why hide me?"

"You know exactly why." I hang my head. "I was only supposed to have you for two months. That was it."

Her face softens. "Do you have real feelings for me?"

To answer her question, I bring her hand to my heart. "I'm in love with you, Ella." The words are faint and vulnerable but not any less meaningful. "I won't ever let you go. You have to know that."

"I don't want you to." Tears spill over her eyelids as she offers me the most beautiful smile I've ever seen. "I'm in love with you too, Thorsen. So much."

Leaning into her, I grab her face and kiss the hell out of her until we're both breathless. When she kisses me back, I feel whole again, and I'm tempted to climb into her bed and fuck hospital rules by fucking her. But not like this. She needs to rest, and we still have something important to discuss. I pull away, reluctantly, and Ella looks up at me with a dazed expression.

"Your turn." I brush her hair back from her face. "Tell me what happened today, *gudinne*. No more lies."

She expels a shaky breath and sinks into her pillow as she stares up at the ceiling. "Lavinia found me at the sanctuary while I was waiting for Olivia. I'd fallen asleep, and when I woke up, she was there. Things got ugly. She'd doused me in lighter fluid, intent on finishing the job. We fought, and she poured the elixir down my throat, thinking it was poison."

An edgy, twitchy feeling takes over me as my vision clouds. What Ella just described is too gruesome to comprehend. And right now, the beast in me is rattling his cage, demanding I let him out. His thoughts are loud, punctuated by violent images of torture and murder. I want them all to pay, and I won't have peace until they do. It's only when Ella reaches out to touch me that I realize I still haven't spoken.

"I'm sorry," I whisper. "I'm sorry I wasn't there to protect you."

"You couldn't have known." She shrugs. "I've made excuses for them for so many years. But there's nothing else to say. She's psychotic."

"Why did you lie to the doctor?" I ask.

"I didn't want the police involved," she says. "I hurt her too, and I was afraid she'd twist everything up to make it all my fault. At the time, I was pretty sure she was engaged to you, and I didn't know what would happen if I had told the truth."

"Do you really think I would allow you to be punished for something like that?" I can't hide the hurt in my voice.

"I didn't know what to think," she answers softly. "All I knew is what she told me and what I'd seen in the article.

You never brought it up with me, so the only conclusion I could make was that it must be true."

"It's my job to protect you," I tell her. "And I can't do that if we both have secrets. You'll only ever have my honesty from now on, and I want the same from you."

"Okay," she agrees. "That's what I want too."

She finally looks at peace, and I don't want to shatter that, but there's one more thing I have to know.

"What about the whipping? Was that Lavinia too?"

"Yes." She touches the scar on her face, absently. "That was her too."

We sit in silence for a few moments, each of us lost in our own thoughts until I kiss her on the forehead and tell her to get some rest.

"Are you going somewhere?" she asks.

"After you go to sleep, but I'll be back before you wake."

"What are you going to do?"

"I'm going to finish this, *gudinne*. It isn't your battle anymore."

34

THORSEN

THE MANOR IS quiet and dim. Narcissa and her daughters have long since gone to bed. I've waited until the early hours of the morning to execute my plan, and for once, the darkness in my mind is a solid companion.

There is no sympathy in my heart for the woman who has coldly refused to acknowledge Ella as her own over the years. As for the spawn she raised to be just like her, they can burn in Hades for all I care. Ella has only ever known suffering at their hands, and tonight, the scales of justice will find balance again.

I work systematically, dousing each window and door frame with petrol. When I'm satisfied with my efforts, I retrieve the bottles I spent the past two hours fashioning. Some call them petrol bombs. Some call them Molotov cocktails. I call them retribution.

There isn't much time for me to do this and get back to the car. While the bombs are incendiary, they aren't explosive, but the glass shattering will make noise, and it won't take long for the smoke alarms to activate. The women will realize as they try to escape, there's only one way out, and it will be straight through the fiery birth canal of hell.

I'm not too concerned about the neighbors hearing the ruckus right away, considering the manor sits on a decent chunk of property. But I don't plan on sticking around either.

One last time, I look over the house that should have been Ella's home. I don't know if she has any happy memories here, but I hope she will forgive me when they go up in flames. I begin my work on the left side of the house, smashing the first bottle through the largest picture window, along with the empty petrol tank for good measure. From there, I methodically work my way around to the back. The entire process probably only takes a couple of minutes, but the adrenaline flooding my body makes it feel like ten.

It isn't long at all before the bloodcurdling screams unfurl inside as the women stir to life and realize what's happening. But I don't have the privilege of a VIP seat for this show. They will have to find their own way out.

Leaving them behind, I walk across the field and return to my car. From my driver's seat, I watch as the first fiery shape leaps from the picture window, spilling onto the grass outside. Two more orange-flamed silhouettes follow, clinging to the earth as they mourn the loss of the only thing they hold dear. Their vanity.

When sirens sound in the distance, I slip back out onto the dark streets and drive to an abandoned petrol station. Parking behind it, I dispose of my shirt in the dumpster and wash myself quickly with a bottle of water and some hand soap. It's already past four in the morning, and I need to get back to Ella.

The hospital is quiet when I arrive. Only a few nurses are hanging around, including the one I spoke with yesterday. She recognizes me right away and stops me on my way to Ella's room.

"Did you leave?" she asks.

"I had to get some things for Ella." I hold up the black bag in my hand.

"That's so thoughtful of you." She smiles, but I'm fairly certain she's already thinking of ways to leak this to the media just as soon as Ella is discharged. Regardless, I don't care about that right now. As long as I take her home with me, I don't really care what the press says anymore.

When I get to Ella's room, she's still fast asleep and stays that way as I take a proper shower in her adjoining bathroom. Once I'm dressed and freshly shaved, the exhaustion hits me all at once, and I barely make it back to the chair beside her before my eyes fall shut, and I drift into the easiest slumber I've had since she left.

The nurse wakes both of us when she comes to check Ella's vitals in the morning. Ella sits up, glancing at me like she's still a bit disoriented.

"You're still here."

"I'm not going anywhere."

The nurse smiles at us and then checks Ella's eyes and asks her to perform a series of tests. When she's done, she types some notes into the computer.

"How are you feeling this morning? Any nausea, dizziness, pain?"

"I'm fine," Ella answers. "Other than feeling a little hungover, I'm totally fine."

"Good." The nurse nods. "Dr. Hobbs is making his rounds now, so he should be here shortly."

"Okay." Ella smooths her finger over the Band-Aid on her hand. "Thank you."

The nurse leaves, and Ella looks at me.

"Did you go somewhere last night, or did I dream that?"

"I had a few errands to run." I keep my answer vague for now. "And I bought you some clothes to go home in today."

"Home?" she murmurs.

"My home, Ella. Our home."

"So you want to take me back to Norway," she says. "And then what?"

"Well... the estate is ours, but we'll need to move into the palace full time."

"You want me to move into the palace?" Her eyes widen.

"Yes."

"And what will I do there?"

"Whatever you want." I offer her what I hope is a reassuring smile. "I thought maybe you'd like to do some charity work with animals since you're fond of them. My secretary can give you some options closer to home."

She's quiet, and I think I know what's holding her back. Olivia was waiting to tell her, but I think now is as good a time as any.

"Of course, we'll have to come back to Cranbrook to visit regularly too."

"We will?" She perks up.

"Considering we're the proud new owners of Hilliard Sanctuary, it might look bad if we don't."

Ella shrieks, and I don't think I've ever seen her so relieved. "Are you serious?"

"I already finalized the deal with Olivia. She's still going to run it, and we can visit whenever you'd like."

She stares at me with watery eyes. "I can't believe you're doing all of this for me."

"I love you," I tell her again. "You've given me something to fight for, and this is me fighting. Come home with me, Ella. Because I really don't want to have to drug you again."

She laughs, and I smile, and it feels so natural between us, I don't know why I resisted it for so long. This woman gets me. We're both fucked up, but together we work somehow. And in spite of everything, she still loves me. Miserable bastard and all.

"I'll come home with you, Thorsen." She leans over to graze my lips with hers. "But you have to promise me that you'll keep fighting. Even on your darkest days. Promise me we'll get through the hard times together. No more pushing me away."

"I promise," I growl into her lips and dig my fingers into her hair. I need to feel her. I need to get inside her again and fuck away the stress of the last two weeks. But before I can even try, the door opens, and Dr. Hobbs enters the room.

"Feeling better, I see?" He arches an eyebrow at us, and Ella blushes as we separate.

"Yes, I'm much better this morning. Thank you."

He glances at her chart and props himself against the counter. "I spoke with Dr. Blom at length yesterday, and he assured me he feels you aren't at risk. So I'm willing to release you on the condition that you meet with him as soon as you get back to Norway for follow up care."

"I will," Ella assures him. "We'll contact him right away."

He nods and scribbles his signature on some papers and sets them on the table beside Ella's bed. "In that case, Miss Laurent, you are free to go. Please take care of yourself."

"Thank you, Doctor." I nod at him, and Ella repeats my sentiments before he leaves.

Once the door's shut, she swings her legs over the bed, and I help her stand even though she looks like she'll be just fine. "I need to call Olivia and Charlotte. And I need to take a shower before we leave."

"I have some clothes for you in the bathroom," I tell her. "Take a shower, and you can call your friends in the car and arrange a visit with them this afternoon."

Her expression warms as she turns to me, and when she reaches up to touch my face, I fall into her lips all over again. But a taste isn't enough, and soon, we're pawing at each other, desperate for more. I'm groping at her tits beneath the gown and grinding my erection against her hip when she eyeballs the door like a little deviant.

"Do you think they'll know?"

I take her by the hand and drag her to the bathroom, locking the door behind us.

"What if they catch us?" she whispers.

"You need assistance in the shower." I turn on the water and help her out of her hospital gown before moving on to my own clothes, stripping them off as efficiently as possible.

Once we're both naked, I haul her up into my arms and step inside the shower, pressing her back against the tile. She arches into me, whimpering as I suck her nipples and slide my cock against her wet pussy.

"Oh, God, Thorsen." She wrecks my hair when I thrust inside her.

"You feel so fucking good," I groan into her neck.

Her nails dig into my back, and I fuck her into the wall, my hands squeezing her ass to hold her up. It's brutal and necessary, both of us racing toward release with a restlessness that betrays how much we need it.

"Oh, shit." Her eyes fly open, and I freeze.

"What?"

"My patch. I haven't worn it since the doctor took it off when he was cleaning my wounds back in Norway."

My dick surges inside her with primal possession as my fingers dig into her body. "*Min gudinne*, I don't care. I'm coming in you."

Her mouth falls open, and I kiss her again, my teeth gnashing against hers as my cock swells within her. She comes around me first, milking my rigid flesh until I bury myself balls deep and flood her womb with my seed. The caveman in me is beating his chest. I don't want to leave the warmth of her body, but more than anything, I want to get her back home, in our bed, where I can do this all over again. When I set her on her feet, Ella peeks down between her thighs, observing the come as it leaks out of her.

"Are you sure about this?" she asks.

I tilt her chin up and force her to look at me so there can be no misunderstanding between us. "More certain than I've ever been. Now, let's get you cleaned up."

35

ELLA

"I WANT to see Narcissa and the girls while we're in Cranbrook."

Thorsen's jaw works as he glances at me from the driver's seat. "Why?"

"I have a few things I want to say to them before I leave."

He's quiet for a long beat, and I'm getting the sense that this is going to be a battle, but he surprises me.

"First, I want to show you something."

"What is it?"

"I'm taking you there now."

That's all I get out of him, and I'm not really sure what to think as he navigates the familiar streets of my old neighborhood. It's strange how I've lived here for most of my life, but now, it feels like anything but home. The closer we get to the manor, the harder it is to breathe. Facing off with Narcissa and the girls isn't going to be easy, but it's long past overdue.

I'm thinking about all the things I want to say when Thorsen stops the car and parks it. We're near the field I usually cut through on my way back from the sanctuary. I've walked this path countless times, but I can't figure out why he stopped here. Not until he looks out across the field, and I follow his gaze. There's a direct view of the manor, but it isn't a manor anymore.

A cold chill shoots up my spine as my eyes move over the blackened shell of what used to be my home. Thorsen won't take his eyes off me. He's watching me too carefully, and I'm still trying to process what I'm seeing. But then his words from last night come back to me. I thought I'd dreamed about him saying he was going to leave. I was exhausted and overwhelmed, but I know now that it wasn't a dream. He doesn't have to tell me what I can see in his eyes. *He did this for me.*

"Are they... dead?" I shudder.

In answer, he unlocks his phone and hands it to me. On the screen is an article about the fire along with a few photos. My eyes move over the text in a daze, and it all seems too surreal. But the details are right there in black and white. Lavinia, Magnolia, and Narcissa have all been badly burned, and they are in the hospital.

"Say something." Thorsen grabs my hand when I give him the phone back.

I lean my head back against the seat and close my eyes. My mind is a tangled mess, and I don't even know where to begin. After everything they've done, I can't find it in me to feel sorry for them, and I think that's what shocks me the most. When I finally release a breath, it feels like a thousand-pound weight has been lifted off my shoulders. Every cruelty they ever doled out, every mocking word. They all break away, unleashing a flood of emotions I've kept buried for so long. My body shakes, and then I start to laugh and cry simultaneously.

"It's what they deserved." Thorsen strokes my cheek, wiping away my tears.

"I know."

He turns my face back to his. "They suffered, Ella. And they will continue to suffer. I want you to understand they can never hurt you again. I will always do what it takes to protect you. From here on out, they will only ever know pain."

My attention drifts back to the house, and the morbid part of me considers what it must have been like to watch them burn. To imagine Lavinia writhing in pain, suffering the same blow she dealt me is almost too poetic for words. Between the three of them, I can't imagine how they'll ever survive such a twist of fate. They'll have no choice now but to live with the scars they mocked me for at every turn.

"I get why you did it," I tell Thorsen. "This is the worst thing that could ever happen to them. Now they will live the rest of their lives as ugly on the outside as they are on the inside."

"It's only the beginning." He offers me a tender kiss.

"What do you mean?"

"Narcissa hasn't carried insurance on the house in years," he says. "It's all gone. They'll have nothing left. Every comfort they ever denied you, every punishment they ever doled out, they will come to know that bitter reality on an intimate level."

"I love you." I lean against his body and breathe him in. "For loving me enough to do something so insane and oddly sweet."

"I love you too, *min gudinne*."

He twists his fingers in my hair, and our lips come together, and I wonder if this intoxicating high will ever end. But in his eyes, I recognize the flame in his soul burning for me too, and I know that it won't. We were always fated to be together. In this life or the next, I would have found him.

"To be continued," he teases as he adjusts the growing erection in his pants.

I smile in agreement. "I'm already looking forward to it."

He releases me and starts the car again. "I'll take you to see them if that's what you want."

"Please."

The drive is quiet, but I'm surprisingly calm when Thorsen parks at the Chelsea and Westminster Hospital in London. For a while, we just sit in the parking lot, neither of us saying a thing. He waits for me to give the final word that I'm ready, and when I do, we walk hand in hand together.

Thorsen leaves me to my thoughts as he takes control of the situation and speaks with the nurse. He explains that I'm family, and she informs us that all three of the women required emergency surgery in the early morning hours. They are conscious but unable to speak.

When he asks about their prognosis, she tells him that barring any infections, they will survive. But they will be physically disfigured for the rest of their lives. Their fate is sealed, and it's a confirmation of Thorsen's promise. It's hard to believe someone would go to these lengths for me, but I know I would do the same for him. When the nurse leads us down the hall to the room, and I finally see them, I don't think justice has ever felt so romantic.

The smell of charred flesh and disinfectant burns my nostrils as I lay eyes on the blood-soaked bandages over their bodies. There isn't a place the fire hasn't touched, and between the lot of them, their features are no longer distinguishable. Three pairs of empty brown eyes stare back at me. The women who never had a kind word to say can't say anything at all right now. They're frozen in this hell. Three gasping sacks of mangled flesh.

I had so much I thought I needed to express when I came here, but I think their misery says it all. They will live and die in the wretched existence they have created for themselves. And I'm certain once I walk out of this room, I'll never have to think of them again. I take a step closer, and then another, until finally, there can be no doubt who they are looking at or what I have to say.

"I hope you remember me," I tell them. "Every time you look in the mirror. Every agonizing bite of pain you feel. Every horrifying stare you'll get when the children scream and run the other way. Remember how you laughed. How you sneered. How you lived your lives with complete disregard for anyone but yourselves. And know this. I will go on with my life, and you won't infect my mind or my heart anymore. The cord is severed, and the only thing you'll have to keep you warm at night is the mark of shame you'll bear for the rest of eternity."

Thorsen wraps his arm around my waist, a steadying presence as I draw the first real breath I feel like I've ever taken. Because now I am free of my chains. Of my guilt. Of these awful women whose names I've already forgotten.

"One more thing," Thorsen tells them, his face as cold and callous as a wintry day. "If you ever try to contact Ella again, I'll kill you myself."

"Ella, how are you feeling?" Olivia pulls me in for a hug as soon as I'm out of the car.

"I'm fine." I squeeze her back and then repeat my assurances to Charlotte next.

After I called them this morning and explained what happened yesterday, we arranged to meet at the sanctuary. Now that we're here, it's a little awkward, to say the least. We had a difficult conversation, and I finally unleashed all my truths about the torment I endured at the hands of Narcissa and the girls. Though Olivia and Charlotte both confirmed they had suspected as much, they're still treating me as if I'm made of glass. And to top things off, Charlotte can't stop staring at Thorsen. She's dying to ask me what the hell is going on, but she's trying to contain herself.

"Have you been to see the manor yet?" Olivia asks carefully.

"We have." I nod. "We saw it before we visited them at the hospital."

"What on earth do you think happened?" Charlotte asks.

"Who knows." I take Thorsen's hand in mine.

"Well, it was no secret that they had more enemies than friends in this neighborhood," Olivia says. "I hear the police have been quite busy fielding calls by every scorned woman Narcissa crossed. I think all three of them must have slept with every husband in Kent. Then, of course, there are rumors that the women had been at odds with each other since their return. Apparently, Narcissa and Lavinia had been going at it like cats and dogs. Some of the neighbors are even speculating that it may have been either of them who torched the place."

"They weren't particularly well-liked," I agree. "I wouldn't put it past them."

"Well, if you ask me, I think they got what they deserved," Charlotte hisses. "Wretched, evil women. After everything they've done to you, and then yesterday—" She shudders. "I can't feel sorry for them. I'm just glad Thorsen asked me to get your things from the manor. At least you still have what's left of your parents' belongings."

"You picked up my things?" I look back and forth between them.

"Yes," Charlotte beams. "It wasn't really that difficult, considering Lavinia had chucked them all onto the lawn. Apparently, you really pissed her off."

"Well, we don't need to give her any more airtime in our lives than she's already had," Olivia says. "Would you like to come inside for a cup of tea?"

"That would be lovely, thank you."

We follow them into Olivia's home, and the overwhelming relief I feel at the familiarity of this place nearly brings me to tears. For so many years, she has provided a sanctuary for me too. The stray neighbor girl who didn't have a family of her own. She let me into this magical space and showed me that kindness still existed, and love could be found for all of us, even in the darkest of times.

When she pulls out a chair at the table for me, I hug her again and nearly break down into a sobbing pile of mush. Nobody says a word as Olivia comforts me, hugging me back with all the strength I've always admired her for.

"It's okay now, Ella," she whispers into my ear. "I think you've found your forever home too."

We both laugh, and I wipe away the moisture leaking from my eyes as I nod. If Thorsen's face is any indication, he's struggling with this new concept of sharing me. He wants to wipe away my tears and take care of me just like he promised. But he also knows I need this.

"Okay, sorry." I wave my hands in front of my face as I sit down. "I just really had to get that out of the way. I'm still trying to process everything. But I'm so glad the sanctuary will live on."

Thorsen drapes his arm over my shoulder, playing with the strands of my hair, and it makes me shiver in all the right places.

"It truly is amazing." Olivia nods at the man I love. "I've never been so blessed."

"It was all Ella," he says, his voice full of warmth for me.

"Yeah, it's really great." Charlotte gives me a look that tells me she's dying for information. "Now, will you please tell us how any of this even happened?"

Olivia chuckles as she heads to the kettle to prepare the tea, leaving us to hash out the details.

"We met at the ball," I admit. "I was too embarrassed to tell you after all the trouble you went through to get me a ticket. I got into the wrong line. Or at least, that's what I thought. But now I know it was definitely the right line."

Thorsen grazes my cheek with a gentle kiss, and I can practically hear Charlotte swooning from here.

"So then you went to work for him?" she asks. "On a ship?"

Crap. I wasn't anticipating how I'd field these questions, and I'm trying to think of a response when Thorsen covers for us smoothly.

"No, it wasn't really on a ship. But Ella had a nondisclosure agreement. She couldn't tell anyone where she was or what she was doing."

"Oh." Charlotte blinks. "I suppose that makes sense."

"And then you two fell in love?" Olivia returns with a handful of cups and saucers, arching her brow at me in question. I know all she really needs to hear is that I'm happy, and this is truly what I want.

"Yes." I sigh happily. "We fell in love, and it's been a crazy ride, but I wouldn't have it any other way."

"What now?" Charlotte asks. "Olivia said you're going back to Norway."

A look passes between Thorsen and Olivia, and I gather they've spoken about more than just the sale of the sanctuary.

"I am going back to Norway with Thor," I answer. "But we'll be back to visit as often as we can."

"Thor." Charlotte blushes. "I can't believe you call the King of Norway Thor. And you're going to live with him at a freaking palace. This is so crazy."

"Charlotte reads all the royal gossip columns," I explain to Thorsen.

"I do not!" Her voice rises, and we all laugh. "Okay, fine, maybe a little. So when can I come visit you then?"

"Any time you'd like," Thorsen says. "As long as Ella approves."

"Of course, I do." My heart soars at the idea. "And the same goes for you too, Olivia."

Then a thought occurs to me, and my stomach flutters with nerves. I'm not sure how to propose this, and I'm not even sure cats are allowed at the palace, but I'm not going anywhere without him.

"Alfred is going to love his new home." Olivia sets the kettle onto the table and prepares the tea.

"What new home?" I frown.

"The palace, obviously." She smiles and shakes her head. "Who would have thought he'd go from the streets to royalty in a matter of a few months."

When I look at Thorsen, he just shrugs. "Apparently, there's a horse coming too."

"Oh, my God!" I shout, startling everyone. "Mabel is coming too?"

"She belongs with you," Olivia says. "She'll be leaving by ship this week with two royal guards watching over her."

I nearly knock over the table as I lunge at Thorsen and throw my arms around his neck. I've never been so elated, and if this is a dream, I don't want to wake up from it.

"I'm so happy for you, Ella." Charlotte wipes a little tear from her eye too. "You deserve this. You deserve the whole world."

36

THORSEN

"Don't be nervous," Calder tells me.

"I'm not."

But I'm lying.

"You are." He laughs. "I've never seen you so uptight, and that's saying a lot. Just try to relax, if nothing else, for *Mor's* sake. Look how happy she is."

My eyes haven't moved from Ella and my mother all night. It's strange how natural it is for her to meet someone, even on their death bed, and put them at ease. This is how it's been every night since I brought her to the palace three weeks ago.

My mother loved Ella the moment she saw her, and I've never felt so right about anything in my life. Every evening, we come to her room for a visit. Sometimes, Calder tells her stories about his latest misadventures, and sometimes, I fill her in on the duties I'm slowly adapting to. But often, when there is a silence, Ella talks to her about the herbal concoctions she's dedicated her life to making. She jots down notes as my mother happily passes on her knowledge. It's bittersweet, but we never miss these opportunities because the doctors tell us it probably won't be long now.

"I think she approves," I tell Calder.

"I think we all do," he says. I'm grateful that both he and Ella have seemingly put the awkwardness of their first interaction behind them, for all our sakes.

"The media perception has taken a turn for the better since you've been in public with her," he adds. "It must be a nice change of pace."

I shudder at the memory of the chaos that ensued when I had to announce that I was not, in fact, engaged to Lavinia. The aftermath was quite the shock to all the media outlets who suspected I'd chased her off too. But when they saw Ella, they were quick to move on, rabid for information about the beautiful French girl who stole my heart and softened the hard edges of my personality.

"She's easy to love," I say. "And I'm a better man for it."

"What are you two whispering about over there?" Ella peeks over at us suspiciously.

"Climate change." Calder smirks, and Ella rolls her eyes.

"You'd better come say good night. Your mother is tired."

We join her at our mother's side, and I think she has never been so at peace. Alfred has decided to take up residence in her bed, which Ella explains is his way of comforting her. Either way, I've become fond of the little gray street cat, and I know Mother has too.

We say our goodbyes and leave her to sleep, and in the hall, Calder informs us he has a hot date. Ella tells him he should try taking her out before he sleeps with her this time. After a bit of grumbling on his part, he finally disappears, leaving us alone for the night.

"What now, my King?" The little fire-breather leans up on her tiptoes and brushes her lips against mine.

"Let's take a walk in the garden."

She kisses her way across my jaw to the beating pulse in my throat as her palm comes to rest on the bulge in my trousers. "Or we could just go to our suite."

My cock stirs to life, and I close my eyes, trying to remember what I was supposed to be doing before she distracted me.

"You've been so busy this week." Ella takes my hand in hers and leads me to our door. "So tense. Surely, there's something I can do to ease your stress."

"What did you have in mind?" I hoist her up into my arms, and she wraps her legs around my back. Her fingers cling to my biceps as I carry her across the threshold of our suite and kick the door shut behind me.

"I don't know, Your Majesty." She teases my ear, biting at it as she grinds against me. "Would you like me to suck your royal cock?"

"You've turned into quite the little deviant," I muse, setting her onto her feet.

"I had a good teacher."

She sinks to her knees before me, and I'm trying to remember my plans as she unbuckles my belt and unzips my pants. It certainly didn't involve her on her knees with a mouth full of my cock, but I'm not about to say no to that either.

Ella pulls my dick free and then pushes me back into the chair as she crawls toward me like a predatory feline. I'm anxious to feel her lips wrapped around me because this never gets old. Her nails scrape over my thighs, and she toys with me for a while, licking me soft and slow. Her eyes hold me hostage as she leans between my parted legs, worshipping me with her mouth. I fall back against the chair, eyes at half-mast, my body relaxing as she gives me exactly what I need.

It would be so easy to blow my load in her mouth right now. It would be pure fucking heaven. But more than anything, I've made it a goal to come inside her at every opportunity until I've claimed her body in an entirely different way. Breeding her until she's round with my child. It stirs a primal possession in me, and that's what has me pulling her hair back until my dick falls out of her mouth.

"What's wrong?" she asks.

"Get on top of me," I command. "Come sit on your throne."

Ella grins and shakes her head. She knows exactly what I'm doing, and she loves every filthy moment of these games. When she stands up and lifts her skirt, she's not wearing any panties, and I'm officially on the fucking edge.

She grips my shoulders as she straddles me, slowly lowering herself onto my shaft until she's so full of me she collapses forward with a faint groan. When she rocks her pelvis into me, I dig my fingers into her hips and thrust her body down. The shock reverberates through both of us, and Ella takes over, fucking me like it's her last day on earth. And I love her like this. Wild for me. Desperately chasing the high that I give her. She is achingly beautiful, and when she breaks apart, crying out in agony, she is mine.

The spasms in her body milk the come from my dick, and still, the little fire-breather hasn't had enough. She grabs my face and continues to kiss me, long after my cock has gone soft inside her. I think we could kiss each other like this forever, and that reminds me, I was supposed to try my hand at being romantic tonight.

I had a walk in the garden planned. A starry night. The scent of roses around us. I even had a speech prepared. But nothing has ever felt as natural or right as this moment does now, with the two of us still intimately connected. When I pull away from her lips and force her to hold still, she pouts.

"Why are we stopping?"

"Marry me, Ella."

Her eyes widen, and she freezes. It takes her a full minute to say anything, but I've come to recognize this is how Ella processes everything. She takes her time, and I've learned not to push her during these moments.

"You want me to marry you?" she whispers.

"More than anything."

She squishes my face between her palms and nods, tears shining in her eyes. "I want that more than anything too, my King. I love you so much."

"I have never felt more like a king than I do right now," I tell her.

She starts pawing at me again, frantically trying to unbutton my shirt and strip me down naked, just how she likes me.

"This week," I murmur against her lips as she fumbles over my buttons. "Marry me this week."

She pauses. "This week?"

"I want my mother to be there."

Her eyes are soft and sad when she nods, her fingers trailing across my jaw. "Of course, my love. This week sounds perfect."

"Good." I sigh into her neck and move her hands back to my shirt. "Now you can fuck me, goddess."

37

THORSEN

"You look so handsome, Thorsen." My mother tries to hold back her tears as Aunt Runa wheels her into position in the garden.

It's the first time she's been out of bed this week, and I was beginning to have my doubts she'd make it down here at all. But she came through, summoning her strength to be here tonight. And after our conversation yesterday, I understand that this is the last of her will. This is what she's been holding on for.

"I love you, *Mor*." I lean down to kiss her on the cheek.

"Oh, my dear, sweet son. I love you too. I'm so proud of you. It's time for you to live your life. You have my blessings of happiness."

My eyes burn, and my voice wavers just a little as I give her the answer she's been waiting for. "You have my blessing too."

Tears leak from her eyes, and she nods, squeezing my hand in hers.

The music begins, and it's time for me to leave her and join Calder. I thank my mother for all her help, and my brother leads me to the ring of glowing candles with a lit torch in hand. As we reach the entrance of the circle, he sets his torch down on one side and leaves me to join the *Gothi* within the sacred space while I wait for my bride. A week wasn't much time to throw everything together, but the benefit of having an entire royal staff at your disposal is that you can make it happen.

Ella got everything she wanted, which wasn't much. It's a small, intimate affair with just my family and Olivia and Charlotte. When I told her how I had meant to propose, she said we should get married that way instead. So that's exactly what we're doing. In the garden, in the middle of the night, among the roses and stars.

My mother was more than happy to be involved in all aspects, telling Ella about the rituals she believes will ensure a long, happy marriage. Scattered around us are flowers, branches, and leaves. Myrtle to symbolize our love, oak for fertility, and willow for protection. Everything has a significance, and Ella was eager to incorporate all of them, much to my mother's pleasure.

Charlotte walks down the aisle next, a nervous smile on her face as she sets her torch down at the entrance to make way for the bride. Outside of the circle, Olivia is next to my mother, Dr. Blom, and Aunt Runa. When Ella appears at the end of the aisle, we all turn our attention to her.

A smile curves across my face when she walks toward me in a dress that's oddly familiar. And while I realize it isn't the same one, she chose a dress just like the one she first met me in. But instead of blue, it's white. The only thing that's missing is her silver heel, which is conveniently tucked into my arm. Even so, she manages her way to me with a grace not many could possess. When she joins me at my side, there is a collaborative resonance of laughter when I kneel before her and place the shoe on her foot.

"I think you left this behind."

"Lucky for me." She beams as I stand and take her hands in mine.

"I like the dress." My eyes move over her with a carnal appreciation only she can see.

"I thought you might." She blushes.

Her face is aglow with happiness, and I recognize it because I feel it too. Her warmth has penetrated the frozen exterior I've flaunted like a weapon for so long. Ella blasted right through those hard outer layers and broke them down inch by inch, chiseling so deep inside me I'd never be able to let her go. And right now, I've never been more grateful for her determination. After today, she will be my wife. My fire goddess. *My Queen.*

The *Gothi* directs our attention to him, opening with a traditional Norse blessing. Facing in each direction as he speaks, he forbids all evil from entering our lives from this point forward. After invoking the gods, our ancestors, and everyone gathered here today as our witnesses, he lights a symbolic candle to purify us so that we may enter our marriage with unadulterated love.

Dipping an evergreen sprig into a bowl of holy water, he anoints Ella and me, offering his blessings before binding our hands together with the rite of the white ribbon. We recite a prayer to Frigga, the goddess of marriage, followed by our vows promising to love, honor, and cherish each other. The rings we exchange were personally chosen by Ella. A moonstone set into oxidized silver for her, and a brushed silver Tungsten band for me.

As the final rite of passage into married life, the *Gothi* pours a goblet of mead wine and brings our free hands together around the stem, encouraging each of us to drink. Once we do, he declares us bound for eternity as husband and wife. He removes the goblet, and I bring my hand to Ella's face, sealing our marriage with a kiss.

Around us, bells begin to ring, a salute from the witnesses. But Ella and I only have eyes for each other as we seal our commitment to one another.

When the *Gothi* opens the circle again with one last symbolic prayer, we exit to our new life amongst our family and friends. Celebrations are in order, and the chef has prepared a feast of traditional foods. Ella and I join our guests in the banquet room, listening and laughing as they each share a toast to our good health and happiness, along with a few embarrassing stories. When my mother begins to fade, Ella and I both offer to take her to her room, but she is quick to dismiss us.

"Enjoy your celebrations, my beautiful children." She offers us each a kiss on the cheek. "I have everything I've ever wanted now. I'm at peace. Now, drink and be happy."

Aunt Runa starts to wheel her away before my mother stops her, offering me a mischievous smile.

"Oh, Thorsen, I almost forgot," she says. "I put a Mandrake Root beneath your bed too. For virility."

Ella and I spend two full days lost in each other, soaking up the moments we have right now. Our honeymoon has been delayed by choice, and on the third day, when her guests have gone back to London, we wake with a somber cloud over our newlywed calm.

"Are you ready for this?" she asks as we step out of the shower, and she dries me with a towel.

"No. But I don't think I'll ever be ready."

"I know." She kisses me softly. "But for what it's worth, I think you're doing the right thing."

Two months ago, I wouldn't have agreed. Even a week ago, it wasn't easy to accept what my mother asked of me. I'm not ready to let her slip away, but she has always been the strongest woman I know, and she wants to be remembered that way. When she came to me, asking me to let her die with dignity while she still could, it broke my fucking heart. But it would be selfish of me to ask her to stay only to prolong her pain and suffering.

She is ready to go before her mind is gone completely, and she can no longer talk or function. When I learned that everyone else had already agreed, the burden fell on me to give her my approval too.

"I'm going to need you." I bow my head to Ella's and breathe her in. "More than I ever have."

"I'll be right here," she whispers.

I bury my face in her neck and hold her, silence enveloping us as I gather the courage to say goodbye. After a few minutes, she untangles us, caressing my face beneath her palm.

"I love you, Thorsen. We'll get through this together."

It's difficult to speak over the overwhelming thoughts in my head. But as long as Ella is by my side, she can keep me calm. She helps me dress for the day, picking out her favorite light blue dress shirt from my closet and a pair of navy trousers.

"We don't wear black today," she tells me as she buttons the shirt for me. "We don't wear black because she'll always be right here."

When she presses her palm against my chest, I nod, enclosing my hand over hers.

Ella dresses herself, and then walks beside me in silence, her hand holding mine as we near my mother's suite. When we step inside, Calder and Runa have already gathered there. It feels like I'm walking to my doom, what I imagine the forest would have been like if I'd ever actually gone.

"There they are." My mother smiles warmly, gesturing for us as we close the door.

She seems so small today, and it's difficult to see her like this. So pale, so thin, so weak. I know we are making the right choice for her, but it doesn't make it any easier.

"Come sit beside me, my loves."

Ella and I take a seat beside Calder and Runa, and the room falls silent, melancholy energy stagnating the air around us.

"Are you still sure about this?" Calder asks.

"Yes, my son." She nods in a way that proves she's still in there, despite her failing body. More determined than ever, she's a shining light in this world who deserves to go in peace.

"I have already spoken with Calder and Runa," she tells us. "But I have a few things I would like to say to both of you. Come to me, please."

Ella and I join her at the bed, each of us taking a side and uniting our hands with hers. She speaks to Ella first, her face full of warmth and love for the woman who has brought me back from the darkness.

"Thank you." Her voice betrays her emotion. "Ella, you are my daughter now, and that doesn't change just because I'm gone. Call on me whenever you need a friend to talk to, and remember everything I taught you. I want you to have my books, my elixirs, and my jewelry. They belong to you now."

"Thank you." Ella's lip trembles, and she nods. "Thank

you for accepting me into your family and for loving me. I can't tell you what it's meant to me."

"That love will never end," mother says. "Please look after my son. Love him as fiercely as I know only you can."

"I will," Ella promises. "I will take care of him always."

My mother nods, and Ella hugs her before taking her leave to sit and wait for me.

"Thorsen." Mother looks up at me, tears gleaming in her eyes. "My dearest Thorsen, how I admire and love you. The depths of which you will someday understand when you are raising your own son."

"I love you too." My voice fractures.

"Remember what I said. I'll never be far away. Speak to me often, tell me how you are, and never stop fighting for the beauty in life. You will find it, even in the darkness, if you choose to look."

"I'll make you proud," I assure her.

A tear splashes onto her cheek. "You already do."

I hug her, and she whispers into my ear that it's going to be okay. That I shouldn't mourn for her because she'll always be right here in the leaves and the wind and the blossoming flowers. I don't want to let her go, but she tells me it's time, and I hold on a little longer until I can't hold onto her anymore. She summons the others back to the bed, and we all gather around her.

"Let us say a prayer to Hekate." She closes her eyes, and we follow suit, repeating her words as she recites a prayer for a safe rite of passage after death.

When we open our eyes again, she has the elixir in her hand, harnessing the last of her energy to bring it to her lips.

"I'm going to sleep now," she says. "It's been a long journey, and I'm very tired. Remove this bottle when I'm gone, and never speak of this moment again. Remember me in the garden, or my herbal room, or spending time with my boys. Remember me only in good ways, and be happy, not sad, when you think of me."

We all promise her that we will, and she drinks the elixir before handing the bottle off to Calder. She smiles, closes her eyes, and goes to sleep.

Just like she said.

EPILOGUE

ELLA

"Hello, my King."

"Good evening, *gudinne.*" Thorsen kisses me on the top of my head as I roll into him. I bury my face into his neck, inhaling the sun and the salt of the sea.

"Nice of you to join me again," he says.

"You wore me out." I yawn as my fingers trail over his beautiful body. "Was I out long?"

"About two hours."

I sigh and close my eyes, content to stay here like this all day. It isn't often we have time to lounge around anymore, but we make the most of the Norwegian summers by taking the yacht out every chance we get. Thorsen is perpetually busy, but he carves out this time in his schedule for us, and it's non-negotiable. He works hard, and he's dedicated to making a lasting impact during his reign. But when it comes to time with his family, we're always his first priority.

Five years ago, we took a late honeymoon on this yacht. Thorsen spent days inside me, and I don't think he'd ever felt more accomplished than when he learned that Atlas and Frey were conceived on that trip. It was the moment I truly saw him break through the clouds of darkness that had plagued him for so long. And when it comes to his sons, his dedication is unwavering. Thorsen told me right away he wanted to be a hands-on father, and I knew it was important to him that they always felt loved. Even with all his responsibilities, he still manages to take the boys to their horseback riding lessons and find the time and new opportunities to teach them.

But today, we are lucky to have Uncle Calder onboard, who never lets them down either. He's on the deck teaching them how to fish, giving Thorsen and me a rare opportunity to spend an afternoon naked under the covers.

"How long do you think he'll last before they tire him out completely?"

Thorsen's chest rumbles with laughter. "I'm surprised he's lasted this long."

"Think we have enough time for round two?" I slip my hand beneath the covers, barely grazing his cock before the sound of laughter spills into the corridor.

"Incoming!" Calder yells before the door bursts open.

Thorsen and I sit up with matching expressions of guilt and amusement as Calder rolls his eyes. "Five years and you two still can't keep your hands off each other. Uncle C is off duty now and in need of a stiff drink."

"Thank you, Calder," Thorsen calls after him as he heads out the door.

I smile as the boys leap onto the bed, jumping up and down without a care in the world as they tell us about the fish they saw. Both their cheeks are flushed from the salty air, and they look just as wild as their father. In fact, the twins could probably pass for his twin in another twenty years. While Thorsen likes to say there are parts of me in there too, I see every detail of my beautiful husband entwined into their features, and I wouldn't have it any other way.

Somehow, at some point, my life turned out to be a fairy tale. It's the type of fairy tale where my husband still spanks me and fucks me like he owns me, but it's a fairy tale just the same. When he isn't busy taking care of us, we're busy taking care of him, and by some miracle, we have found balance in this crazy world.

There are still dark days, and I think there always will be, but we get through them together. Our pasts can't haunt us as long as we keep looking forward to the future together. Dr. Blom is quick to remind us of that during our weekly visits. To this day, Thorsen doesn't miss his appointments, and over the years, he's managed to build to completion an entire fleet of model ships in the hours we've spent at sessions. We keep them as reminders that even when they are imperfect, they are still worth saving.

I stay busy doing charity work and occasionally fly back to London to help Olivia at the sanctuary. It's one of the boys' favorite things to do, and it always amazes me to watch them as the smart, compassionate beings they are.

During one of our visits a few years back, Thorsen and I stumbled across a group of transients digging through the local rubbish bin. They were eating a moldy loaf of bread, fighting over the crumbs, when one of them looked over at us. It caught me off guard when I saw the horrifically scarred face. In place of her shiny blonde hair was patchy, greasy strings that hung from her head. I wouldn't have even recognized her if it hadn't been for their presence in Cranbrook. The three women were the most horrific sight I'd ever witnessed.

The experience shook me, and I couldn't really explain why. I hadn't expected to see them, and it left me unsettled for days. It wasn't long after that when Thorsen started to tell me a story as I was drifting off to sleep. The story was about three women who haunted the forest of Aokigahara. According to legend, the trio had been dropped so deep into the vast, dense forest that they could never find their way out. The only souls they ever stumbled across were those who came there to die, and even those dark souls were so terrified of their hideous faces, they refused to speak with them. For the rest of their days, they were doomed to wander the sea of trees, surrounded by death and sorrow.

Oddly enough, I never saw Narcissa, Lavinia, or Magnolia again. And a part of me suspects that the legend woven by my god of thunder might not be such a legend after all.

"It's almost bedtime for you two." Thorsen ruffles the boys' hair as they snuggle in beside us.

"Can you tell us a story?" They beg in unison. "Please?"

Thorsen looks at me, and we all settle into our spaces on the bed, the boys curling up beside their father as he covers them over with the top blanket.

"What story would you like to hear?" he asks.

"The god of thunder!" Atlas shouts.

My lips tilt up in amusement as I lay my head back against the pillow and listen to Thorsen tell this tale for the thousandth time. As the story goes, a dark lonely god locked himself up in his castle, swearing that he would never let anyone in. He was angry, and he didn't like to venture outside of his fortress, but one day, he was forced to. The god attended a ball, where he met a goddess of fire who wanted to save her furry friends. She was pure-hearted, but he thought she was deceiving him like everyone else. When his thunderous moods caused a hundred storms that shook the earth, somehow, the goddess survived them all. And when he saw that she was indestructible in the face of his thunder, the clouds began to clear, and the sun began to shine on the land that had been cast in darkness for so long. The god immediately fell in love with the goddess, and they created two perfect boys in their likeness. Their names, coincidentally, were Atlas and Frey.

I think I like Thorsen's version of events the best, and it never fails to make the boys gasp during all the same parts even though they've heard it countless times. I'd be lying if I said my pulse wasn't racing, too, every time he confessed the depth of his love for me this way.

When the boys fall asleep, Thorsen reaches out and presses his palm against my heart. "I feel you, *min gudinne.*"

I kiss him, thanking the gods that I was indestructible to his thunder as my fingers crawl to his beating heart. "I feel you too, my King. Forever."

The End.

BOOKS BY A. ZAVARELLI

For a complete list of books and audios, visit http://www.
azavarelli.com/books

ABOUT THE AUTHOR

A. Zavarelli is a USA Today and Amazon bestselling author of dark and contemporary romance.

When she's not putting her characters through hell, she can usually be found watching bizarre and twisted documentaries in the name of research.

She currently lives in the Northwest with her lumberjack and an entire brood of fur babies.

Sign Up for A. Zavarelli's Newsletter:
www.subscribepage.com/AZavarelli

Like A. Zavarelli on Facebook:
www.facebook.com/azavarelliauthor

Join A. Zavarelli's Reader Group:
www.facebook.com/femmefatales

Follow A. Zavarelli on Instagram:
www.instagram.com/azavarelli